DEAD TO THE WORLD

Francis Henry Durbridge was born in Hull, Yorkshire, in 1912 and was educated at Bradford Grammar School. He was encouraged at an early age to write by his English teacher and went on to read English at Birmingham University. At the age of twenty-one he sold a radio play to the BBC and continued to write following his graduation whilst working as a stockbroker's clerk.

In 1938, he created the character Paul Temple, a crime novelist and detective. For thirty years the radio serials were hugely successful until the last of the series was completed in 1968. In 1969, Paul Temple was adapted for television and four of the adventures prior to this had been adapted for cinema, albeit with less success than radio and TV. Francis Durbridge also wrote for the stage and continued doing so up until 1991, when *Sweet Revenge* was completed. Additionally, he wrote over twenty other well-received novels, most of which were on the general subject of crime. The last, *Fatal Encounter*, was published after his death in 1998.

Also in this series

FRANCIS DURBRIDGE

Dead to the World

PLUS

The Ventriloquist's Doll

WITH AN INTRODUCTION BY
MELVYN BARNES

COLLINS
CRIME
CLUB

COLLINS CRIME CLUB
An imprint of HarperCollins*Publishers*
1 London Bridge Street
London SE1 9GF
www.harpercollins.co.uk

This paperback edition 2018
1

First published in Great Britain by Hodder & Stoughton 1965
'The Ventriloquist's Doll' first published by Associated Newspapers in
the *Daily Mail Annual for Boys and Girls* 1952

A catalogue record for this book is
available from the British Library

ISBN 978–0–00–827635–5

Typeset in Sabon LT Std by Palimpsest Book Production Ltd, Falkirk, Stirlingshire

Printed and bound in Great Britain by CPI Group (UK) Ltd, Croydon CR0 4YY

MIX
Paper from
responsible sources
FSC® C007454

This book is produced from independently certified FSC™ paper
to ensure responsible forest management.

For more information visit: www.harpercollins.co.uk/green

Introduction

Wealthy American Robert Scranton asks Philip Holt to investigate the murder of his son at an English university, with the only leads being a postcard signed 'Christopher' and a missing signet ring . . .

When *Dead to the World* was published in March 1967, regular listeners to Francis Durbridge's radio serials featuring Paul Temple could hardly have failed to be reminded of the plot of *Paul Temple and the Jonathan Mystery*, particularly as a new production had been broadcast less than four years earlier. *Dead to the World* was indeed the novelisation of that radio serial, but with Paul and Steve Temple replaced by photographer Philip Holt, his secretary Ruth Sanders and Detective Inspector Hyde. It was Durbridge's second novel to feature these characters, their having debuted in his previous book *The Desperate People*, the novelisation of his 1963 television serial of the same name.

At that time, Francis Durbridge (1912–1998) was a longstanding, popular and distinctive writer of mystery thrillers for BBC radio and television who was soon to dominate the professional and amateur theatrical stage. Today he remains best known as the creator of the novelist-detective

Francis Durbridge

Paul Temple, whose first appearance in the 1938 BBC radio serial *Send for Paul Temple* led to Paul and his wife Steve becoming cult figures of the airwaves, with further serials running on radio throughout the 1940s, '50s and '60s. There were also books, four black-and-white feature films and two spin-off BBC television series. But while the radio serials have enjoyed a twenty-first century renaissance on CD thanks to the efforts of the BBC's audio publishers, and the films and TV episodes have appeared on DVD, some of the books, including *Dead to the World*, have until now been sadly neglected.

The radio serial *Paul Temple and the Jonathan Mystery* was first broadcast in eight episodes from 10 May to 28 June 1951, with Kim Peacock as Paul Temple. By the time of the new production (14 October to 2 December 1963) Peacock had long been succeeded by Peter Coke, who made the role his own with eleven appearances from 1954 to 1968. But the actress Marjorie Westbury warranted the label 'definitive' even more than Coke, given her twenty-three outings as Steve Temple from 1945 to 1968 opposite four different actors: Barry Morse, Howard Marion-Crawford, Kim Peacock and Peter Coke.

Paul Temple and the Jonathan Mystery begins when the Temples meet an American couple, Robert and Helen Ferguson, on a flight from New York. Soon afterwards they learn that the Fergusons' son Richard has been murdered at his Oxford college, and that the only clues are a postcard from Harrogate signed 'Jonathan' and the disappearance of Richard's signet ring. The ensuing plot was typical Durbridge fare and resulted in yet another international success, with European broadcasters using their own actors in translations that included the Dutch *Paul Vlaanderen en het Jonathan*

vi

mysterie (25 January to 29 March 1953), the German *Paul Temple und der Fall Jonathan* (17 September to 5 November 1954) and the Italian *Chi è Jonathan?* almost twenty years later (12 to 23 April 1971).

So what inclined Durbridge, relatively soon after the second UK radio production of *Paul Temple and the Jonathan Mystery*, to recycle this serial as the novel *Dead to the World* and in the process change the character names and replace his popular duo the Temples? It was by no means the first time he had done this, leaving his fans to ponder a question that has never been authoritatively answered. Although his radio serials firmly maintained his reputation over a period of thirty years, he probably wanted to be acknowledged as something more than the creator of Paul and Steve Temple and therefore deliberately set out to broaden his appeal to the reading public by providing a little variety. The first five Temple novels had faithfully followed his radio scripts, but he broke the mould by substituting different protagonists in *Beware of Johnny Washington* and *Design for Murder* (both 1951), even though both had begun life as the radio serials *Send for Paul Temple* (1938) and *Paul Temple and the Gregory Affair* (1946) respectively.

However, having then returned to writing Paul Temple into short stories, newspaper serials, novelisations and even an original novel, it was not until 1965 that Durbridge again took one of his own radio plots, *Paul Temple and the Gilbert Case* (1954), as the basis for a new standalone book, *Another Woman's Shoes*, which was followed two years later by *Dead to the World* as the only other example of him recycling his own material in this way.

Looking back, one wonders if Durbridge's occasional penchant for replacing the Temples, while retaining the typical elements of his radio plots, was considered an affront to his loyal audience? I doubt it, as the books still delivered a generous helping of what they had always expected of him – complications, twists and cliff-hangers galore, and the obligatory sting in the tail. *Dead to the World* again proved to be as popular as ever throughout Europe, in such translations as *Der Siegelring* in Germany, *Sous le signe du dollar* in France, *Morto per il mondo* in Italy, *De zegelring* in the Netherlands and *Umarly dla świata* in Poland.

Following *Dead to the World*, Durbridge produced fifteen more books. Apart from his non-series title *The Pig-Tail Murder* (1969), they were either novelisations of his iconic television serials or Paul Temple mysteries: eight of his TV serials were novelised between 1967 and 1982, and there were six more Paul Temple titles up to 1988, of which two were original novels and four were based on radio serials. (Although some bibliographies list an additional novelisation, *Paul Temple and the Conrad Case* (1989), this appears to be a mistaken reference to the first BBC Radio Collection release on cassette tape of the 1959 radio episodes and not a book after all.)

Whereas Durbridge's books featuring the Temples have been reprinted over the years, *Beware of Johnny Washington, Design for Murder, Another Woman's Shoes* and *Dead to the World* have all been out of print for more than fifty years. Perhaps a less ignominious fate would have befallen them had they been published as *bona fide* Paul Temple novelisations rather than with new characters! Their republication by Collins Crime Club, along with Durbridge's first standalone novel *Back Room Girl* (1950), finally allows new fans to enjoy these thrilling stories in book form. Of similar vintage is the bonus Paul Temple short story 'The Ventriloquist's Doll', which originally appeared in 1952 in the *Daily Mail Annual for Boys and Girls* and shows Durbridge's more playful side when using his central character to appeal to a younger audience.

MELVYN BARNES
September 2017

Chapter One

The wind that came up from the sea that night was ideal for a murderer's purpose.

It crept over the Downs towards Deanfriston College on talons of ice, probing through chinks in ill-fitting doors and windows, taking possession of the night. On its heels came swirling shards of mist, in places thin as gossamer, in others thick as swansdown, enough to swallow the outline of a murderer and dull the soft tread of footsteps on springy turf up the hill to the College.

The murderer's sole risk – that of being seen – had been eliminated. Deanfriston's single street was swept of all life, its inhabitants imprisoned by the bitter cold, glad of a warm fireside and a television screen. Fog and cold were the murderer's handmaidens: there was little risk.

The killer's plan was simple . . .

The young victim looked up with a pleasant, expectant smile as the heavy wooden door of the study opened; trust and welcome were on his face as he took out a bottle of 'students' port and two glasses and turned for the last three seconds of his life to stare briefly and uncomprehendingly down the muzzle of a heavy-bore gun.

1

Despite the silencer with which the gun was fitted, the muffled explosion in the small room was considerable, and the damage done to the victim at such short range was appalling. For a few seconds the assailant's nerves tottered on the edge of panic.

Then the echoes died, and nothing stirred down the long, cell-like corridor called Scholars' Row, built of huge blocks of stone cut in a slower, more opulent age.

The killer quickly set to work arranging the body. The details had been mentally rehearsed a hundred times and the sequence of action now had a remorseless, computer-like quality, as though some disembodied agent were executing the complicated moves. There was no room for mistakes, and none would be made. Twenty minutes later the mutilated corpse was in position. Every detail was perfect; nothing had been forgotten.

Turning to leave, the assassin's eye was caught by a bikini-clad pin-up who smiled from the top of a page-a-day calendar on the wall. Yes, that would be rather a nice touch! Swiftly the current date was ripped from the calendar, and the date for the morrow lay revealed. It was ringed with red ink and had been jubilantly inscribed, many months before, with the words: 'My twenty-first birthday – everyone please note!' On the mantelpiece stood two birthday greetings cards. They had arrived early and had already been opened. One was from Julie, the other from Antoinette. How very ironical.

The newspapers would love it, the murderer reflected, picturing the headlines. No editor would be able to resist such a perfect tearjerker. 'STUDENT MURDERED ON EVE OF 21st.' No, they would surely add the word 'brilliant' – only 'brilliant' or 'gifted' students were ever killed. 'LIFE ENDS FOR GIFTED STUDENT ON EVE OF MANHOOD.' That was better. It was too late for the morning papers, but the evening editions would carry it. They would make interesting reading.

With an inner chuckle the murderer buttoned the high collar of a thick coat and strode out on to the mist-shrouded Downs.

'What I like about modern air travel,' growled Philip Holt, 'is the speed, comfort, and convenience with which one is whisked from continent to continent! – Like now, for example!'

The crowded perimeter-bus in which they had been standing for nearly ten minutes gave a lurch, jolted forward a few yards, and jerked to an abrupt standstill on the tarmac again.

'I expect we're having to wait whilst another plane lands,' said his secretary, Ruth Sanders, in a soothing voice. Ruth possessed an irrepressible enthusiasm for everything, which seemed to keep her strikingly bright and pretty throughout the most exacting day.

The young photographer ignored her attempt to placate him. 'We've been hurled across the Atlantic at twice the speed of sound,' he complained, 'and since we touched down on British soil twenty minutes ago we've moved precisely four yards!' He sighed, dragging his palm impatiently over the back of his head and ruffling his chestnut hair. 'When we do eventually get to the main terminal we'll probably have to wait half an hour while they find our luggage, and then—'

The bus gave a sudden jerk, preparatory to moving off, which sent Holt bumping into the man strap-hanging next to him.

'Oh! My apologies, Mr Scranton. I really wasn't expecting this thing to move!'

Scranton laughed. 'It's the same the world over, Mr Holt,'

he said in the pleasant drawl of Mid-Western America. 'Like it was in the Army – hurry up and wait, men – hurry up and wait!'

'You're not being at all helpful,' Ruth put in with a mischievous grin. 'You mustn't stop the boss here enjoying a good old British grumble.'

The American chuckled and turned attentively to his wife, a little woman in a mauve hat who had managed to gain a seat.

A little later the bus slid to a standstill and, in the mild confusion of getting out, Holt and Ruth became separated from the American couple.

'Who's your new buddy?' Ruth asked as they trailed in the wake of a stewardess down endless corridors towards the arrival lounge.

'The American? Oh, he's from Minnesota. His name's Robert Scranton. We got talking over a drink when you were sleeping on the flight. He manufactures washing machines. Nice chap – only he will refer to his wife as "Mother".'

'A lot of Americans do.'

'I know; it's an appalling habit. If I were a wife I'd rebel! It must make a woman feel so ancient.'

'Perhaps Mrs Scranton *is* a mother,' Ruth suggested.

'As a matter of fact she is – he mentioned two daughters and a son. But that's not the point! She's Scranton's *wife*, not his mother, and she probably likes to think of herself as still a young girl with—'

He was cut short by the announcement that passengers on the flight from New York should proceed at once to the Customs Hall.

They stood alongside the mechanical moving band and waited for their luggage to appear. For a long time nothing came up and it was obvious they had been called prematurely, before unloading had been completed.

Holt looked around irritably, anxious to be on the move again. 'There'll be a stack of work for us to catch up on when we get back to the Studio,' he said dismally. 'Another time I'll think twice before going off to New York to give an exhibition of my work.'

'Nonsense!' said Ruth cheerfully. 'Your photographs are absolutely super and the trip was a huge success! The publicity will do you no end of good.'

'Then at least I'll take care to leave my secretary in London to get on with the work while I'm away.'

'Not on your life!' she declared emphatically. 'You know you couldn't manage without me.'

'Now what on earth makes you think that?' he asked mildly, looking down at her and knowing it was true. There was no doubt about it, Ruth was an excellent secretary and a very capable photographic assistant, even if her efficiency was sometimes a little overpowering.

She began to enlighten him. '. . . Because you'd have been sure to lose your plane tickets – and been late for all your press shows – and you'd have been eaten alive by all those fabulous women who were prowling round the studios waiting to pounce on helpless males!'

Holt grinned suddenly, his ill-humour beginning to disperse. He turned, and caught the eye of Robert Scranton standing with his wife not far away. 'As you said,' he called pleasantly, 'hurry up and wait!'

Scranton smiled patiently. 'That's how it goes!' He looked at his wife. 'Say, why don't you step aside, Mother, and take it easy while I stay here and watch out for our bags? See if you can sit down someplace.'

Mrs Scranton nodded gratefully and moved away. She looked tired and none too strong, Holt thought.

'Are you staying in London, Mr Scranton?' he asked.

'Yeah. Booked in at the Savoy.'

'I've got my car here; can I offer you a lift up to Town? The Savoy isn't very far from my Studio in Westminster.'

'That's real nice of you, Mr Holt! . . . I'll have to ask Mother, though – there's just a chance we may be met. I'll go see what she thinks.'

Holt turned as the luggage from their flight began to tumble from the well below, on to the moving band, and climb slowly up towards them. He was concentrating on his search for their suitcases when Ruth gave a little squeal of excitement and grabbed his arm. She was staring beyond him towards the exit.

'Look – isn't that Inspector Hyde out there?'

'Inspector Hyde?' Holt peered in the same direction. 'Yes, you're right, it is.' He waved his hand but the police officer did not respond. 'I don't think he's seen us.'

'Oh, how disappointing,' Ruth said. 'I wonder what he's doing here. Maybe he's come to arrest a dangerous criminal! Oh, Philip, how thrilling! You'll be able to get some on-the-spot pictures, and Hyde might even ask us to help him again. Wouldn't it be exciting if we could solve another mystery for him . . . ?' Her eyes sparkled at the prospect as she let her imagination run riot.

'Oh, I shouldn't think that's likely, Ruth,' Holt said soberly, recalling the events which had led to their being involved in the Maidenhead affair.* 'That was more than twelve months

* See *The Desperate People*, 1966.

ago. I'm sure Scotland Yard can function quite well without us.'

'Hold it! I think the Inspector's seen us,' Ruth cut in. 'What's more, he's coming in here! And there's a fat man with a press camera trotting behind him.'

Holt vaguely registered the thought that perhaps Ruth was right and that something unusual might be about to happen. It was strictly against the rules for anyone to contact air passengers before they had been cleared at the Customs Hall. There was no time for further thought, however; Hyde was only a few paces away.

'Hello, Inspector! What brings you here? You haven't come to arrest us, I hope?'

Holt noted that the older man had not changed much since their last meeting; his thick hair was just a trifle greyer at the temples perhaps. But he thought he detected a slight sense of urgency behind the habitually quiet and courteous manner as Hyde gave a tight smile and the three of them exchanged brief greetings.

'This is an odd coincidence, meeting you here,' the Inspector said. 'But I must be quick! As it happens, you may be able to help me. That man you were talking to just now – the tall fellow with the lady in the violet hat – do you happen to know his name?'

'Yes, we got friendly on the plane. I've just offered them a lift up to Town.'

The Inspector glanced at a photograph which he held in his hand. 'Well, if he's Mr Robert Scranton from Minnesota—'

'Yes, that's right.'

'Then I've got some bad news for him.'

The Scrantons started to thread their way through the crush, towards Holt, tentative smiles of gratitude on their

7

faces. It was obvious that they had decided to accept his offer of a lift.

'Miss Sanders,' Hyde said quietly, 'do you think you could get Mrs Scranton out of the way for the moment? I'd like to break the news to her husband first.'

Ruth's reactions were split-second fast. She broke away from the group and headed Mrs Scranton off with an admiring comment on her hat. In a moment they had been swallowed up by the crowd.

'Mr Robert Scranton?' asked Hyde politely as the American reached them.

'Sure. That's me!'

'I'm Detective-Inspector Hyde from Scotland Yard. I don't want to make a mistake, so may I ask you if you have a son in this country, Mr Scranton?'

'Yes, I have . . . Why, is there anything wrong?' Scranton turned pale. 'He's a student at University over here – Deanfriston College, down on the south coast. As a matter of fact we're over here to celebrate his twenty-first birthday.'

Hyde cleared his throat. 'I'm afraid I have something very unfortunate to tell you, sir. It's . . . it's bad news.'

Scranton steeled himself. 'Go on, Inspector.'

'Your son was found dead in his study at Deanfriston early this morning. There seems little doubt that he was murdered.'

'Oh, my God!' Scranton began to sway, his face assuming a deathly pallor. He looked as though he were about to crumple and Holt jumped forward to steady him. At that precise moment a press camera flashed.

Hyde's face registered intense anger as he whirled on the press photographer behind him. 'How the hell did you get in here, Jenkins?'

'It's a free press, Inspector,' said Jenkins smugly, fitting another bulb into his camera and beating a cautious retreat.

Hyde suppressed his annoyance and turned again to Robert Scranton who asked for a glass of water and felt in his waistcoat pocket for a small silver capsule which contained pills.

'Be . . . okay in a moment . . . It's my heart . . .'

Presently a girl in uniform hurried over to him with the water, and as he took the pills he gave them all a beseeching glance. 'Don't tell Mother about this – not yet. Leave it to me . . . She's not very strong, you know.'

Holt nodded, and refrained from saying the obvious – that Scranton himself did not appear to be very strong either. To the Inspector Holt said quietly, 'Is there anything I can do to help? I expect you'll want them to accompany you up to Town now.'

'Quite so,' Hyde replied. 'There is one thing, though. I'd be most grateful if you could steer Mrs Scranton to the upstairs lounge and give her some strong tea. Just say her husband isn't feeling too well but will be joining her shortly. We'll take over from there.'

'You're sure that's all we can do?'

'I think so. Many thanks to you, Mr Holt. And please convey my thanks to Miss Sanders.'

Although Holt and Ruth discussed the incident on their way up to Town they did not seriously imagine that it would ever again touch their lives. It was only a chance drink on board a transatlantic plane that had brought Holt and Scranton together, and it was pure coincidence that Detective-Inspector Hyde had been put in charge of the case; had it been any other police officer it was unlikely that they would have been involved in the matter at all.

By the time Ruth had arrived at the Studio the following morning and they had begun to tackle the arrears of work, the previous day's events had been practically forgotten.

It was early afternoon, after a hurried lunch of sandwiches and milk, when the telephone rang.

Ruth answered it, then placed her hand over the mouthpiece and said with mild surprise, 'It's Robert Scranton. Are you at home?'

Holt looked at his half-cleared desk, made a wry face, then reached for the receiver.

'Mr Scranton? . . . Yes, this is Holt speaking. How did you know where to find me? . . . Oh, the telephone directory, of course! What can I do for you?'

A short conversation followed, in which Holt said little but continued to look perplexed. When he rang off Ruth looked at him expectantly, but he made no comment and stretched out his arm towards the cigarette box on the far side of his desk. He was attempting to cut down on smoking, if not to give it up entirely, but had soon discovered that Ruth's enthusiasm for this project was greater than his own. When she was present, abstinence usually triumphed, if only temporarily. She slid the box out of reach, silently, and waited for him to speak.

'Scranton wants to see me,' he said at last. 'At the Savoy.'

'On business? Does he want you to photograph his washing machines?'

'I don't think so. It's got something to do with his son. He says he has something to show me. Why me, I wonder?'

'Perhaps he needs a friend. Maybe he doesn't know anyone else in London.'

'I don't think that's the answer. He told me he comes over here pretty often, travels all over Europe, in fact.'

'Are you going?'

'What else could I say? I can't really spare the time, but somehow he made it sound quite urgent. His wife chipped in a word, too. Said she'd be eternally grateful if I'd spare them ten minutes. I could hardly refuse.'

He took his raincoat and hat from the hook and glanced at Ruth's desk. 'You've got enough to get on with till I get back?'

'Not if you're going to be away longer than three weeks,' came the dry reply.

Holt's laugh was a shade embarrassed as he descended the narrow staircase and let himself out through the street door. He sometimes wondered if he drove Ruth too hard. If so, she seemed to thrive on it. Women were funny creatures. On the whole, since his divorce, he had been happier without them. The trouble was, of course, he didn't really understand them . . .

Now a *car*, he thought, as he swung open the garage door and gazed with pride at his gleaming red Mustang – a car was something a man really *could* understand. No tantrums, no coy or inexplicable moods about those sleek and splendid beasts!

It was only a month or two since he had parted with his Lancia Flaminia, after barely a year's ownership, in favour of the Mustang, and he still experienced a feeling of exultation as he slid behind the wheel and fastened his safety belt. It was great to be back with the Mustang! . . . Now to the Savoy . . . Turn left, swing round beneath Big Ben, down on to the embankment, and a nice straight run to a parking spot near Waterloo Bridge. It would take him five minutes – well, it rather depended on police speed patrols . . .

He backed out carefully and then flicked on the specially-fitted racing speedometer with its wide sweeping secondhand. Say, four-and-a-half minutes!

Robert Scranton opened the door to his hotel suite almost immediately after Holt had knocked. He must have been waiting in the near vicinity.

They shook hands and Scranton offered Holt a drink. Then Mrs Scranton, dressed in severe black, came out of the adjoining room. She was very pale, but seemed composed and well able to help Holt over the awkward hurdle of expressing his condolences.

'Mr Holt, I won't try and describe to you what it means to lose your only son,' she said. 'We have two married daughters in the States, but a son . . . Anyway, we didn't bring you here to inflict our burden on you. Do sit down.'

'Mother's right,' Scranton said, handing Holt his drink. 'We've no right to waste your time. They say you're one of the most successful photographers in the country, so you must be a very busy man. I'll come straight to the point!' He strode to a table in the middle of the room and picked up a magazine. 'This is what I wanted to show you. It came by post this morning, just before lunch. It was addressed to us care of the hotel. I'll show you the wrapper – it's got a London postmark – but I don't think there's anything on it to help us.'

The magazine was called the *New Feature*. Holt knew of it, though he seldom read it. He looked at Scranton inquiringly.

'It's page eighteen that we're supposed to read,' Scranton said tensely.

Holt flicked over the pages, aware how intently they were

12

regarding him. Page eighteen carried only one article, with the heading 'Britain and Europe'. He scanned the paragraphs hurriedly, then his eye jumped to the author's name printed in discreet type at the foot of the page: PROSPERO.

Holt had no idea who Prospero might be, but the person who had sent the magazine evidently knew; the *nom de plume* had been underlined twice in green ink, and alongside was written the cryptic sentence:

If you want to know who murdered your son, ask Prospero.

Holt studied the handwriting for a moment, then asked, 'Was this all you received?'

'Yes, just that,' Scranton replied. 'We're been through it from cover to cover, haven't we, Mother? As for the article itself, it's kinda heavy going, if you know what I mean – politics, economics, and all that sort of thing. I don't think there's anything of significance in it for us.'

'And who is Prospero?'

'That's just it – we haven't been able to find out. I tried phoning this morning, but the magazine won't play. They seemed to be scared I wanted to challenge Prospero to a duel or something – maybe slap a libel suit on him.'

'How about the police, Mr Scranton? Shouldn't this copy of the magazine go to them anyway?'

Scranton, who had been sitting next to Holt as they studied the magazine, now stirred uneasily and glanced across at his wife sitting very erect in a highbacked armchair. She gave him a little nod of encouragement and he uncoiled his long, bony body and stood up.

He wore a dark suit, well-cut but of rather poor cloth, a

smart white shirt, and a dark tie. The face was lean, angular, and close shaven, and his iron-grey hair was cropped close to the skull. Holt got the impression of a pleasant, unpretentious businessman with little physical or intellectual vanity but plenty of shrewd commercial acumen.

With long, easy strides Scranton began pacing the room. 'I'll lay my cards on the table, Mr Holt, without any evasion – that way you can say straight out whether you like the proposition or not. The fact is, I want your help. *We* want it, Mother and me. We want your help and we're prepared to pay for it.'

'My help? In finding out who Prospero is?' asked Holt, puzzled. 'Well, I don't suppose that will be very difficult.'

'No, it's much more than that. I want to hire your services as a private investigator. I want you to find out who murdered my son. Isn't that right, Mother?'

Holt looked astounded and Mrs Scranton blushed slightly. 'Robert is very blunt, Mr Holt, you mustn't mind, it's just his way. But I can't tell you how grateful we'd be if we could enlist your help in getting to the bottom of this dreadful business.'

'But, Mrs Scranton, here in Britain we have an excellent police force and I'm sure they'll do everything necessary to find out—'

'Oh, they're doubtless very painstaking and honest,' Scranton interjected. 'If I'd lost a diamond ring or a pet poodle I'd be perfectly willing to leave things in their hands. But I haven't – I've lost a son! Brutally murdered as he sat at his books, boning up hard, trying to be a credit to us and the Faculty that awarded him that Exchange Scholarship from the States. Vance was a fine boy, Mr Holt, he had a big future ahead of him as a writer . . .'

'As a writer? Was that what he was studying?'

'No, not exactly. But that's how it turned out. He was doing courses in history, philosophy, economics – the whole works. I don't know if he would ever have made the grade as a writer; we never shall know now. To tell the honest truth, I'd always hoped he might get his feed-bag full and come back to the States one day, maybe help out on the sales side of our business . . . But we're getting off the point! Vance was our only son and we want to find out who shot him, and why. The police have got the case in hand, but those boys have got their hands full. They're swamped by the crime wave. Am I right?'

'What you say is true, but—'

'It's the same back in the States. There's someone murdered every few minutes, and half the crimes are never solved. The cops just can't keep pace with it all.'

'We'll co-operate all we can with the British police, and we know they'll do their best,' put in Mrs Scranton. 'But that's not enough. We want a private investigator who's only got one job on his hands – the job of nailing the man who shot Vance.'

Scranton stopped his pacing and turned to face Holt. 'Well, what do you say? Will you take the job?'

Holt chose his words carefully. 'You have my fullest sympathy, both of you – but . . . well, I'm afraid my answer has to be no. You see, I'm not a private investigator; I don't know who told you to the contrary. My business is photography. I dare say I could find out for you who this fellow Prospero is, but after that I can't imagine how I could help you.'

Robert Scranton smiled and took Holt's glass to the cocktail cabinet to replenish it. Over his shoulder he said, 'If I've never encountered the famous British reticence before I sure have run full tilt into it now! I can see I shall have to lay some more cards on the table. I don't have the full details, Mr Holt, but I heard you'd been pretty smart in solving a murder case last year, and—'

'Where did you hear that?' Holt asked sharply.

'Well, that's what Abe Jenkins told me.'

Holt sat up straight, genuinely puzzled. 'Who's Abe Jenkins?'

It was the American's turn to look surprised. 'You mean to say you don't know Abe Jenkins? He sure knows all about you – and not just the fact that you're a wow with a camera, either! He's the guy who got into the Customs Hall at the airport and took my picture, just when the Inspector broke the news.'

'And you liked that?' Holt said a trifle thinly.

'No, sir, not at all! Not at all! I felt good and mad when I realised what was going on, but by that time it was too late. Believe me, I was in no hurry to meet up with that guy again, but there he was at the morgue this morning when I was driven there to identify Vance's body. Jenkins is a crime reporter working for one of your big newspapers. He saw me talking to you at the airport yesterday, and this morning he asked me if I was thinking of hiring you.'

'Really, Robert! What a clumsy phrase!' Mrs Scranton reproved.

Her husband looked slightly abashed and mumbled an apology. 'That's how Jenkins said it, not me. I asked him what he meant and – well, he kinda led me to believe you were a private investigator.'

Abe Jenkins had evidently done a good deal of nosing around, Holt reflected, for the part he and Ruth had played in the case had been given little or no publicity, owing to its rather unorthodox character. 'Remarkable,' he said bitterly. 'Tell me, Mr Scranton: did this Abe Jenkins chap pass himself off as a friend of mine?'

'No, as a matter of fact he did not! To tell the truth, I almost got the impression that he doesn't like you at all.'

'But I've never done him any harm – I don't even know the fellow!'

'Could it be professional jealousy, Mr Holt? You've reached the top of your profession in the photographic world, whereas he still appears to be lugging a press camera around in search of lucky snapshots. He also seems to fancy himself as a crime reporter and amateur sleuth, so it isn't hard to understand his feelings when one Philip Holt beat him to it in that field as well.'

'I begin to see a little more daylight,' said Holt slowly. He reached into his pocket for his cigarette case, then thought better of it and thrust it resolutely back. 'I wonder how Jenkins happened to be at the airport yesterday. Was that pure chance, do you think?'

'No, his editor sent him down to Deanfriston because he thought the story was right up Jenkins' alley. Now we'd sent Vance a cable telling him what flight we were coming on, and Jenkins somehow got a look at that cable. We'd kinda hoped Vance would be at the airport to meet us . . .' He broke off as he glanced at his wife and noticed the effect his words had had upon her. 'Now then, Mother,' he began soothingly, '. . . you promised yourself no tears, remember . . . ?'

To avoid the pitiful and embarrassing scene, Holt rose quietly, took the copy of the *New Feature*, and discreetly said his farewells. 'I'll do what I can with regard to this Prospero business,' he promised.

Scranton accompanied him to the door. His tone was low and serious as they shook hands. 'Think my offer over, Mr Holt. You can go places where the police can't – you're an outsider, an unknown, a sort of lone agent, if you see what I mean. If it's money you're worried about, just name your own price. Mother and I will go to any lengths to find out who did this terrible thing to our son.'

Awkwardly Holt released his hand from the American's powerful grip. 'I'll make no promises, but I'll certainly think it over. You'll hear from me very soon.'

'Thanks a million, Mr Holt!'

Chapter Two

Inspector Hyde settled himself comfortably at his desk and lit his pipe. 'I'm very glad that you've decided to come in on the case, Mr Holt,' he said between puffs. 'You were a great help to us last time and your assistance would be very welcome, certainly.'

'Well – I haven't finally decided,' Holt told him. 'My chief reason for coming here this morning is to hand you this copy of the *New Feature* I mentioned on the telephone. The poison-pen insinuation is on page eighteen.'

The Inspector took the magazine and with the aid of a large magnifying-glass examined the sentence written in green ink. Then he took something from a file on his desk and made a further study of that through the glass. From where Holt sat, it looked as if it might be a greetings card of some kind.

'H'm . . . Yes . . .' Hyde mumbled to himself. 'There's certainly a similarity. Of course, I'm not an expert in these things but I should think we're on to something there.'

'On to what?'

'M'm . . . ?' the Inspector murmured absently, locking the file in a drawer. Holt fidgeted in his seat. 'Now come off it,

Inspector!' he said with a smile. 'Don't try that hoary old cat-and-mouse game with me.'

'I thought you hadn't decided to come in on the case, Mr Holt.'

'I hardly know anything about it yet,' Holt protested.

'Quite so . . . Now why not listen to a short summary of the facts as we've so far been able to assemble them, and then – well, let us say, favour me with your observations?'

'Fair enough!'

'Good! We'll begin with the murder itself. Last Monday, some time between ten o'clock and midnight, or maybe a little after, an unknown assailant walked into the study where Vance Scranton was sitting at his books and shot him at very close range with a weapon of heavy calibre. The boy must have been killed instantly; most of his head was blown off. There were two unused glasses and an unopened bottle of port lying on the carpet near him.'

'Unopened?' Holt interrupted. 'And the glasses were dry? It sounds as if he'd been expecting someone – either the murderer or a friend.'

'There's a third possibility: that the murderer *was* a friend. Whoever it was must have known that Vance was studying late and been reasonably sure that all the other students' rooms in the passage – they call it Scholars' Row – were empty. So chance murder, or an assailant unknown to Vance, can be ruled out almost entirely. There were no signs of violence other than the ghastly effects of the gunshot – the room wasn't ransacked, the boy's wallet was intact. The only thing that appears to be missing is a signet ring which he generally wore on his left hand. We're checking up as to whether he'd been wearing it at the time or whether he'd simply lost it.'

'I see,' said Holt. 'Now if I may pop in a question – what was he studying at the time of the murder? I mean, what was on his desk?'

'That's an interesting point,' Hyde said with approval. 'He was writing a piece of fiction, a short story I should imagine. He was supposed to be reading History and Economics but his inclinations seem to have been on the literary side. Some of his stories have even been accepted, by rather *avant-garde* magazines. Frankly, I can't make head nor tail of them myself, but a chap on the Assistant Commissioner's staff tells me they belong to the "stream of consciousness" school, whatever that may be.'

Holt nodded. 'I know what you mean. I'm afraid it's not my cup of tea, though. Let's get back to Monday night. How did the murderer get into the College?'

'It was simple. The wing they call Scholars' Row is never locked. We imagine that the murderer just walked in, opened Vance's door, and as the boy straightened up from getting out the port and glasses for his visitor our murderer fired at point blank range. Then the murderer had only to pocket the gun, walk out of Scholars' Row, and disappear into the fog.'

'There was fog? Don't forget, I was out of the country at the time.'

'Oh, yes, it was a filthy night. No one was about. Traffic along the coast between Hastings and Brighton came to a complete standstill, so the reports say.'

'I wonder if that affected our murderer. Did he drive away from the scene of his crime, or leave on foot?'

Hyde shook his head. 'That line of inquiry is a dead loss, we've tried it. By the way, don't be too sure the murderer was masculine. There's absolutely nothing to confirm that. It could just as easily have been a woman.'

21

'I'd have thought Deanfriston would be out of bounds to women; it's an all-male College.'

'So it is. But Monday night was an exception. There was a piano recital and some of the students had invited their girlfriends along for the evening. The sight of a girl in Scholars' Row wouldn't have been especially remarkable.'

'Did Vance Scranton have any girlfriends?'

'Two, apparently. And they both hated each other! He had two girlfriends but he doesn't appear to have had any real friends amongst the young men at the College. This strikes me as rather unusual. We haven't had time yet to check on all possible alibis, but on the face of it it looks as though Vance's fellow-students were all at the concert. That he was alone and still working seems to be rather typical of his character – an odd ball, a "loner" as I think the Americans put it. A loner and an intellectual.'

'I wonder why he had no friends. Was he unhappy over here? I suppose he didn't commit suicide, by any chance?'

Inspector Hyde shook his head. 'You forget – no weapon was found.'

'Of course. Stupid of me.'

'No, I don't think there's any evidence to show that Vance was unhappy. It seems more likely that his manner tended to repel friendship. As far as I can make out, he was a rather arrogant sort of fellow. Two or three students I questioned called him an intellectual snob, and his Professor described him as a neo-Fascist. No, I think Vance Scranton was a loner because he wanted to be, because he just didn't care for the company of his fellow-men.'

'But he did have two girlfriends?'

'Yes. Julie Benson and Antoinette Sheen.'

'Have you met them?'

'Yes. They were called to identify the body. Julie Benson fainted. She's a blonde – pretty, fluffy little thing, about eighteen or nineteen. She was engaged to Vance at one time; it seems he discarded her rather brutally.'

'Which she didn't like at all, I suppose?'

'When I could get her between fainting fits she seemed pretty bitter about the affair, yes.'

'Well, that has been known to be a motive for murder . . . But surely a fluffy little blonde given to fainting couldn't be capable of a gruesome shooting like this?'

Hyde shrugged his shoulders and a tiny smile played at the corners of his mouth. 'When I was a young man, Mr Holt – when I was a young man, it was often my experience that the fluffy, blue-eyed little blondes were the most cruel and calculating wenches of them all!' Holt laughed, and Hyde hastened to add, 'Now don't misunderstand me – at this stage I'm definitely not suggesting anything other than keeping an open mind about *all* possibilities and a sharp look-out for a *motive*.'

'Fair enough. Why was the engagement broken off?'

'Antoinette Sheen,' Hyde replied succinctly.

'I see. And what is she like – also blonde and fluffy?'

The Inspector smiled, broadly this time, and rolled his eyes in an unexpectedly frivolous gesture. 'She's neither! She's about as different from Julie as chalk from cheese. Very beautiful, very poised, and will definitely not see twenty-five again.'

'Antoinette Sheen . . .' Holt mused. 'That name rings a bell, but I can't quite place it.'

'By profession she's a novelist,' Hyde explained. 'Somewhat lurid historical romances, I gather.'

'Ah, yes, of course. Are they successful?'

'That would appear to be the case. At any rate, she supports herself by her writing. She has a mind of her own, she knows what she wants out of life, and I should guess she gets it. By hobby she's a painter. She says her friendship with Vance was based purely on their common interest in the Arts. Myself – well, I'm a staid old married man, of course, but I must say if I'd been in Vance's shoes I'd have been interested in other aspects of Miss Sheen's personality! To be perfectly frank, she's really rather stunning!'

'H'm . . .' Holt said, raising his eyebrows. 'And what does Julie Benson do for a living?'

'She's secretary to Professor Harold Dalesford, lecturer in Political Economy up at the College.'

'Does that mean Vance was one of his students?'

'Yes, he was.'

'What about their alibis? The two girls, I mean.'

'Well . . .' Hyde paused and fiddled with the orderly row of pencils lined up on his neat and impersonal desk. 'As you may remember, I prefer to proceed cautiously in these matters; it never pays to jump to conclusions. But I'll commit myself so far as to say that I don't like either of their stories. Julie Benson claimed that she was working late for Professor Dalesford on the night of the murder – which he denies. He was at the piano recital. Julie's the sweet-voiced, English rose type, but I'm afraid that doesn't prevent her from being a very bad liar.'

'Interesting,' observed Holt. 'And Miss Sheen?'

'She was at the College that night too. She attended the piano recital.'

'Alone, or with someone?'

'With Professor Dalesford.'

'With her rival's boss? Funny set-up. One more question:

how far from Scholars' Row is the room or hall where this piano recital was held?'

Hyde said, completely wooden-faced, 'It would take you about four or five minutes to get from one to the other.'

A silence followed, whilst the Inspector cleaned and refilled his pipe and Holt pondered on the problem. The younger man was obviously intrigued, and Hyde judged that very little more would be needed to succeed in trapping his interest entirely.

'The boy would have celebrated his twenty-first birthday if he'd lived another day. I think it shows what a loner he was, that on this day of all days there were only two birthday cards for him.' He got out the Scranton file once more. 'Perhaps you'd like to have a look at those greetings cards?'

Holt examined them carefully. 'From Antoinette . . . My, what a lot of flourishes! The card's in good taste, though. And Julie . . . a forlorn attempt to attract her ex-fiancé's attention maybe? . . . But wait a moment! I wonder . . . Could I have a look at the . . .'

The Inspector was already sliding his magnifying glass and the *New Feature*, opened at page eighteen, across the desk.

Holt compared the signature on Julie Benson's card with the handwriting at the foot of the Prospero article. 'You're right,' he said after a moment. 'I should think we're definitely on to something there! It'll be interesting to see what your calligraphy experts have to say.'

'And while they're at it,' Hyde said, holding out a postcard, 'they can take a look at this too.'

It was a plain postcard of the type that can be bought in a sixpenny packet at any stationer's. It was postmarked

Harrogate and had been sent to Vance Scranton at the College. The message, printed in neat, well-spaced block capitals, was simple; all it said was:

HAVING A WONDERFUL TIME.
REGARDS FROM CHRISTOPHER.

'Well, at least Vance had a friend somewhere.'

Hyde shook his head. 'That's just where the mystery starts. There *is* no Christopher – or at least, we can't trace him.'

'That's odd.'

'Nobody we've questioned – and we've been through just about the entire student body – has ever heard him mention anyone by the name of Christopher. Julie Benson doesn't know him, nor does Miss Sheen; we drew a blank with all the professors and lecturers on the teaching faculty, and his parents can't throw any light on the matter either.'

'That's strange. Do you think it's important?'

'It's too early to say. We'll have to wait for the lab's report on the postcard.'

'You begin to intrigue me, Inspector.'

'I was hoping I would. To be quite frank, I'd be very glad of your help. The Scranton case isn't the only one I have on my plate at the moment. We're just about snowed under.' He paused for a fraction of a second, then went on, 'I don't want to ask for too much of your time; you're a very busy man, I know. But – well, there is one specific job – a very small job – it shouldn't take up a great deal of . . .'

'Perhaps you'd tell me what it is?'

Now that he had reached the point in the conversation at which he had been aiming, the Inspector became surprisingly hesitant. Clearing his throat he muttered, 'This is

all very unorthodox, of course, and if you should get into
trouble there's no guarantee that the Yard would be able
to . . .'

'What do I have to do, Inspector?'

'Talk to Curly,' was the unexpected reply.

'Curly? Who's Curly?'

'He's an old lag. If he or any of his pals saw me coming
they'd take off faster than a space rocket from Cape Kennedy!
But he owes me a good turn. He was up on a charge of
receiving stolen goods some years ago, and I didn't feel it
was entirely his fault so I used my influence to get him off
a very stiff sentence. I've never asked a favour in return, and
he isn't one of our regular informers.'

'But you think he might be of some use in this particular
case?'

Hyde raised his hands and made a grimace of despair.
'What is one to do? There has to be a starting point some-
where. And Curly *was* caught in the net.'

'What net?'

Hyde crossed to the window, which commanded a some-
what cheerless view of an inner courtyard. 'Look at it from
the police point of view, Holt. A perfectly innocuous American
student gets his face blown off and the murderer slips out
unseen into thick mist, leaving no clues. No fingerprints, no
weapon, no witnesses, no motive. There are some shaky alibis
on the part of two girls, but otherwise there's absolutely
nothing for the police to go on. But we've got to start our
investigations somewhere, so we throw out a net and haul
into it all the dubious characters who were within a short
radius of Deanfriston on the night of the murder. Naturally,
not one in a hundred actually has anything to do with the
crime, but they talk – they talk amongst themselves, little

splinters of information pass from mouth to mouth . . . Now, in that net there are one or two characters with a foot in both camps.'

'Your informers?'

'Quite so.'

Holt nodded. 'So Curly, who owes you a favour from times gone by, was caught in the net the night Vance Scranton was murdered, and you have an idea that he knows something about the case?'

'Correct. Unfortunately, Curly is sitting on his tongue. He refuses to talk. But they tell me he looks very uncomfortable whenever anyone mentions Vance Scranton or Deanfriston College.

'And what's Curly's alibi?'

'Oh, he's too much of a professional to let us catch him out. His alibi's no better and no worse than that of twenty others we pulled in. But he knows something, I'm certain.'

'And you'd like me to find out what it is – by jogging his memory and reminding him that he's still morally in your debt?'

'Exactly. You see how unorthodox it is – you see why it's something I can't undertake myself?' There was a pause. 'Will you do it?'

Holt nodded. 'I'll do it!'

'Right! I'll give you the details of Curly's background in a moment,' Hyde said briskly. 'Now, how to find Curly and how to recognise him. His passion is horse racing. He spends most of his time in racing circles – stables, pubs favoured by jockeys and trainers, betting shops, and so on. On the night after the murder we picked him up in Brighton, but he's back in London now, so the grapevine has it. I don't think he'll be hard to find, but he may be devilish hard to pin down. He's as slippery as a weasel, and he can move incredibly fast despite his size.'

'He's a big man, I gather. How else can I recognise him?'

For answer Inspector Hyde produced a yellow envelope and extracted three photographs: full face, left profile, and right profile.

'Good grief!' Holt exclaimed. 'Now I know why he's called Curly!'

Chapter Three

No one looked up or paid them any attention as they entered the betting parlour in Tottenham Court Road. Holt wore his oldest flannels and a faded sports jacket repaired with leather at cuffs and elbows, and Ruth had taken special pains to look dowdy, which was no easy task for one of her bright colouring and sparkling personality.

When they had started their tour of the betting parlours they had felt acutely self-conscious and as a result had attracted much unwanted attention. But now, at their fourth attempt, they had grown accustomed to the seedy, half-feverish and half-weary atmosphere of a betting shop, to the smell of stale cigarette smoke and body-sweat, the petty triumphs and minor tragedies, the raucous clerks in shirt-sleeves, and the incessant jangling of the telephone. With the nonchalance of seasoned gamblers they strolled in, pulled crumpled newspapers from under their arms, and leaned against the wall, alongside unshaven taxi-drivers, barrow boys, shop assistants, petty crooks, and aimless drifters. Folding their newspapers into professionally neat squares, they took out pencils and 'studied form'.

This was an occasion when Ruth even went so far as to approve of Holt smoking. He lit a cigarette and squinted through a haze at a man chalking up runners' names and their odds on a greasy blackboard which ran the width of the far wall. Now and again Holt jotted down figures, and his head jerked with interest whenever the loudspeaker crackled and news from the track was announced. His performance was masterly and for a moment Ruth almost believed her boss had developed a genuine interest in betting.

Then he nudged her carelessly and tapped his paper. 'Seen anything you like?'

'Not really. Have you?'

'Yes, I reckon so!'

'Which race?'

He pointed at the newspaper with his pencil.

He had drawn some kind of diagram, Ruth realised. She took the paper from him. 'I just hope you're right, that's all,' she said woodenly. 'We've wasted enough time as it is.'

'Not any more, we haven't!' Holt ground out his cigarette on the filthy floor and strolled towards the blackboard as if for a closer look at the columns of odds.

Though outwardly calm, Ruth's heart was beating rapidly. The diagram indicated that the man they were looking for, Curly the ex-convict, was seated less than two yards away. Holt had sketched a bird's-eye plan of the betting parlour and marked a bench on which sat four men. He had picked out the nearest with an arrow and the letter C.

Ruth did not dare to look directly at the bench. For a moment she pretended to search for Holt, now realising that he had gone to the blackboard in order to get a better view of their quarry as he made his return. Then, with her back

31

to the bench, she took out her compact and peered into it, dabbling crudely at her face with the powder puff. Presently, Curly came into view through the mirror.

He wore no hat, and his huge head was shaped like a bladder of lard, utterly devoid of hair. The great dome of skin did not gleam; it had a curious, unhealthy colour resembling putty. The rest of the features were on a scale commensurate: staring eyes, flaring nostrils, and large ears lying like flaps close to the skull. A pair of deathly-pale hands the size of North Sea haddock hung listlessly over his knee-caps. They were the biggest hands Ruth had ever seen in her life. Despite his attitude of placid disinterest, she sensed a tense watchfulness just beneath the surface. The total effect of the man was frightening, and she knew that if she had bumped into him under a lamp-post on a dark night she would have screamed and run.

Holt wandered back, a fresh cigarette in his mouth; it flapped crudely up and down as he spoke. 'Well, girl, what you think?'

'Could be. Shall we take a risk?'

'I reckon we can't lose.'

'I hope you're right.'

'Don't worry, girl! It's a dead cert!'

At the precise moment when Holt turned and was making a determined move towards Curly a taxi-driver in a voluminous coat barged past and the two collided.

'Ain't yer got no eyes, mate?' the driver bawled.

'Oh – I'm dreadfully sorry, I'm afraid I was—' Holt began, then checked himself.

The cab-driver swore, Holt bent to pick up the newspaper that had been knocked out of his hand, and when he straightened up Curly was nowhere to be seen.

'Quick!' Holt directed, and thrust his way out, Ruth hard on his heels.

They were just in time to see Curly's bulk spring with astonishing agility onto a passing bus. For a matter of two or three seconds, until his view was blocked by another vehicle, Curly stood on the conductor's platform, looking back at them with pale, piercing eyes. Then he was gone.

Holt stood at the pavement edge and swore quietly.

'What on earth do you suppose frightened him off?' Ruth asked.

'God knows,' Holt muttered through his teeth, 'but we certainly muffed that one, didn't we!'

'Where will he head for, do you think?'

'Out of Town, I imagine. Hyde said he takes off like a space rocket when he smells trouble. Obviously he smelt trouble. Hey, where are you going?'

Ruth gave no answer, but herself took off like a space rocket and disappeared into the betting shop once more. Holt hesitated, then decided not to follow her; she was obviously following a hunch of her own.

A few moments later she came out, radiant, and swung off towards Oxford Street. He hurried to join her.

'Don't call a cab!' she commanded airily. 'We might be followed! Let's take the Tube.'

'Okay, Ruth – whatever you say!' Holt's tense features relaxed into a smile. 'I can see you've achieved something by going back into that revolting place. What is it?'

'Yes, they are depressing, aren't they?' she said loftily, deliberately ignoring his question. 'Fancy calling it "the Sport of Kings". I've never seen anything less royal or sporting in my life! Give me a real live horse race any day, but betting by remote control – well, it's simply—'

'Ruth! You're holding out on me!'

She relented and grew serious. She said quietly, 'Curly will be at the Brighton Races tomorrow. I'm willing to stake a month's salary on it.'

'How on earth do you know that?' he asked, astounded.

Ruth grinned, and adopting an appalling accent said, 'I just went in and yelled, "Anyone 'ere know where that swine Curly's got to? I'll boil 'im in oil when I find 'im!" – Men like those deadbeats in there are quite used to the sight of a screaming shrew hunting for her bloke. – "Try the Brighton track tomorrow, darlin'. 'E's bound to be there." And look, Philip, just to clinch matters, I found this betting sheet on the bench where he was sitting. It lists the runners at Brighton tomorrow. Curly seems to have marked some of his favourites. So, it's a fair bet, don't you think?'

'My word! You really are rather bright at times, Miss Sanders,' said Holt with amusement.

'I try to please,' she answered with an impudent grin.

The rest of the day was devoted to hard work at the Studio in Westminster; Holt in the dark-room, Ruth retouching black and white prints under a powerful desk lamp. It was getting late when they decided to pack up.

'Get your coat and I'll drive you home,' Holt said.

'No, don't bother. I can easily get a bus.'

The ringing of the street door bell forestalled any further argument.

'Who the heck can that be at this time?' Holt sighed.

Ruth ran down the steep stairs and opened the door to the street. A dapper little man with a neat moustache and a flashing smile whipped off his bowler hat and said with studied politeness, 'My name is Wade. Jimmy Wade. I must apologise for calling so late, but I wonder if Mr Holt is at home?'

'Well . . .' Ruth hesitated. 'Is it about a portrait?'

'No. Oh, no. Perhaps I may be so blunt as to say straight out that it has to do with Vance Scranton.'

There was a pregnant pause, then Holt's voice came crisply from the top of the stairs. 'Ruth, please show Mr Wade up.'

A brief pantomine took place in which Ruth tried to persuade Mr Wade to enter so that she could shut the door behind him, whilst he insisted with a series of gallant bows that ladies should go first.

When the visitor finally reached the head of the stairs Holt greeted him a little coolly. He did not offer to shake hands but asked bluntly, 'Are you a friend of Vance Scranton's, Mr Wade?'

'Well, no, not really. But I knew him quite well, in a manner of speaking, and—'

'Well I never met the boy, so perhaps you'd tell me how you happened to connect him with me?'

Jimmy Wade gave a quick, nervous smile and darted a hand into his breast pocket for his wallet. 'It's very simple, Mr Holt. This postcard came to my flat this morning and I took it at once to the Scrantons, whom I knew were staying at the Savoy. They suggested I showed it at once to you. If I may say so, it seemed at the time rather a sensible suggestion.'

'I see.'

Holt took the proffered postcard. It was addressed to Julie Benson, but was in all other respects similar to the card which Inspector Hyde had shown him the day before, and the message was identical:

HAVING A WONDERFUL TIME.
REGARDS FROM CHRISTOPHER.

The postmark was Harrogate, and it had been stamped on the previous day.

'Who is this Christopher?' Holt asked casually.

Mr Wade's rubicund features creased into an apologetic smile. 'I only wish I could tell you. Nobody seems to know. The police have given poor Julie a dreadful time, hammering away at her about that wretched name.'

'How do you know that?' Holt asked.

Mr Wade blinked, somewhat taken aback. But in a moment he was all smiles again. 'Oh, I must apologise – I should have explained. Julie Benson is my sister-in-law. I really should have begun there, I suppose.' He glanced from Holt to Ruth and back again. He had liquid dark eyes like a thrush and all his movements were bird-like – a quick peck at some tasty morsel, a rapid glance to left and right. 'I married Julie's sister – or you could say her sister married me. They say it's generally the lady who really makes the decisions, don't they?'

Ruth gave him a cosy smile and offered him a chair. 'May I ask you, Mr Wade,' she said, at the same time taking his raincoat and hat, 'is it common knowledge that your sister-in-law is staying with you? Or is this only known to a limited number of people?'

For some curious reason this question, which Ruth had intended quite harmlessly, seemed to throw Wade into a mild state of consternation. His complexion turned even redder, the wallet he was holding slipped to the floor, and he muttered a series of incoherent phrases which totally failed to make a sentence.

Holt came to the rescue. 'My secretary has a point there, Mr Wade; I can see what she's aiming at. From what I've been given to understand, Julie lives in Deanfriston and works for a Professor at the College there. How did Christopher know she was to be reached at your London address?'

'Ah! Ah, yes – yes, indeed! Well, you see, whenever Julie's in Town she stays with me – I mean with us, at Honor Oak.'

'Where is Honor Oak, exactly?'

'Just next door to Lewisham – a very different class of locality, if I may say so.'

'Yes, yes, of course,' Holt soothed in an attempt to dismiss the matter of the area's prestige. 'Now, if we can narrow the field down to those people who know Miss Benson stays with you at Honor Oak, then it might help us to run the elusive Christopher to earth.'

Wade blinked rapidly. His hand dived into his pocket and whipped out a silver cigarette case. Everything was done at top speed, and accompanied by a bewildering variety of ingratiating smiles. 'I follow you, Mr Holt, indeed I do! Oh yes, I'm with you all the way. I only wish I could be more helpful. But the trouble is, if I may say so, that literally scores of people know that Julie is to be found with her sister when she's not at Deanfriston. Just about everyone at the College, for a start. I'm afraid there's nothing much to help us there.'

Mr Wade offered his cigarette case. Ruth refused with a smile and, as he turned to Holt, she added sternly, 'Mr Holt is trying to give it up – aren't you, Mr Holt?'

Holt gave a brief acknowledgement to Wade and went on, 'Tell me: what does your sister-in-law make of this post-card from Harrogate?'

'Julie? Well – er – I trust you'll pardon my somewhat high-handed action, but as a matter of fact I haven't shown it to her.'

'*You haven't shown it to her?* But it's addressed to her!'

'No, well, you see . . . Julie wasn't there this morning

when . . . Yes, well – I saw the mail before anyone else and . . . if I may say so, there's no point in causing additional worry, is there?'

Holt frowned. 'I don't quite understand you. What were your reasons for not showing Miss Benson the card?'

'If you'll pardon the expression, Julie's had enough!'

Both Holt and Ruth stiffened. There was a perceptible change in Wade's manner; he had grown firm and even a little pompous.

'She's really been through the mill!' he went on. 'The police gave her a dreadful time on Tuesday, trying to trip her up over her alibi. If you ask me, they're a lot of blundering idiots, throwing their weight around and trying to scare an innocent girl into saying something foolish! . . . It's quite ridiculous – Julie wouldn't hurt a fly! The police ought to have the decency to see that and leave her alone!' Wade's face was now brick-red with anger and he puffed at his cigarette in short, aggressive bursts.

Ruth spoke to him soothingly. 'I'm sure you're right, Mr Wade. I don't suppose the police really meant to cause her any distress.'

Mr Wade was not listening. '. . . As if she'd go and shoot the chap she was once in love with!'

'It has been known,' Holt commented quietly.

Wade turned to protest and Ruth slipped in quickly, 'I agree with Mr Wade – the idea's unthinkable. But the police have to do their job, you know. It's their duty to check everyone's alibi.'

He began to cool down and tossed a thankful smile in her direction. 'I must say, I wish you were the one who had carried out the police interrogation, my dear. I can see you wouldn't have upset her. As it is, the poor girl's just a bundle of nerves. First Vance breaks off the engagement, then he gets himself killed, and then the police practically put her through the third degree. She's absolutely innocent, she was nowhere near Vance's study when he was shot.'

'But how do you *know* that?' Holt asked again.

'How do I know? Well, because she said so, that's enough for me! A pretty little thing like that doesn't go around telling lies, that I can assure you.' His smile flashed on and off like a neon sign.

'I see.' Holt's tone was thin. 'And so, to save her further worry, you intercepted her post and took it straight to the Scrantons?'

'Yes. I thought they ought to see it. Also, in that way no one could accuse me of trying to conceal evidence, or anything like that. I've always been very careful where the law's concerned. You have to be, in my profession.'

'What is your profession, if I may ask?'

'I'm a representative.'

'For whom?'

Mr Wade coughed and two or three conflicting expressions fought for pride of place on his cherubic face. 'I represent one of the largest firms of funeral directors in the country. We arrange everything, from floral tributes to a wide choice of tasteful gravestones and suitable inscriptions. Here's my card.' His hand sped to his wallet and a visiting card appeared at conjuror's speed. 'Well, I think I'll be running along.' He stood up. 'Perhaps you'd care to take possession of the post-card, Mr Holt?'

'Yes, I'll look after it. Just let me ask you a couple of questions before you go, Mr Wade. You mentioned that Vance Scranton broke off his engagement with Miss Benson. What happened – was there a quarrel?'

'It's perfectly simple. Vance was a pleasant enough lad until he met Antoinette Sheen. He and Julie always got on well together. But this sophisticated painter-woman soon changed all that. She's ten years older, for one thing. He became harsh and cynical – a sort of worldly cynicism that just didn't sit well on a twenty-year-old boy.'

'And you put down this change to Miss Sheen's influence?'

'There's no doubt about it! From the moment he met her Vance was a changed person. In a very short time he'd broken off his engagement to Julie and after that you just couldn't talk to him. He'd always been, if you'll pardon the expression, rather a self-opinionated young man. Of course, one expects a certain amount of that in undergraduates, and they generally get away with it because they have the natural charm of youth at the same time. But Vance wasn't in the least charming once he came under Antoinette Sheen's spell.'

Ruth held Wade's coat ready for him to slip into and another pantomime followed before he could be persuaded to accept this simple courtesy from a lady; and a subsequent polite argument as to who should be allowed to open the street door took all of three or four minutes.

'What an extraordinary little man!' observed Ruth as she climbed the stairs after seeing him off the premises. 'I almost expected him to drive away in a hearse, but he runs a Volkswagen of a particularly nauseating shade of blue.'

'If I may say so, and if you'll pardon the expression, I should have thought black would be more suitable,' Holt said in fair mimicry of their visitor's ingratiating tones.

'And if I may say so,' Ruth imitated, 'isn't it a pity that Mr Jimmy Wade is such a terrible liar!'

The smile left Holt's face abruptly. 'Go on, Ruth . . .'

'Well, I don't know if he's lying about the Christopher

postcard – he could quite easily have written it himself – but I'm sure he hasn't told a fraction of the truth about his sister-in-law's alibi.'

'My, you're on form tonight, aren't you? I spotted that myself. It's much too glib to say that because she's a sweet little thing and the police are a lot of boorish oafs, Julie always tells the truth. For my money, Jimmy Wade *knows* where she was at the time of Vance Scranton's death.'

'Then why the dickens doesn't he tell Hyde and clear the girl?'

'That, if I may use the expression, is the sixty-four thousand dollar question! And who is this Christopher fellow? Come to that – who killed Vance Scranton?'

'All of which we're determined to find out!'

'Yes. Yes, indeed.'

'Well, what's the first move?'

'I'm not sure. We'll start by asking Curly at Brighton tomorrow.'

Chapter Four

The 'Sport of Kings', in crisp autumnal sunshine at Brighton the following afternoon, seemed much more royal and exhilarating than in the seedy London betting shop. Ruth had won five pounds at the Tote and was in high spirits. So engrossed had she become in the colourful spectacle around her that the object of their journey – the search for Curly – had very nearly slipped her mind. She was to be forgiven, however, for it was her first visit to a large race-track.

Holt was content to let her display her enthusiasm, for her genuine interest in the races served to disguise his own preoccupation. They had dressed in sporty tweeds and Holt wore a powerful pair of field-glasses slung around his neck in addition to his usual photographic equipment. Ostensibly he used the binoculars to follow the horses as they rounded distant bends in the track, but in fact he more often trained them on the faces of the crowd in the Grandstand and the various enclosures. And although he went to the paddock at the beginning of each race, apparently to form an opinion of the runners, he spent more time glancing idly at the spectators than in appraising horse or jockey.

It was just after the start of the fourth race that he

announced suddenly in a low, tense murmur, 'Got him!'

'Where?' asked Ruth without taking her eyes off the horses as they swept in a tight pack into the first bend.

'The last place you'd expect. He must have come into money recently. He's sitting in the Grandstand – fairly high, near the back – at about two o'clock from the centre. Here, take my glasses.'

Ruth adjusted the binoculars and scanned the Grandstand slowly. Her heart gave a queer leap as the dull white expanse of Curly's head swam into focus. Suddenly he turned and his pale eyes seemed to stare straight at her. Startled, she lowered the binoculars and pretended to engage Holt in lively conversation. It was ridiculous – he was at least five hundred yards away – and yet she had the uncanny feeling that those great eyes were boring into the back of her neck.

'What do we do now?' she whispered.

'We watch the race,' replied Holt calmly, retrieving the binoculars. 'I've placed two pounds for you on a French nag. It's an outsider, but I liked the look of it in the paddock. Number Seven. There she goes, look – moving up on the inside rail!'

Ruth was drawn back into the surging excitement of the race. Order was emerging from the confusion of brilliant jockey colours, flying hooves, the gleam of equine muscle strained to the uttermost. Three runners began to press to the front of the tight field, and the crowd rose with a mounting wave of excitement. Ruth found herself waving and shouting for Number Seven. The horses thundered round the final bend and down the home stretch. Number Seven inched forward – first a nose, then a neck, then half a length, and by the time it had flashed past the finishing post it was showing a wild pair of heels to its two nearest rivals.

'Philip, you're fantastic!' Ruth cried, quite forgetting herself and throwing her arms round his neck. 'You must have a nose for winners! How much is my booty?'

'Something in the neighbourhood of forty pounds, I think. And what's more,' he added, turning from the Grandstand and lowering his glasses, 'Curly's looking pleased with himself too. I think this is the right moment for us to get chummy! Let's get your money and then we'll seek him out.'

They jostled their way through the crowd towards the Totalisator and stood in the queue at one of the windows. They had barely reached the head of the queue and collected Ruth's winnings when Holt stiffened, gave a tense, silent nod of the head, and broke from the line.

'Philip, wait for me!' Ruth wailed, scurrying after him.

'Come on! I've just spotted Curly!'

Holt was tall enough to keep his target in sight as they weaved through the crowd, but for Ruth it was simply a question of hanging on to her boss's sleeve.

'Hold it! He's stopping. Don't let him see us!' Holt rapped out urgently.

They took cover in the lee of a programme seller as Curly went up to a thin, raffish-looking man somehow clearly stamped with the hallmark of a bookmaker. Reluctantly the bookie produced his wallet and took out several five-pound notes. Curly's great hand closed over the money like a bull-dozer's grab. For a few moments the two men remained in conversation, just out of earshot, and Holt discreetly slipped his Olympus Pen F camera from his pocket and took a snap of the couple; then Curly slapped the bookie on the back, glanced furtively around him, and strode with giant steps into the crowd where only the putty-coloured dome of his head remained visible.

'Where's he going, I wonder?' Holt set off in pusuit. 'This isn't the way back to the Grandstand.'

'As far as I can see it'll take us to the car park.'

It was indeed the car park for which Curly was aiming. Had he won such a large sum on the last race that he was content for the day? What if he drove off before they could pin him down? . . . Holt quickened his pace – only to realise with sudden dismay that Curly was no longer in sight. One moment he had been there, towering above the ranks of parked cars, and the next instant he had vanished.

'Now how the hell did that happen! Hyde said he was as slippery as a weasel, but that beats everything!'

Ruth shook her head in bewilderment. 'What do we do now?'

From the distance came the excited roar of the crowd at the race-course, but in the vast car park there was not a soul to be seen.

Despondently they stared around them and discussed the situation, reaching no decision. Holt lit a cigarette, without protest from Ruth. He threw away the match and thrust his hands deep into his coat pockets . . .

'Lookin' for someone?' a deep voice growled from behind them.

They whirled round. Ten paces away, leaning nonchalantly against a mini-bus, stood Curly with a gun in his hand.

Ruth choked back a cry of alarm.

Holt gripped her elbow and said coolly, 'Yes, Curly. We were looking for you.'

'Thought so. Smelt it yesterday, when you was nosin' round Tottenham Court Road. A couple o' phonies, that's what you are!'

'Go on, Curly.'

'Just a couple o' phonies,' he repeated. 'You should 'ave kept yer mouth shut, mate, when that cabbie knocked the paper out yer 'and – you should 'ave kept yer mouth shut.'

'Thanks for the advice. I'll be more careful next time.'

'If there *is* a next time. Get in!' He jerked the muzzle of the gun towards the mini-bus.

'Oh, are we – er – going somewhere?' Holt appeared more self-possessed than he felt as he steered Ruth towards the bus.

'S'right, mate! You said you was lookin' for me, didn't you? You and me and the bird 'ere's going for a little ride. – Ah no, not that side, matey! You get in behind the wheel with the bird beside yer. I'm lazy, see? I prefer to sit in the back and watch while you keep yer mind on the traffic.'

'Driving with a gun in my back is liable to make me nervous,' Holt said.

'I dare say. But don't worry, chum,' Curly replied, slipping the gun into his raincoat pocket.

'I wasn't plannin' to wave it at them fancy coppers on the Royal Parade.' Idly he picked up a thick piece of wood that lay on the ground. It was a sawn-off stump as thick as a fence-post. 'Shouldn't think it'll be necessary, would you?' he said, snapping the stump with his enormous hands as though it were a twig. Then he slid into the mini-bus behind Holt and rested his arms along the back of the driver's seat with the huge hands clearly in view. They got the point.

Holt started the engine and backed carefully.

Once out of the car park Curly gave clear instructions for the route he wanted to take. Holt said nothing, giving all his attention to getting the feel of the vehicle. It might prove useful to be able to handle her well, in the event of a chance of getting rid of Curly. Driving the mini-bus was not quite like handling the controls of the Mustang, but the brakes seemed good and the second gear unusually powerful.

Curly obviously knew Brighton like the back of his hand. He seemed anxious to get clear of the centre of the town as quickly as possible. They soon found themselves on the high cliff road out of Brighton that led eastward towards Newhaven. On a long, lonely stretch with green turf to their left, and on their right frequent glimpses of steep white cliffs dropping vertically to the sea, Curly gave the order to halt. He sat back and produced his revolver, evidently considering Holt a potential danger now that he was no longer occupied with the wheel.

'All right, out with it! What is it yer want?'

'Just a little information, Curly.'

'Such as?'

'What you know about the Vance Scranton murder.'

Holt was watching him in the rear-view mirror. Curly was a poor actor. He turned even paler than normal, licked his flabby lips with a dry tongue, then struggled to assume a truculent air. 'Sorry, mate! You're on the wrong number.'

'Are you sure?'

'Dead sure.'

'And if I offer to buy the information?'

'I tell yer, you got the wrong number! I ain't got nothin' to sell.'

'Would forty pounds make you change your mind?'

Curly gave a hollow laugh. 'Made more'n that on the fourth race this afternoon. Anyway, I got nothin' to sell. My 'ands is clean.'

'Nobody's accusing *you* of murder, Curly. We just want a tip as to where to start looking, that's all.'

'I don't know nothin', mate.'

'But it's true, isn't it, that you were in the neighbourhood on the night this American student was murdered? – No, don't bother to stall, Curly, we've got our information from top sources. Inspector Hyde sends his regards, by the way.'

'So that's who you're workin' for. Well you can just tell 'im from me that I ain't—'

'Let me bring you up to date, Curly. It's Mr and Mrs Robert Scranton that I'm working for – the murdered boy's parents. They're rich Americans and they'll pay a good price to anyone who's helpful. They've asked me to investigate their son's death.'

''Fraid you've taken on a very nasty job, mate.'

'I thought you said you knew nothing about it!' Holt put in swiftly.

A slow smile spread over the ex-convict's features. 'So I did . . . Pretty quick, aren't yer? . . . Well, you might prove a bit too quick for your own good one o' these days. Take my advice and keep out o' this Scranton business. From what I've 'eard it's not the sort of thing for a toff like you to get mixed up in. And you wouldn't want this little bird of yours to get hurt neither, now would you?'

'I'm not so fragile,' Ruth retorted. 'Listen, Curly, aren't you forgetting something?'

'What's that?'

'Muswell Hill – six years ago?'

'What . . . what the hell's Muswell Hill got to do with it?'

Holt said, bitingly, 'Inspector Hyde leaned over backwards to help you then, because he thought you'd had a hard break. I think he saved you about four years in clink, didn't he?'

Curly was silent.

'Have you forgotten, Curly?' Ruth insisted. 'I don't think you have.'

48

'What you drivin' at?'

'It's perfectly simple,' she said briskly. 'Now's your chance to pay back that favour.'

'Why don't he ask me hisself?'

'Because he knows you wouldn't be seen dead talking to him! He's had to ask you through us.'

Curly's Adam's apple worked convulsively and his hulking body seemed to screw itself into knots as he fought a battle with his conscience. Then a curtain of fear seemed to draw over his eyes and his voice was harsh as he declared, 'We're wastin' time! Let's get back to the nags, shall we? You got nothin' for me, an' I got nothin for you – nor Inspector Hyde neither. So let's just part friends, shall we?'

Holt began to protest but Curly cut him short. 'Turn 'er round and drive back! And look sharp!'

There seemed no point in arguing; Curly was flourishing the revolver in an ugly manner. Holt started up the engine again. He glanced in the rear mirror and waited for a small delivery van to overtake him, experiencing a motorist's twinge of annoyance at the way it crawled past. When it had gone the path was clear for Holt to swing in a U-turn to the other side of the road.

Curly had not seen the van; he had been busy stuffing the gun into his raincoat pocket. He looked up just as Holt was pulling out of the turn. Instantly, he hurled himself over the back of the seat, swearing vehemently, and peered out of the rear window. 'Look out – he's stopping! . . . He's goin' into a turn! . . . For Christ's sake step on it!'

Holt slipped into second gear and thrust his foot down, uncomprehending, but recognising fear in Curly's voice. In the rear mirror he saw the van swing into a U-turn just as he had done. A second later it was in swift pursuit and, judging by the speed at which it began to catch up with them, this was no ordinary delivery van but a harmless looking exterior containing a hotted-up engine.

'What's all this about, Curly?' Holt shouted.

'Keep yer 'ead down! Just keep yer bloody 'ead down!' came the hoarse reply.

Ruth was scrambling over the seat, clutching Holt's pocket camera. A great hand flattened her to the floor. 'Lie flat, you little idiot! D'you want to get killed?'

There was the ring of splintering glass as Curly smashed out the rear window with the butt of his revolver, and an instant later came the crack of a bullet.

'Curly – you fool! If you kill anyone—' roared Holt.

'The tyres, mate, that's all I want! The tyres – same as them.'

Further shots were exchanged, then the van changed tactics. With a surge of speed it bore in from the side and began to force Holt off the road. This was the manoeuvre he had anticipated; the men in the van were not shooting to kill, they wanted to promote an 'accident' the kind of accident which, with steep cliffs dropping to stony beaches fifty feet below, could only result in a burst of flame from the petrol tank and instant death for all three of them. Holt was ready.

'Hold tight, everybody!' he yelled.

With exquisite timing he waited until the very last second before metal scraped on metal, then slammed on his brakes, lunged with a fearful grinding into bottom gear, and hauled for all he was worth on the hand-brake. The attacking van had been swerving in hard, intent on forcing him over the cliff. Holt's action, though it caused the mini-bus to swerve wildly for a moment, had successfully dropped him 'into the slot' like a racing driver just behind his opponent. When the van lay almost broadside on Holt changed like lightning into second gear and stamped on the accelerator. The front bumper of the bus caught the van like a cowcatcher on an American train; the van lifted clear off the road, overturned, and, bouncing and slithering over the turf, disappeared over the rim of the white cliff. There followed a violent explosion and a sheet of blinding flame.

The impact slewed the bus into a wild slalom, but Holt fought it viciously and finally forced it to a standstill on the grass verge within a few feet of the jagged cliff edge.

From a call-box on Brighton station Holt telephoned his report to Inspector Hyde.

'The one thing I'm not too happy about, Inspector, is that we didn't stop to see what had happened to those thugs in the van.'

'You said the petrol tank exploded,' said Hyde reasonably. 'What was there for you to do? I haven't had the official report through yet, of course, but I imagine they were killed instantaneously.'

'Yes, but perhaps we ought to have . . . Yes, I suppose it does seem a bit ridiculous to talk about first aid when a vanload of ruffians have done their level best to kill you. Anyway, Curly wouldn't hear of our going back. He brandished his damned gun and insisted we drive him to Brighton railway station. He was in a tearing hurry to get on the train – just couldn't wait to shake the dust of Brighton off his heels.'

'That's not hard to understand. His cronies are evidently gunning for him. Did he take the London train?' Hyde asked.

'No, Chichester. Are you going to pick him up?'

'Not yet. I'll have him followed. He might lead us in the right direction. He knows *something*, I'm sure of it. Didn't you get anything useful out of him at all?'

'Yes; but I don't know yet what it means. He warned me to keep my nose out of the Scranton murder, said it was an ugly business. And then he said, "I reckon I owe my life to you, the way you handled this bus just now. So here's my message to Inspector Hyde. Then nobody won't owe nobody no favours."'

'Yes – go on, Holt.'

'He said: "Tell him, they forgot the ring". That's all – just "tell him *they forgot the ring*."'

Hyde was silent for a moment. Then he said, 'It's rather a cryptic message. What do you make of it?'

'I told you, I don't know. I haven't really had time to collect my wits yet, but I'll think about it on my way up to Town. I had been planning to drive over to Deanfriston as it's only fifteen miles away, but this little drama needs a bit of digesting, I feel. And anyway, I think Ruth ought to have a break.'

'Quite so, quite so. Drop in at the Yard when you can, Holt. The labs may have turned up something on those Christopher postcards by then. By the way, did you or Ruth get a good look at the men in the van?'

Holt gave a dry laugh. 'I was rather busy trying not to be stampeded off the edge of the cliff! But Ruth was very smart – she grabbed my camera and managed to get two or three shots out of the rear window, and one from the side when they came level with us. Goodness knows if they'll develop, she's not a professional.'

'It sounds professional enough to me! Bring in the film as soon as you can. Wonderful girl, Ruth! I don't think you really value her enough, you know.'

'I seem to have heard that before,' Holt said a trifle stiffly, and rang off.

Through the darkening afternoon Holt drove the Mustang back to London as though the engine were new and required to be run in. Once, on an open stretch of road near Crawley, a butcher's errand-boy on a moped overtook them; it was probably the supreme moment of his life.

'Now this is what driving must have been like round about the turn of the century,' Ruth said. 'Peaceful, smooth . . .'

'Please be quiet, Ruth. I'm thinking.'

Ruth's mischievous grin faded. '"They forgot the ring"?'

'"They forgot the ring". Whose ring? Vance Scranton's obviously. It was the only thing that was missing from the body. A simple signet ring, of no great value, apparently. Yet somebody stole it . . . And yet if they *stole* it, they didn't *forget* it, did they?'

'It doesn't make sense. Perhaps Curly's just hanging a red herring in front of our noses.'

Holt frowned. 'Do you really think that?'

Ruth did not reply immediately. Then at last she said, 'No. As a matter of fact, I think he was telling the truth. That incident up on the cliff top shook him to the core; and when a person gets scared – really scared – they don't pretend. I think he meant what he said.'

'That was my impression too. But it still doesn't make sense.'

Holt said no more but continued to drive northwards at the same leisurely speed. Then, without warning, an exclamation sprang from his lips and he slid through a rapid change of gears until the Mustang was showing its taillights to everything else on the road.

Ruth sat upright, on the alert at once. 'Something has bitten you?' she asked eagerly.

'Something has! Something so fantastic that . . .'

'Well, what is it?'

'. . . I wonder . . . It's impossible! . . . Or is it?'

'Fascinating conversation,' Ruth said dryly, almost bursting with curiosity but quite determined not to betray it. 'No doubt you'll tell me, in your own good time . . .'

Miraculously they avoided all speed traps and drew up outside Holt's yellow front door as Big Ben announced that it was eight o'clock. Without stopping to garage the car he thrust the key into the lock and bounded up the stairs to the studio.

A quick search through a notebook revealed Inspector Hyde's private number, and just as he stretched out his hand towards the telephone it startled him by ringing.

The conversation which followed was brief and he had hung up by the time Ruth strolled in with the Olympus Pen F in her hand. 'Who was that?'

'Scranton from the Savoy. He says he's been trying to get me all afternoon. Sounds pretty het-up about something. He wants me to go round right away.'

'Has someone sent him another issue of the *New Feature*?'

'No, I don't think so, not this time. Come on, let's go.'

Ruth indicated the camera she was holding. 'What about this film?'

'We'll do that when we get back.'

In the Mustang they threaded their way through light evening traffic and Ruth asked, 'Is this likely to affect your brilliant new theory, Philip?'

'Unless I'm very much mistaken, it may even confirm it,' was the enigmatic reply.

Ruth had not long to wait before she learnt the answer. When they arrived at the Savoy Robert Scranton was pacing up and down near the Reception Desk. He hurried them to the lift.

'I'll let Mother tell you in her own words,' he said as they travelled smoothly upwards. 'I must warn you, though, she's kinda hysterical right now. I don't ever remember her being so worked up! I'd have sent for a doc, but she insisted on seeing you first.'

Holt nodded, making no comment.

They crossed soft carpets to the door of Scranton's suite. He took out his key and let them in.

Mrs Scranton lay on a couch in front of an electric fire. She looked frailer than ever, and deep shock was evident in her features. Yet, also, in her eyes there was something resembling elation; it frightened Ruth by its unexpectedness.

'Please forgive me if I don't get up,' Mrs Scranton said. 'I have the most fantastic thing to tell you – I guess it's shaken me up.'

'I think I know what you're going to tell me,' Holt said calmly. Robert Scranton was at his wife's side, holding her hand. They both stared in silent astonishment, and Holt continued, 'Have you, by any chance, heard from or seen your son recently, Mrs Scranton?'

Ruth let out a tiny gasp as Mrs Scranton nodded slowly and answered in little more than a whisper, 'Yes. I saw Vance this morning. How did you know?'

Chapter Five

In his office at Scotland Yard Inspector Hyde waved Philip Holt to the visitor's chair. 'You're looking very fit, despite yesterday's excitement,' he said.

'Yes. I've just been taking my Sunday morning constitutional. I've been to the Savoy, and then walked all the way here – that's quite a step!'

'What's happened – has the Mustang broken down?'

'No, no – she's in great shape!'

'Now don't tell me you're between cars again!' the Inspector smiled, recalling Holt's weakness for changing his personal transport whenever a new design took his fancy.

Holt laughed. 'At the moment I'm absolutely faithful to the Mustang! – Well, let's say just an occasional flirtatious glance at the new Coronado. It's got a fascinating front-wheel—'

'Quite so. But you didn't drag me here on a Sunday morning in order to talk cars. How are the Scrantons this morning?'

'I don't know. You see, I didn't go into the Savoy itself. I stayed outside and checked up on Mrs Scranton's story.'

Hyde leaned forward sharply. 'Wait a moment – don't go too fast for this poor old brainbox! Let's get this clear. When you phoned me at home last night and told me she'd seen Vance you seemed perfectly prepared to accept her story. In fact, you said it fitted in with a new theory of your own – a theory which was prompted by Curly's cryptic reference to a ring. Am I right so far?'

'Yes, that's perfectly correct.'

'Robert Scranton may have thought his wife was having hallucinations, but you were inclined to believe her?'

'Yes.'

'Then what's all this about "checking up" on her story. Have you had doubts about it since?'

'I wanted to check up on it because there was just one aspect of the story that didn't fit.'

'Go on, Holt.'

Holt took a deep breath. 'Let's go over it, step by step . . . Yesterday morning, at about eleven o'clock, the Scrantons were just going out of the hotel, through the swing doors of the Strand exit, when Robert Scranton remembered something and went back. His wife waited for him outside. She happened to glance up, and there – about fifty yards away on the street corner – stood her son Vance. Or so she says.'

'On which corner? By the bank or the men's outfitters?'

'On the bank corner. There are traffic lights there; her son was leaning against them, gazing towards the Savoy and twiddling his hat round and round on one finger. Apparently that was a typical mannerism of his and it convinced Mrs Scranton that she wasn't having hallucinations. But even so, it took her a few seconds to get over the shock, as you can imagine.'

'Yes, indeed. I suppose she didn't attempt to call out to him; the mere fact of seeing him there probably made her speechless.'

'That in itself would be perfectly understandable – but in any case one wouldn't call out to someone standing fifty yards away; twenty – even thirty, at a pinch – but not fifty, in a crowded London street. It all happened pretty quickly, according to Mrs Scranton, and by the time she'd recovered her senses and her husband had come out of the hotel the boy had gone. Scranton himself says he thought his wife had gone "mental", but just to humour her he ran out into the Strand and searched in both directions. There was no sign of Vance. Whoever it was had been swallowed up by the crowd.'

Holt paused for a moment, allowing time for Hyde to take in the details so far, then he went on, 'If we assume that Vance is alive, then the question is, *why didn't he acknowledge his mother*? She saw him clearly enough, and she says he was looking straight at her. Why didn't he greet her?'

'It would be rather illuminating to know the answer to that one, certainly.'

'I think I have it!' Holt replied. 'I stood at the traffic lights on that particular corner this morning, just after eleven o'clock. I looked across at the Savoy and had a perfectly clear view of the commissionaire at the swing doors. I must admit I was completely baffled by the problem. Then, quite suddenly, the sun came out – from *behind* the hotel. It was shining right in my eyes and I couldn't see a thing! I spoke to the commissionaire afterwards and he said he'd noticed me standing there on the corner, the sun had picked me out like a floodlight. Then I asked him what sort of day it had been in Town yesterday – Ruth and I were driving down to the coast, you remember. He said it had been a lovely autumn day with brilliant sunshine.'

'Yes, that's right, it was,' Hyde confirmed. For a moment

or two he occupied himself with his pipe, then he summed up briefly. 'So let's say that young Scranton, for reasons of his own, came and gazed at the hotel where he knew his parents would be staying, and that he failed to see his mother because the sun was in his eyes.'

'Yes. I'd say that was a fair enough assumption.'

'Now what about the father? Does he really think his wife is nuts, or does he believe it possible that Vance is alive?'

'Last night, when he phoned me, he obviously didn't believe it. After all, he'd identified the body. He'd actually seen a corpse, whereas his wife hadn't! That makes a big difference. It took me a long time to convince him that it might be possible.'

'Did you succeed in convincing him?'

'Of the *possibility*, yes – but I don't think he believes it really was his son that his wife saw. Of course, we haven't anything definite to go on, either, but an idea drifted into my mind as I was driving up from Brighton. Curly said, "They forgot the ring". By "they" I assume he meant the people, the gang, the organisation behind this strange business. Could it be, I wondered, that they'd killed a man of Vance's stature and colouring, rigged up his body very carefully in some stolen clothes of Vance's, and then made one tiny slip – they forgot to put Vance's signet ring on the dead man's finger? That seems to be the only possible interpretation of Curly's tantalising remark. Though, even if it's true, it still doesn't explain *why* they did it.'

'H'm . . . You put this point of view to Scranton?'

'Yes. He was pretty sceptical. So I put it to him this way: I said, "Mr Scranton, you were met at London Airport and told that your son had been murdered. You were driven down to Sussex to identify a body – a body with most of the features blown off – which several people had already confirmed as your son's. In other words, you went there expecting to see your son and there was no earthly reason to assume that the body might have been anyone else's!"'

'But how do you account for other people making the same mistake – Julie Benson, Antoinette Sheen, for instance?'

'For exactly the same reason!' Holt insisted. 'If they'd seen a body in Vance's study, wearing Vance's clothes, sprawled over a desk with one of Vance's short stories on it, then obviously it would never enter their heads that it *wasn't* Vance!'

'That's true enough,' agreed Hyde. 'Especially as there doesn't appear to have been anything very striking about the boy. He had no outstanding physical features or birthmarks, it seems.'

'And another thing to be taken into consideration is the fact that his father lives in America and very rarely saw his son. No, to put it bluntly, the one person who knew him most intimately and might perhaps have noticed something – Julie Benson – fainted on the spot, I believe you said?'

'Yes, she did. So in the light of these latest theories, it doesn't add much weight to the value of her identification.'

There was an awkward pause, sensed by both men.

Reluctantly, the Inspector filled it. 'You're being very tactful, Holt – refraining from asking how it was that the police slipped up too . . .'

'Always assuming this new idea holds water,' Holt hastened to point out.

Hyde cleared his throat uncomfortably and fiddled with the pencils and memo pad on his desk. 'My investigation squad were led up the garden path just like everyone else – only in our case it was quite inexcusable. But there it is;

even the police are fallible human beings. We were summoned to Deanfriston College because the local police reported that a student named Vance Scranton had been murdered. We went, expecting to find Vance Scranton, and when we got there we found a boy sprawled over a desk, too badly mutilated to identify from photographs. We checked his clothes, his wallet, the articles in the room, the story on the desk, and then, just as a formality, we made the customary fingerprint check.'

'What exactly does that consist of?'

'Taking the prints of the dead man and comparing them with those of Vance Scranton. Everything seemed perfectly in order.'

'But surely you didn't possess a set of Vance's fingerprints, did you?'

'Oh, no.'

'Then how were you able to compare them?'

'It's a standard routine. We tested various objects in the study. Scranton's cigarette case, wallet, books and papers, ornaments on the shelves, his typewriter. The prints on every one of these articles were the prints of the dead man. Of course, I could kick myself now, but that's merely being wise after the event. I can see that they must have deliberately planted the fingerprints on Vance's personal effects, knowing full well that everything would tally and that the police would believe it was Vance Scranton and start looking for his murderer.'

'Instead of which we should now be looking for Vance Scranton himself, as well as finding out who was killed, who killed him, and why!'

'It's getting complicated, isn't it?' commented Hyde.

'Complicated,' Holt mused, 'but intriguing . . . I warned

the Scrantons that they aren't out of the wood yet, by the way. They were so overjoyed to think their son might be alive that it took some time for the ugly penny to drop.'

'What do you mean? That Vance himself could be the killer, trying to cover his own tracks by pretending he's dead? Yes, it's obvious, isn't it? I don't expect they liked hearing that. How have you left matters with them?'

'The important thing now seems to be to get in touch with Vance Scranton. Everything else is secondary. So I told the parents to put on a front; to stay at the Savoy, and try to lead a perfectly normal life, neither too dazed with joy nor too deep in mourning – go shopping, sightseeing, making business calls, and so on. I'm convinced it won't be too long before Vance contacts them. The father's promised to ring me the moment he does.'

Hyde walked to the window and gazed unseeingly at the dismal view. When he eventually spoke his voice was heavy and somewhat despondent. 'Provided, of course, we've got our major premise right: that the boy is alive.'

'You mean you're doubtful yourself?'

'. . . A missing ring? . . . A mother's wishful thinking? . . . A cryptic sentence extracted from an old lag in a moment of fear? . . . It's not very much to go on, is it?'

The telephone rang before Holt could reply. The Inspector returned to his desk.

'Hyde speaking . . . Why, hello, Ruth! How very nice to hear your voice . . . Don't tell me Mr Holt makes you work on Sundays too! An attractive young lady like you should be out enjoying herself . . .'

Holt leant forward automatically and reached for the phone.

'Certainly, my dear,' Hyde said into the receiver. He grinned at Holt and waved him aside. 'No, she wants to speak to me. Go on, Ruth, I'm listening.'

The Inspector's side of the conversation was monosyllabic, but he was evidently intrigued by the message. 'By the way,' he said at last, 'we were very pleased with the snapshots you took of those two beauties in the van yesterday. You did a good job there, they may be very helpful. I'm having them checked in the Rogues' Gallery. I'll let you know if they're identified . . . Now don't let Mr Holt overwork you. And thank you for phoning, Ruth. Goodbye.' He replaced the receiver and leaned back in his chair.

Holt said, somewhat thinly, 'You two form an excellent mutual admiration society, don't you?'

Hyde gave a sugary smile. 'Don't we just! Remarkable girl, that! . . . Well, Holt, you'll be interested to know that there's been fresh confirmation that Vance is alive. Someone else has apparently seen him!'

'Who's seen him? Where?'

'A man called Jimmy Wade. He's an undertaker.'

'Funeral director, if you'll pardon my saying so,' said Holt slyly. 'I've met him. I wonder what the devil he's up to? I take it he's been to the Studio again?'

'Yes. Ruth says he was tremendously excited. He claims to have seen Vance in the Underground at Piccadilly Circus. They were on the escalator; Vance was going up and Wade was going down. Wade couldn't believe his eyes, and by the time he'd realised who it was it was too late to do anything about it.'

Holt took out his cigarette case, then returned it to his pocket. He would have one later, he decided. 'Now you *have* got me worried,' he said.

Hyde looked at the younger man in astonishment. 'But

63

this is a tremendous stroke of luck, Holt! It confirms your theory that Vance is—'

'It confirms nothing, I'm afraid. For the simple reason that both Ruth and I are convinced that Jimmy Wade is a born liar!'

Holt took a taxi back to Westminster and, after a brief discussion with Ruth about Wade's visit, he said with a slight twinge of conscience, 'You push off now, Ruth. It was good of you to come in this morning.'

'Are you sure you don't want me to stay, Philip? There's still plenty to do and—'

'No, no – I can manage now. You run along. See you tomorrow.'

When she had gone he allowed himself the promised cigarette and settled down to catching up with some of his paperwork, but his mind strayed continually to the Scranton case.

The following afternoon, with heavy rain splashing against the bay window, and the intermittent hiss of passing traffic slitting a curtain of rain outside, Ruth brought in the tea tray and called Holt from the Studio where he was setting up lamps for a tobacco advertisement. Dusk was falling, the blurred lights from the Embankment keeping the night temporarily at bay, and as she poured the steaming tea and they relaxed for a while in the pleasant warmth of the office all thoughts of the murder were momentarily forgotten.

Then the ringing of the telephone shattered the peaceful atmosphere and started a train of events which left no room for detachment.

It was Robert Scranton, almost breathless with excitement.

'Mr Holt? . . . I've got some news . . . but I must be quick because I don't want Mother to overhear me . . .'

'Yes, what is it?'

'I've heard from Vance! He's just called me!'

'Have you seen him? Where is he?'

'No, no, he telephoned. Just under an hour ago.'

'But, Mr Scranton, you promised to contact me immediately he—'

'I know I did, but . . . Listen, Mr Holt, can I have your word that you won't get in touch with the police yet? Give the boy a chance to explain. I think he's in trouble, real bad trouble.'

'But where *is* he, Scranton – where is he?'

'I don't dare tell you over the phone, Mr Holt. You never know when these things have been bugged. He wants to meet me – he needs money badly. I can fix that all right, the hotel will cash me a traveller's cheque. But I'd like you to come with me.'

'Yes, all right. When?'

'Right now, if you can make it.'

Holt glanced at his watch. 'I'll be at the hotel inside ten minutes. Is that soon enough?'

'Great, just great! Meet me at the back entrance, facing the Embankment. Okay? – Bring your car, and perhaps that cute little secretary of yours as well. I'd sure be grateful if you could bring her. If Vance is hurt or ill it may need a woman's touch and I just don't dare take the risk of telling Mother . . .'

'Quite. I understand.'

Holt hung up and turned to Ruth. 'Now the ball is really rolling! Get your brolly and coat, it's raining like hell. We're on our way to meet the elusive Mr Scranton Junior!'

Ruth's eyes gleamed and in a few moments she was ready.

Robert Scranton was waiting at the hotel doorway as Holt swung the Mustang into the crescent of Victoria Embankment Gardens. The American did not appear to notice their approach, so Holt tapped his horn lightly. Scranton still took no notice.

Ruth lowered her window and leaned out. Rain was pouring down with torrential force. 'Hey – Mr Scranton!'

'Ruth! You'll get drenched!' Holt remonstrated. He pressed more firmly on the horn.

The figure in the doorway made a feeble gesture with one hand and began to walk very slowly over to the car.

'What on earth's the matter with him, is he ill?'

'Something must have happened. Just look at him!' said Ruth, opening the car door as Scranton reached them.

'It's my heart,' he muttered, sliding into the rear seat. 'Often . . . often plays me up . . . Get too excited . . . Guess it was Vance's call that did it.'

Holt eyed him with alarm. Scranton felt in his pocket for his tube of pills. By the inner light of the car he certainly looked ghastly; he was obviously having great difficulty with his breathing.

'Are you sure you're well enough for this?' asked Ruth. 'Perhaps we'd better take you up to your room?'

'No . . . I'll be all right . . . in a minute. I must get to Vance . . . he needs me . . . Sounded real strange on the phone . . .'

'Tell us where he is,' insisted Ruth. 'We'll take care of things. You don't look fit to go out on a terrible night like this.'

'No. You'd only go straight to the police,' Scranton said in a weak, accusing whisper.

'No, we wouldn't,' Ruth assured him gently. 'Whatever

has to be done in the end, we'll make you a promise: you can see him first.' She turned anxiously to Holt. 'We can promise that, can't we, Philip? It's only human decency. We'll take Vance the money, Mr Scranton, or tell him you'll send it. Where is he?'

Scranton looked at her, uncertain whether to trust them, then he reached for his American-type billfold and extracted a wad of ten-pound notes. 'I feel bad about this,' he said, 'but I guess I won't be able to make it. And if I should pass out on you at a critical moment, that won't help Vance much.'

'Exactly!' Ruth agreed, taking the money. 'Now then, where do we find him?'

With shaking fingers Scranton dug once more into his billfold and produced a scrap of paper on which an address had been scribbled. 'Sure hope you can read it. It's a place called Lewisham. Ask for John Griffiths, that's the name he's using – he didn't say why.'

Scranton made to open the car door but had to clutch suddenly at his breast and struggle for breath. Ruth jumped out, ignoring the pelting rain, and helped him out of the car. She shepherded him to the hotel entrance and they disappeared from sight. Two minutes later she reappeared and dashed back to Holt.

'That was quick. Did you take him to his room?'

'No, he insisted on being left in the hall – didn't want to upset "Mother". I got a waiter to bring him a brandy.'

'And you think he'll be all right?'

'Goodness knows. He looks dreadful, but I think it'll set his mind at rest if we go and find this son of his. He'd be in a far worse shape if we hadn't said we'd go.'

Holt debated the issue in silence, whilst the rain drummed with tremendous force on the Mustang's bonnet.

Ruth asked, 'Do you think we shouldn't go?'

'Well . . . it's not very ethical, what we propose doing. Young Scranton's a wanted man, you realise – a suspect for murder. I ought to contact Hyde.'

'We can do that from Lewisham. Supposing it's a false alarm? We'd look pretty stupid, wouldn't we? Let's get a bird in the hand, and then make our decision.'

After a moment Holt nodded. 'You're right! How do we get to Lewisham?'

'That's your department. The place rings a bell somewhere, though . . . Wait a minute – didn't Jimmy Wade say he lived near there?'

'Yes. Honor Oak, just next door.' Holt started the engine. 'A very different class of locality, if I may say so.'

Ruth grinned at Holt's mimicry. 'Will Honor Oak be on our route?'

'No. We'll take the Old Kent Road and then the A.20. Good grief, what a night!'

He drove carefully, his nerves taut but under control. If they found Vance Scranton a very difficult decision would have to be made. The boy was wanted by the police and Hyde would have to be told. Nevertheless, Holt was working for the Scrantons and had promised not to go straight to the police. He quietened his conscience with the thought that Robert Scranton would never have parted with the Lewisham address without this promise so there had been no alternative.

They crawled behind slow traffic into the main Lewisham High Street, where a policeman on point duty gave them directions for reaching the address on the paper.

It proved to be a narrow, evil-smelling lane in a bleak slum quarter. Holt felt conspicuous in his scarlet Mustang.

Eventually they located the grime-covered two-storey house which bore the number they wanted and Holt drove past and parked his car some distance away: They dashed back through the downpour and stood gasping for breath under an inadequate porch cluttered with empty milk bottles.

Holt pressed the chipped door bell but no sound came. There was a knocker blackened with dust and soot, which he thumped resoundingly, and after a while they heard heavy, shuffling footsteps and the door creaked open.

'You come about the telly, man?' The voice was a deep contralto and appeared to come from black space, completely disembodied. 'You come about the telly?' the voice repeated in a monotone.

'No, actually we've come to see Mr Griffiths, please.'

Their eyes were becoming accustomed to the sepulchral darkness and it was just possible to make out the silhouette of a very large body standing in the doorway.

'He doan have no telly, man,' the voice droned. 'I'm the one with the broken telly. You come right on in and fix it, man. I'm lost without the telly.'

As the body moved a faint gleam of light from a street lamp caught the outline of a coal-black shining face and eyes with enormous whites, and they realised they were talking to a Negress.

'We haven't come about the television, Mrs . . . er . . .' Ruth said in a brave attempt to apply a little charm to the chilly scene.

The huge woman swayed forward to look at them more closely, bathing them in fumes of strong alcohol.

Ruth blenched but stood her ground. 'Is Mr Griffiths in? We'd like to see him, please. It's raining rather hard; do you think we might come in?'

'Man, doan I know it's raining! I got soaked coming from the boozer.'

The Negress moved on squelching feet to the wall and fumbled for the switch. The weak light of a naked twenty-five-watt bulb revealed a cramped hall almost entirely blocked by bicycles and prams.

'He's one of my coloured gentlemen, this Griffiths, is he?' asked the woman, staring at them and knocking some of the rain off her clothes.

'No, he's . . . he's not coloured.'

'Ain't no white folks here, 'cepting that feller that come day 'fore yesterday. You go up and see, if you like – third floor, second door on the left . . . My ole legs is tired. I just wanna curl right up like a cat in front of that telly – you sure you ain't gonna fix it, man?'

Holt muttered an apology and started climbing the poorly lit staircase. Ruth followed. When the fumes of gin and rum had receded other aromas crowded in. Stale odours of food, inadequate sanitation, and damp laundry hanging out to dry assailed their nostrils, but the stairs were too steep for them to hold their breath in self-protection.

After the second floor the illumination ceased and they groped their way up the last flight in the diminishing glimmer coming from the landing below. When they reached the third floor, in almost total darkness, Holt had to enlist the aid of his pocket torch.

'You stay there, Ruth,' he said. 'I'll find the room.'

She waited at the head of the stairs while he crept along the passage and located the second door on the left, in a recess where the roof sloped at a steep angle. With his head and shoulders bowed he rapped firmly. But there was no answer.

He called 'Griffiths!' several times, then changed to calling 'Vance!' Still there was no reply.

He tried the door handle. It turned and he faced an unlighted room. When he found the light-switch he saw that it appeared empty except for an unmade bed and a battered chest of drawers.

'No one here,' Holt said, stepping across the threshold.

As he did so, the door swung slowly to, behind him, cutting off all light to the landing and leaving Ruth enveloped by the blackness.

'Philip! I can't see a thing! Open the door so I can find my way.'

'Just a minute, Ruth,' he said gently, ominously. 'I'll be with you in a minute.'

He had spotted the hand on the far side of the bed. It was the size of a North Sea haddock.

He leapt round the brass bedstead. Curly's great bulk lay on the floor, partly hidden by the bedclothes, one arm flung backwards in a mutely defensive gesture. The knife-wound in his throat was half covered by the strands of a black wig. The wig sat lopsided on his skull, like an awkward joke: it had been the pitiful best he could think of to try to disguise the great putty-coloured beacon of his bald head.

The murderer had added a small macabre touch. Where the wig had slipped as Curly had slid to the floor an expanse of skin had been revealed. On this patch a cruel wit had drawn a question-mark in scarlet lipstick.

'I don't think I quite follow,' said Ruth shakily as they drove back to Town, leaving Inspector Hyde and a team of experts to seal off the Lewisham boarding-house and start their investigations. 'Why Curly?'

'Because he knew too much, I suppose,' Holt answered. 'Don't ask me *what* he knew. Probably he was seen talking to us at the Brighton car park and that's why that delivery van went for us. I dare say he decided to go into hiding until the heat was off. Taking the Chichester train was evidently just a blind. He must have doubled back on his tracks and then gone to earth in that foul-smelling hole.'

'What about the landlady? You don't think—'

'Not for one moment. In the first place she was as drunk as a lord. In the second place, it was true that she'd been out – her clothes were steaming wet. No, it's my guess that someone sneaked in while she was out at the pub and slit poor Curly's throat, and then phoned Scranton, pretending to be his son. Scranton did say Vance sounded strange on the phone, if you remember.'

'Yes, so he did. But why should the murderer do that?'

'To lure Scranton out there with a lot of cash in his pocket, I suppose. There's about two hundred pounds in that pile he gave us.'

'What do you think would have happened if Mr Scranton had come?'

'Someone would probably have slugged him in that dark passage, stolen the cash, and cleared off. It could also have been intended as a profitable way of warning Scranton to keep his nose out of the affair.'

'Then why didn't they slug us when we turned up?'

'Well, for one thing, I don't suppose they were expecting us – they'd have been on the look-out for Scranton himself and they wouldn't have known we were carrying the money. And in any case, there were two of us. If he'd gone for me, you'd have set up such a caterwauling that all Lewisham—'

'All right, I get the picture!' She was silent for a moment, then she said quietly, 'He must have been in that house, Philip – in that passage while I was waiting for you, in the dark.'

He felt slightly guilty. His hand left the wheel for a second to give hers a reassuring squeeze. 'Try not to think about it, Ruth.'

Then, eternally buoyant, her spirits brightened. 'Well, what's our next move?' she asked.

He navigated a sharp turn, put his foot down hard on the accelerator, and shot some lights that were turning from amber to red.

'What's your hurry? Where are we going now?'

'You are going home, young lady! Get a good night's sleep, and be at the Studio early tomorrow morning. Bring a suitcase packed with enough things for three or four days.'

She turned to stare at him for a moment, then gave an impish grin. 'Philip, are you inviting me to stay at your flat for three or four days?'

'The suitcase is for Deanfriston,' Holt announced firmly.

'Oh.'

'Unless I'm very much mistaken, Deanfriston is the place where the hard nuts in this case are to be cracked!'

Chapter Six

Deanfriston College stood on a windswept ridge of the South Downs, commanding a fine view of the English Channel and of the charming Sussex village nestling at its foot.

The College, relatively new, specialised in the Arts and Political Science. Professor Harold Dalesford held the Chair of Political Science, and it was in this field that Vance Scranton had been awarded an exchange scholarship at his university in America.

A little over a week had gone by since the night of the murder. The shock waves had not yet ceased to reverberate along the corridors, lecture halls, and quadrangle of the College, and Professor Dalesford found difficulty in concentrating on his work.

Laying aside the latest issue of the *New Feature* he took out a pair of field-glasses from his desk and walked to the window. His hobby was bird-watching and he knew of no finer way to relax a worried and overworked mind.

He focused the glasses and viewed the copse of elms to the right of the road which curved through chalk-white banks down to the village. There was a light tap on his door and someone came into the room. He knew the step and did not bother to look round.

'What is it, my dear?' he said.

The girl who had entered was tall, slim, and strikingly beautiful. Thick tawny hair with elusive rich glints hung down to her shoulders in a perfect blend of care and disarray. A pencil-slim skirt of chocolate brown hugged her slender hips, and a cream turtle-necked pullover swelled decisively over firm breasts. She wore no jewellery and very little make-up, and her skin glowed with a natural honey-gold tan.

Antoinette Sheen picked up the Professor's copy of the *New Feature* and started to say something, but she was halted by a startled exclamation from the window.

'Damnation! I think we've got a visitor. And I'm afraid it's the one we were expecting.'

Antoinette went to the window and took the binoculars. She focused them on a scarlet car which was sweeping up the hill.

'A red Mustang. That will be him,' she murmured.

'Is he alone?'

'Does that matter? . . . No, as a matter of fact I think there's someone in the passenger seat.'

Dalesford made a grimace of annoyance. 'If it's that dull-witted policeman Hyde again . . .'

'It isn't. It's a woman.'

The Mustang turned the corner into the quadrangle and came to a halt.

Antoinette's voice took on a lilt of subdued amusement. 'I do believe he's brought his little doxy with him . . . Pretty little thing, too,' she added as Ruth got out of the car. A moment later, when Holt stood beside his secretary, Antoinette's eyes widened and she gave an appreciative murmur. 'So that's the celebrated Philip Holt, top-flight photographer and amateur sleuth! My, what an attractive hunk of a man! This could prove to be very interesting.'

'I'm glad you think so!' Dalesford snapped with considerable venom.

'Aren't you going down to meet them?'

'No. Julie can play the reception hostess. I suggest you make yourself scarce.'

Antoinette gave a mocking smile. 'Don't you want me to meet the remarkable Mr Holt?'

'I don't consider it wise for our names to be linked, that's all. Now run along, Antoinette, please.'

'Run? In this skirt? Impossible!'

The Professor watched her glide from the room. It was something well worth watching. Then he hastened to his desk and began strewing it impressively with papers.

When the buzzer on his internal phone rang and, a few moments later, Philip Holt and Ruth were shown into the room, the Professor was giving a convincing performance of a scholar up to his eyes in work. Peering over thick hornrimmed spectacles he greeted his visitors and waved them towards two chairs. The young blonde girl, in heavy mourning, who had shown them in started to leave, but Dalesford stopped her.

'This is my secretary, Julie Benson. We've been expecting you sooner or later, Mr Holt. As I expect you know, Julie was engaged to be married to Vance Scranton.'

The pretty, fluffy little thing (as Inspector Hyde had very aptly described her) blushed and shook hands with them. Ruth moved particularly close to the younger girl and held her outstretched hand rather longer than was usual.

Holt frowned at Dalesford's words. 'I don't quite follow. How could you have been expecting us, Professor?'

'Well, Julie's brother-in-law, Mr Wade, mentioned that the Scrantons had put you on this case, so naturally we've been expecting you here any day.'

Dalesford had a confident, ringing voice, ideal for addressing a lecture hall full of students. Holt judged his age as about forty-five. He was fairly tall, thin and stooping, and untidily dressed in a baggy tweed suit. There was a slightly bad-tempered expression on his otherwise quite handsome, large-boned face.

'Has Mr Wade been in touch with you recently?' Ruth enquired innocently of Julie Benson.

'Yes. You see . . . he's my sister's husband, you understand,' she ended rather lamely.

Ruth gave a sweet smile which seemed to set Julie at ease.

'I hope your brother-in-law hasn't been telling too many people that I'm helping Mr Scranton,' Holt said evenly. 'My investigations are of a very private nature; I'd much prefer to work without fuss or publicity of any kind.'

'Don't worry about Jimmy, he's the soul of discretion,' Dalesford assured him in hearty tones. 'He has to be, in his line of business. No, the chappie who needs watching is this Abe Jenkins reporter fellow. That's obviously his work in this morning's paper. I expect you've seen it?'

'No,' said Holt. 'Have you got a copy?'

'Yes, I think it's here on my desk somewhere.' The Professor rummaged around, nearly knocking over a clay jar stuffed with pencils and pens, and succeeded in dislodging a pile of magazines. Despite his protests Ruth went on her hands and knees to help him pick them up. They were all different issues of the *New Feature*.

She favoured him with her guileless smile. 'Do you take this magazine, Professor?'

77

His reply was oddly confused. 'Yes, I . . . er . . . I take it. That is to say . . . Ah, here's the Abe Jenkins article. I've marked it – there, in green ink. Of course, it's a tremendous sensation for a tiny hamlet like Deanfriston to have its own murder. Frankly, the people down here just love it!'

Holt nodded as he took the newspaper. 'It can't have been very pleasant for you, though.'

'Well, there's been a lot of publicity, of course, but I don't know that it's so very harmful. It might even do a bit of good in some circles – may make a few nabobs sit up and realise we do have a branch of the University here. I'm almost inclined to say that any publicity is better than none, as far as our neglected part of the backwoods is concerned.'

'I wasn't thinking so much of the notoriety as—'

'Ah, you mean the police? Yes, of course, they were an infernal nuisance, quite disrupted the lecture rota.'

'No,' persisted Holt, 'I was thinking more of what it must have meant to you, personally, to lose a brilliant scholar like Vance Scranton.'

'Oh. Oh yes, I see what you mean . . . Yes. Yes, indeed . . .'

'He came directly under your tuition, didn't he? And by all accounts he was pretty bright.'

Dalesford cleared his throat importantly; it was as though he were about to make the Chairman's speech to a full Board meeting.

'Nature abhors a vacuum, and Professor Dalesford abhors hypocrisy, Mr Holt. So I must warn you, in case you're expecting me to cry on your shoulder, that this young American was never exactly a favourite of mine. In fact, if you want my unvarnished verdict, he was a self-opinionated young bastard! Clever, I'll grant you, but practically a Fascist in his ideas. There are many other students whose minds I prefer, and whose future careers interest me to a far greater degree. Forgive me if I speak too candidly – I'm afraid I'm rather well known for it.'

He ended his speech with a self-indulgent chuckle.

Ruth had been watching Julie Benson while the Professor's voice droned confidently on. The young girl had a blank, uninterestingly pretty face, for the most part devoid of emotion. But suddenly, half-way through Dalesford's speech, a spasm of hatred darted across her features like a streak of summer lightning. Ruth was shocked by its intensity. Then, as swiftly as it came, the hatred faded.

Holt unfolded the newspaper and began to read the article by Abe Jenkins. His brow darkened and with difficulty he held himself in check till he had reached the end. 'How the devil does this fellow get his information?' he exploded at last.

Dalesford adjusted his spectacles and gave a wordly-wise smile. 'I can't imagine,' he said. 'Unless he has a friend in the police force?'

Holt shook his head. 'I doubt that, but I must admit I don't see how he could have linked the Lewisham murder with the Brighton cliff crash and the Scranton case.'

He banged the newspaper down on the desk and Julie pounced on it. 'Is there something new in it about Vance?' she asked fearfully.

Dalesford looked surprised. 'You mean you haven't read it yet? You'd better sit down, my girl, before you read the last paragraph.'

Julie Benson immediately scanned the final paragraph and its effect on her was dynamic. She gave a short, choking cry and crumbled to the floor.

As Ruth hastened towards her the Professor stood to one side with a complacent, detached smile on his face. 'I warned her, didn't I? I said she ought to sit down before she read this piece of nonsense about Scranton being alive.'

A sharp retort was on the tip of Holt's tongue, but he bit it back.

'Well, Mr Holt, I expect you'd like to see the scene of the crime, wouldn't you? Isn't that where all good detectives start?'

'I'd like to see Vance's study, if I may?'

'Naturally – the now-famous study in the now-famous Scholars' Row. Many is the litre of midnight oil that has been burnt there, many the hours of studious scholarship. But it took a murder to put us on the map, Mr Holt. Come alone, I'll take you on the Grand Tour . . .'

Holt and Ruth stood leaning into the wind as they stopped to admire the marvellous view of the Channel and the Seven Sisters.

'What a remarkable bunch of characters this case seems to involve,' he had said as they drove away from Deanfriston. 'I feel I need a good clean through with a stiff Channel breeze. Let's go for a walk along the Downs.'

They had driven down to the sea and parked the Mustang in the hollow of Birling Gap.

'Well, Ruth, what do you make of it all?' he asked as they turned from the seven white cliffs and continued over the soft green turf.

She summed up her impressions briefly. 'Liars, knaves, ex-convicts, intellectual snobs! Even little Julie Benson could turn out to be a vicious piece of goods, I imagine.'

'Really? What makes you say that?'

Ruth described the frightening look of hatred that had passed across the secretary's blue eyes.

Holt laughed.

'What's so funny?' Ruth asked.

'It's only that, quite independently of each other, you and Hyde have come up with the same verdict on fluffy blue-eyed blondes. I begin to wonder what the other one will be like.'

'Which other one?'

'Antoinette Sheen.'

'Oh, she's not in the least fluffy.'

'How do you know?'

'I've seen her – I think.'

'You've *what*?'

'She was there, at the College.'

'Nonsense! I asked Dalesford if he knew where we could get in touch with her and he was hopelessly vague. He said he hadn't seen her since the night of the murder.

'Professor Dalesford,' said Ruth, with very precise diction, 'was lying. Add that to his other charms – such as his odious candour, his thirst for publicity, and that ugly chip on his shoulder at not being Master of some Cambridge College . . .'

'Steady on, Ruth! I didn't much take to him myself, but we've no reason to suppose . . . Anyway, to get back to Antoinette Sheen. How do you know she was there? And where was she?'

'She was in Dalesford's office, just before we arrived.'

'Have you got second sight, or do your eyes penetrate walls?'

'No, but I've got a darn good nose. I smelt her perfume. The room was strong with it as we came in.'

'Perhaps it was Julie Benson's.'

'No. I got up close to Julie Benson, just to make sure.'

'M'm . . . It's still only a hunch, though. The trace of perfume in Dalesford's room doesn't mean it was necessarily Antoinette.'

81

'All right, I can't prove it, Philip. But in my bones I'm not only certain she was there, but I'm positive we've actually seen her.'

'Ruth! Where?'

'I don't suppose you noticed her, because you never do notice women until they're right in front of your eyes, but we passed a tall girl with a superb figure as we came up the stairs. I hate to admit it, but she really was rather super. I caught a faint whiff of her scent as we passed, and that same scent was lingering in Dalesford's office when we arrived a minute later.'

Holt burst into a peal of laughter. 'You really are quite a girl at times! Supposing you're right: why should Dalesford deny it?' He glanced at her sleeve. 'And what else did you notice?'

'That pile of *New Features*. Judging by the size of it, the Professor must have been a reader for quite some time. But if he's just a reader why keep such a large number of back numbers?'

'Well, it's not all that unusual. In fact, it's quite reasonable for a man in his position. But I see what you're getting at. You think he's a contributor? In other words, that he's Prospero. "If you want to know who murdered your son ask Prospero."' He paused to give it thought. 'It's a possibility. Political Science is his field, and that's what Prospero's articles are about. Also he made no bones about disliking Vance Scranton.'

'He also goes in for green ink,' Ruth observed. 'I noticed that. It wouldn't have been hard for his secretary to pinch his pen and scribble her insinuations on the magazine, then send it to the Scrantons whom she presumably knew always stayed at the Savoy.'

'One thing doesn't fit,' Ruth pointed out. 'She was surely at Deanfriston when that magazine was posted.'

'Yes, that much has been confirmed. But perhaps Jimmy Wade, that soul of discretion, posted it for her.'

'Perhaps he did. They seem rather chummy, don't they?'

Holt nodded. 'Jimmy Wade and Julie Benson. Does your woman's intuition detect a liaison there?'

'It stands out a mile,' said Ruth. 'I wonder what Mrs Wade thinks about the arrangement?'

'She's a wheel-chair cripple, so the Inspector was telling me.'

'Oh. If Julie *is* having an affair with her brother-in-law, why does she try to give the impression that she's still in love with her ex-fiancé – dead or alive?'

'To cover up, perhaps?' suggested Holt. 'Don't forget, fainting isn't necessarily a sign of true love. Perhaps Julie was horrified by the idea of Vance being alive. She would be, for instance, if the murderer had told her he'd done a good job and blown her ex-fiancé's head to bits.'

'Using the current lover to get rid of the discarded one? What a morbid mind you have, Mr Holt! I admit I don't trust Jimmy Wade, but that would make him not merely in the undertaking business but actually supplying his own customers! Aren't we going a little too fast?'

'Walking too fast, do you mean – or theorising?'

'Well, both.'

They stopped again to admire the view and Holt took off his jacket and loosened his tie. It was surprisingly warm for the time of year. Below and stretching out in front of them the English Channel was steel-blue, whipped into a curious pattern like pages of shorthand by the rhythm of the wind on white-tipped waves. Gulls circled above their heads, white against the cobalt sky. Holt found it hard to reconcile the beauty of the scene with the ugly events occurring only a few miles inland.

Ruth broke into his thoughts. 'What impressions did you get out of Vance's study?'

'The Professor made pretty certain that I didn't get any.'

'How do you mean?'

'Oh, he took me down to Scholars' Row all right. But he never left my side! I wanted to look around, get the feel of the place, examine Vance's books, and so on. I needed peace and quiet to breathe in the atmosphere of the place and wait for a flash of inspiration about what really happened that night. But it was quite out of the question with Dalesford buzzing about like a zoo keeper showing off his favourite animal. Honestly, I don't think he cares sixpence who's been murdered as long as he gets his name mentioned in the press. One thing's certain: I shall have to go back again.'

'Won't Dalesford always be there to show you around?'

'Not after midnight,' said Holt tersely.

Ruth looked awed. 'You mean you're going prowling?'

He nodded.

'When?'

'Tonight.'

Within sight of Belle Tout lighthouse and a glimpse of Beachy Head they decided it was time to turn back. On the return half of the walk, with a strong wind behind them, they made rapid progress. Soon the full curve of the Seven Sisters came into view again, and then the lonely hotel, closed for the winter, which nestled in the hollow of Birling Gap.

Ruth, who was marching ahead, called out as she breasted the final slope, 'There's someone down there on horseback, Philip – poking round the car.'

Despite the distance, it seemed almost as if her voice had carried on the wind. The rider looked up in their direction, then moved away from the Mustang and cantered out of sight. Clad in jodhpurs, with a flash of yellow which might or might not have been long hair, neither Ruth nor Holt could decide afterwards if the lone horse-rider had been a man or a woman.

Some five or six minutes later they descended the last stretch and hastened to the parked car. Holt circled it cautiously, examining the bodywork for scratches; it was not unknown for car-haters whose minds were unhinged to do stupid, superficial damage to cars parked in lonely spots, sometimes going so far as to slash tyres and break windows. But there seemed nothing amiss with the Mustang. Perhaps it had simply invited admiration from a car enthusiast. However, remembering Curly's acquaintances at Brighton, Holt took the precaution of opening the bonnet and taking a brief look at the engine.

'Searching for time bombs?' asked Ruth.

He grinned and somewhat shamefacedly shut the bonnet. He slid behind the wheel and the great engine sprang into life at the first touch of the ignition.

'Must be getting windy in my old age,' he remarked as they drove slowly inland along the narrow lane.

. . . It happened very swiftly, despite the fact that they were dawdling . . .

A flock of sheep broke unexpectedly from the steep hedge-rows and spread across their path. Holt gasped with fear, stamped on his brakes, and swung the wheel hard in a frantic attempt to avoid them. Two of the animals bleated their disapproval and just managed to jump out of the way as the car ran with a soft, crunching thud into the bank, half climbed it, then tilted at a sharp angle and stalled its engine.

Neither of them was hurt. They were just blinking at one another in surprise when a farmer's lad came bursting through the hedge to help. By good luck he was a frustrated car-fan. Swearing roundly at his sheep and uttering a series of commands and piercing whistles to a bright-eyed dog, he bent his brawny shoulders to the task of righting the Mustang and getting it back on to the road.

His Sussex brogue was almost unintelligible to Holt and Ruth, but it was obvious, once he had satisfied himself that neither of the car's occupants was hurt, that his chief concern was for the car's damaged bumper and mudguard.

It did not take Holt long to discover the cause of the accident. After squirming briefly under the nose and examining both wheels from the inside, he rose to his feet, a thunderous expression on his face.

The farmhand looked at him anxiously. 'Yew reckon someone been tinkerin' with her, guv'nor?'

'See for yourself. Some bright character has taken a stout pair of wire-clippers and cut through the hydraulic brake tubes on both sides. A nice clean incision with practically no oil drops to show for it. Might have been done by a surgeon!'

The farmhand squatted down to confirm this, then gave a slow, significant whistle as he straightened up. 'Which way was yew thinkin' of takin' up at the crossroads, guv'nor? Newhaven or Eastbourne?'

'Well, I'm not sure really . . .'

'It don't make no difference, anyway. There's terrible steep hills immediate, whichever way yew was goin'. Just like switchbacks at the fairground, they are. Either way yew'd have been killed for sure.'

Chapter Seven

There was a message in Philip Holt's pigeon-hole at the reception desk when they got back to their hotel in Eastbourne. It was a simple request to ring a local number as soon as possible.

'No name?' Holt asked.

'Apparently not, sir.'

Holt frowned, feeling rather irritable after a bumpy return journey on the top of a double-decker bus. 'Well, was it a lady or a gentleman?'

'I'm afraid I don't know, sir. I've only just come on duty. Would you like to telephone from the desk here? I can get the number for you straightaway.'

Holt agreed and a few moments later the clerk nodded to him to pick up the receiver.

'Hello,' said a female voice.

'This is Philip Holt speaking.'

'Oh, Mr Holt, how very kind of you to ring. I tried to get you earlier but it seems you were out.'

'Your voice is charming but it would help if I knew your name.'

There came an infectious chuckle from the other end of the line. 'How stupid of me! This is Antoinette Sheen.'

'Indeed?'

'I heard you were in these parts. I think we ought to meet.'

Holt shared her opinion but was curious to know what her motives might be. 'May I ask *why* you think we ought to meet, Miss Sheen?'

'Certainly, you may,' the husky voice answered pleasantly. 'I have two very good reasons. Firstly, I've something to give you – something in connection with Vance Scranton. And secondly, as I imagine you've been told a pack of lies about me and my relationship with the boy, I think it's only fair that I should be given a chance to defend myself.'

'I see. That sounds reasonable enough. Where can we meet?'

'Could you possibly come out to my bungalow? I'm on a painting jag and if I have to leave it means cleaning myself up and all that bore.'

'Very well. What's the address?'

'I live at East Dean. The bungalow is painted a dreadful shade of salmon pink – it stands alone in the middle of a field . . .' She gave an ironic laugh and added, 'Ideal for amateur burglaries.'

'What makes you say that? Are you a victim?'

'You could put it like that. Someone broke into my bedroom the other day when I was out, but nothing was stolen. Now, do you think you can find the way? It's just before the road branches off for Birling Gap. You have a car, I take it?'

'I had a car, but now I shall have to hire one. My own got buckled up this morning. Oddly enough, Miss Sheen, the accident took place near Birling Gap, not far from East Dean.'

'Really? How strange. I haven't heard anything about it. But then, I've only just got back from my daily ride.'

'Your daily ride, did you say?' Holt said quickly. 'Do you mean – er – horses?'

She chuckled delightedly. 'Of course, Mr Holt. What did you think I meant – bicycles?'

Over lunch at the hotel Holt told Ruth about the invitation.

'She said she'd heard I was down here,' he added. 'News certainly travels fast.'

'It always does in small communities,' Ruth reminded him. 'We've been here nearly twenty-four hours, remember – plenty of time for our whereabouts to have been circulated to the College and East Dean and half-way round the Sussex coast by now.'

'It probably just confirms what you said about Antoinette Sheen being at the College this morning,' Holt conceded.

'So now we're going to meet the gorgeous Antoinette! What time do we leave?'

'Not *we*, my dear. The invitation was only for one.' He held up his hand to cut off her protests.

'But she'll eat you alive!' Ruth exclaimed.

'I'm remarkably indigestible,' he said happily. 'Ask my ex-wife. Besides, it would look ridiculous if I had to lug you along as a kind of chaperone or nanny!'

Ruth looked miserable. 'How do you suggest I spend my time this afternoon while you're being seduced by this . . . this lethal charmer?'

'Ring up Inspector Hyde and tell him what happened to the Mustang's brakes. Give him an account of our visit to the College and ask him to check up on Professor Dalesford's background. And you can ask him when the devil he's going to come up with some facts about the Prospero article and the Christopher postcards . . . and those photographs you so cleverly took of Curly's pals in the delivery van.' Holt beamed at her as he rose to his feet.

She retorted with heavy sarcasm, 'I'm *so* touched by the last remark. It makes me feel really wanted.'

Holt set off alone for the bungalow, in a hired Cortina. Driving down the exceptionally steep hill which dropped with switchback suddenness into East Dean he was forcibly reminded of the farmhand's prediction: 'Yew'd have been killed for sure.' He had escaped one trap; was he walking wide-eyed into another? It seemed that Miss Sheen's residence was conveniently close to the spot where he had parked the car that morning. Quite possibly she could have followed them from the College, then saddled her horse and . . . But, in that case, why admit she had been riding? And what about that glimpse of blonde hair? Antoinette was not a blonde, that much he knew even though he had never met her. A blonde wig? A yellow hat or scarf? Rule out the first two, but a scarf was quite a possibility . . .

He soon spotted the bungalow, salmon-pink in a blaze of sunshine in the middle of a field ('ideal for amateur burglaries' – what an odd remark). He parked the car in a small copse some distance away and completed the journey on foot. He did not actually intend spying on the girl, but on the other hand there seemed no point in announcing his presence too far in advance.

As a result, Antoinette Sheen was too engrossed in her work to notice his approach across the field. The 'painting jag' she had spoken of was apparently in full swing; she had her back to him as she stood at an oil-painting propped on an easel. Soft autumnal sunlight flooded in through the open French windows and rimmed her long, tawny hair with golden fire. He noticed she was wearing jodhpurs and a thin yellow shirt with sleeves rolled up. It was tied with a sash in a knot at the back and emphasised the striking slimness of her waist.

Holt's eyes widened when he saw what she was painting. It was a copy of one of his favourite pictures, Vermeer's *The Kitchen Maid*. The painting was almost completed; only the bread and a corner of the table had yet to be tackled. It was clear that the finished result would be a remarkably accurate reproduction of the great Dutchman's original work.

He was startled when, without turning round, she spoke to him.

'Do you like it, Mr Holt?'

'I . . . I really must apologise,' he began.

'Whatever for? Let's say, my painting was so arresting that it halted you in mid-stride!' There was an unmistakable lilt of amusement in her voice. She turned to face him. 'Or were you admiring my figure? I'm told it's pretty good, even in this Farmer Giles outfit.'

She took down a mirror which was perched on top of the easel and, with no attempt to hide her vanity, pushed and prodded at her hair with the handle of a paintbrush. The yellow shirt was cut alarmingly low and seemed to have been designed without the use of buttons; fold-over lapels which met in the sash at the back were supposed to take care of the proprieties. They did not do a very secure job.

'Your figure is undoubtedly very attractive,' Holt said. 'But to tell the truth it *was* the canvas that stopped me. Vermeer happens to be a minor passion of mine.'

She gave a peal of laughter. 'How refreshing to find an honest man. Most men would have settled for easy flattery.'

Holt went closer to the easel and looked carefully at her work. 'The biggest test still lies ahead of you.'

A worried frown crossed her face. 'What do you mean, exactly?'

'The bread on the table. Vermeer painted those loaves three hundred years ago and—'

'I know what you're going to say!' she cut in with genuine enthusiasm. 'Three centuries ago – yet if you walk into the Rijks Museum today and go straight to Room 225 you feel you can almost snatch the bread off the table and eat it, it looks so crisp and appetising.'

'Exactly! That's your challenge! Flunk that, and you may as well take up pop art.'

For some minutes of animated conversation they continued to explore their common interest in art. It was a chance remark of Antoinette's which brought the ugly present back into the room.

'I don't remember having such a good natter about painting since Vance was last here,' she said.

There was a pregnant silence.

'Did he paint too?' Holt asked.

'No, he couldn't handle a brush very well, but he was tremendously knowledgeable about art, its techniques, history, and so on. He was very knowledgeable about everything, to tell the truth. His real talent lay in writing: queer, twisted stuff, but I think he had in him the makings of something good. I notice, by the way, that you still speak of him in the past tense, as though you really believe he's dead.'

'And I notice that you do, too,' he said.

'*Touché.* You don't believe this red herring of a newspaper rumour about Vance being alive?'

'I don't believe everything I see in print,' said Holt noncommittally.

'It's an absurd story, written by an irresponsible journalist!'

She sounded angry. 'Why try and give hope to the bereaved parents?'

'You're quite certain it was Vance who was killed?'

'Of course. I identified the body.'

'Did you look at it for long?'

Antoinette pursed her lips. 'Hardly. It was a terrible sight.'

Holt said, 'Mistakes sometimes happen in such cases, you know. Nobody looked for more than a few seconds – Julie Benson fainted, I believe.'

'She always does, it's standard routine with her,' The girl laughed. 'No wonder Vance grew out of her, she's so determinedly helpless and still so wet behind the ears.'

'Forgive me for putting it bluntly, Miss Sheen, but when Vance grew out of Julie, he – grew into you, didn't he?'

Antoinette's beautiful eyes sparkled with controlled anger. 'I rather imagined that's what they've been telling you – how I seduced him, twisted his innocent mind, perverted his golden youth. *Jeunesse doré* indeed! Is that what you've heard?'

'Something like that.'

'What a cartload of rubbish! Vance was *born* with a twisted mind, a mind ten times more cynical and bitter than yours or mine will ever be. He was a little evil old man, right from the womb.'

Holt regarded her intently, allowing her full rein.

'Oh, his brain was keen enough,' she went on, 'but only keen to see the black side of human nature, never the good. Voltaire and the other humanists he laughed at, yet someone like Talleyrand was ideal, with his theory that diplomacy was the art of finding your opponent's weaknesses and applying the all-powerful pressure of money at the weak spots.'

'He knew the price of everything and the value of nothing?'

93

'Yes, he admired Wilde too. Vance was crazy about money and said everyone could be bought, from a High Court Judge downwards. Heaven knows, Mr Holt, I'm no angel – I like men, I like sex, I like my freedom – but I refused to accept his cynicism. It upset me to see such good material going to rot.'

'May I ask, were you lovers?' Holt said.

She hesitated a moment before replying, but she met his level gaze without flinching. 'You do go in for plain speaking, don't you?' she said.

'The habit is catching,' Holt replied.

'Fair enough. Yes, we were lovers, for a while. He was handsome and virile. I liked him physically and he seemed to like me. I thought love might . . . I know this sounds corny, but I thought it might thaw him out, if you see what I mean.'

'Yes, I do see. And did it – thaw him out?'

'No. The idea was naïve and quite useless.'

'So you ceased to be lovers?'

Antoinette shrugged her shoulders. *'C'est la vie.'*

'Did he like that – being rejected, I mean?'

'I'm several steps ahead of you, Mr Holt,' she said, softening a little and crossing towards him. 'Yes, I rejected him . . . but no, we didn't have a quarrel.' She smiled. 'No, I did not present him with a rival . . . and no, I did not steal out of the piano recital that night and shoot him because he was pestering me . . . I've had all this out before with Inspector Hyde, you know.' She was standing close to him now, her hands slowly reaching up to his shoulders, her eyes staring up at him, compelling him to believe her. 'Whatever else you may think about me, Philip – and I've admitted I'm no angel – I want you to believe one thing. I didn't kill Vance Scranton . . .'

For a moment Holt did not move; his mind warned him that Mata Hari had used the identical technique. But his pounding blood forced him to admit that even if the wool was being pulled over his eyes it was being done in an entrancing fashion. He would think about Mata Hari afterwards . . .

'At such close quarters . . . it's rather hard not to believe you . . .' he said as his arms folded over her superb body.

'And I want you to continue in that belief, Philip, when we're no longer at . . . quite such close quarters,' she said softly, and raised her lips to his.

After a very long time Antoinette released herself and stepped back. 'I was quite right!' she said. 'When I saw you this morning I said, "There's one hunk of a man!"'

Most of Holt's senses were still surging in the land where Antoinette's splendid attractions had led them, but his mind reacted swiftly enough. 'I thought you said you knew nothing about my accident?'

'What accident?'

'To my car, between here and Birling Gap this morning.'

'But I don't know anything about it! I was out riding, I go out riding most mornings. No, I saw you up at the College. In fact, I even passed you and that little popsy of yours on the steps.'

'But Professor Dalesford told me—'

'He's an old booby who's afraid of his own shadow! He probably said he hadn't seen me for days. Am I right? He doesn't like to have our names linked too much in public, and he doesn't really like me going up to the College at all.'

'For fear you will pervert the entire youth of Southern England?'

They both laughed.

Then Holt asked, 'Why do you go up there? You're not on the staff, are you?'

'No, but I have permission from the College Secretary to use the library.' She pointed casually at the bookshelves which ran the length of one wall. 'I need it, for research on those things.' She laughed again. 'Bottom row, far corner – push those canvases out of the way and you'll soon see who my favourite author is.'

Holt followed her suggestion and examined the shelves. Tumbled in complete disorder, some in paperbacks and some in hard covers, were nine or ten historical novels, all written by Antoinette Sheen. He took out two and glanced at their contents. Deep-bosomed Plantaganet beauties and impossibly muscular French musketeers gleamed from the glossy dust-jackets very much as he had anticipated; but the books bore the imprint of a good publishing house. He was also surprised to see how wide a range of history the novels covered and what excellent reviews some of them had received, to judge by the critics' quotes which the jackets carried.

'Don't embarrass me by looking at them too long,' she said. 'They're just my bread and butter. A girl has to live.'

Holt stood up. An interesting new theory was beginning to form at the back of his mind. As he turned to face Antoinette he found that she was holding out an envelope. 'What's this?' he asked.

'I mentioned on the phone that I had something to give you – something in connection with Vance's death. You'll see now why I can't believe in this fairy story that he's still alive. This is a letter from the man who murdered him. I got it yesterday.'

Holt opened the envelope. Inside was a typewritten note, and a small object wrapped in tissue paper. He read the message aloud: '*Dear Miss Sheen, I feel quite sure that you, more than anyone else, would like to have the enclosed. It belonged to Vance Scranton.*'

Carefully he unfolded the tissue paper and held the contents in the palm of his hand.

'And this *did* belong to Vance?' he said at length.

'Yes, that was his signet ring.'

Back in Eastbourne, Holt turned the Cortina into the hotel drive and found a place to park. In a deeply pensive mood he approached the entrance to the hotel, where a young man with flaxen hair blocked his way.

'Monsieur Holt?' asked the stranger, with a slight foreign accent.

'Yes, that's right.'

'Please forgive me for stopping you like this. The hotel concierge pointed you out to me. My name is Henri Legere. I am a student at Deanfriston College. Please tell me,' he went on, producing a copy of the newspaper which contained Abe Jenkins' article, 'is it true that Vance may be alive?'

'I wish I could answer that question, Monsieur Legere. The writer of that article seems to know more than I do.'

The young French student was not really listening, he was anxious to continue with his own story. 'I must tell you – I am not absolutely certain – but I think I saw Vance myself this morning.'

'Where was this?'

'Here in Eastbourne.'

'Did he see you?'

'No, I was up in my room. I did not go to the College today.'

'Oh, you have lodgings in the town, then?'

97

'Lodgings? . . . Ah, *oui, ma chambre*! Yes, I share rooms with another student called Graham Brown. We have a window that looks out onto the back of a restaurant – The Golden Peacock, it is called. The door to the kitchens is in a narrow alley which is nearly always dark. That is why I am not sure that it is Vance I see. But it looked much like him. Please tell me, Monsieur Holt: is it possible that he still lives?'

'I'm afraid I can't answer that one. Does this friend of yours – Graham Brown – also think he saw Vance?'

'Ah no . . . Graham is in Scotland, visiting his parents.'

'I see. So we only have your word for it. Well, keep your eyes skinned, Monsieur Legere!'

'*Comment?*'

'Keep a sharp look-out and communicate immediately with me or with the police if you think you see him again.'

'Very well, Monsieur Holt. *Au revoir.*'

The fair-haired student bowed, walked quickly down the drive, and pedalled away on an old bicycle which had been propped at the kerbside.

Holt was stopped by the reception clerk when he entered the hotel. Once satisfied that Holt had encountered the young man with the foreign accent who had just been asking for him, the clerk passed on one other message. Would Mr Holt please contact Miss Sanders as soon as he got in?

Holt smiled to himself. She wants to see how much is left of me after being 'eaten alive' by Antoinette Sheen, he thought. With a slight twinge of pique at Ruth's shrewd prediction of events he hurried to his room to wash faint traces of lipstick from his face and brush the collar of his jacket before striding down the corridor and tapping on Ruth's door.

He scowled when a male voice called out, inviting him to enter.

'Don't glare at me like that, Holt,' said Inspector Hyde jovially when Holt turned the door handle and looked in. 'Ruth's room is far more comfortable than mine.'

Holt's scowl dissolved into a grin and he stepped inside, shutting the door firmly behind him.

'I got down here soon after lunch,' the Inspector explained. 'There's nothing new on the Curly murder, I'm afraid. Ruth's been filling me in on your visit to the College and the brake-cutting at Birling Gap. I'm very glad to see you both alive.'

Holt nodded grimly. 'It was a neat job, done by an expert. Both the hydraulic tubes had been cut – if only one had been done we'd still have been able to brake.'

Ruth was scrutinising him. 'What does Miss Sheen have to say about the accident?'

'She claims to know nothing about it.'

'Even though she lives right near by?'

'Well, to be fair, it wasn't a very noisy accident, was it?'

'I see,' Ruth said dryly. 'And I suppose she also claims to know nothing whatsoever about what happened in Vance Scranton's study last week?'

Holt took out a cigarette, caught Ruth's eye again, and did not light it. 'I haven't quite weighed her up yet. She's convinced that it was Vance who was killed, but she swears black and blue she had no part in it.'

It was obvious from Ruth's expression that she had already weighed up Miss Sheen and was forming a pretty accurate reconstruction of the recent scene at the bungalow. She managed to convey her disapproval without saying anything more cutting than, 'And did the curvaceous Antoinette manage to convince you of that, Philip?'

'Spare the chap's blushes!' Hyde intervened. 'Your boss may be of the male sex, but he's nobody's fool. Tell us what you found out, dear chap.'

'Before I do that, I must tell you about something odd that happened in the hotel drive just now.'

The Inspector and Ruth craned forward as he recounted his meeting with Henri Legere.

'That makes three people who claim they've seen him,' Hyde said. 'The boy's mother, Mr Wade the undertaker, and now a College friend. And yet Antoinette, you say, is quite sure he's dead. I wonder *why* she's so sure?'

'I can think of a very good reason,' suggested Ruth with meaning.

Ignoring her, the Inspector said, 'Well, now, Holt, you were going to give us an account of your visit and your impressions of the lady.'

Holt nodded and now lit his cigarette in silence. Then he began ticking off each item on his fingers. 'My impressions are as follows: One: she's stunning to look at. Two: she's astoundingly frank. Three: she's a first-class painter and knows a lot about art. Four: she's got an excellent brain; I'd almost guess an academically-trained brain. She can quote Talleyrand and Voltaire without seeming pompous. And another thing – those books she writes. I haven't read any of them, but I admit I had some pre-conceived notions about her. A quick perusal of her bookshelf rather changed all that.'

'Heavens above!' Ruth interrupted, her face flushed. 'She really has twirled you around her little finger, hasn't she?'

Hyde attempted to be constructive. 'So you think she's in the clear so far as the murder is concerned, and you don't think she had anything to do with the brake-fixing?'

'She may quite well have done both – especially the latter,'

Holt said unexpectedly. He described the clothes Antoinette had been wearing.

'Well,' Ruth burst out, 'what more evidence do you want!'

'All right!' he snapped. 'So we saw someone in jodhpurs and a flash of yellow! But if she did it, why didn't she bother to change before I called on her?'

'Bluff! Pure bluff!' said Ruth heatedly.

'Wait a moment,' the Inspector interrupted diplomatically. 'You said she might have an academically-trained mind, Holt. Was that pure guesswork, or did you know that she has two University degrees?'

Holt sat up straight. 'In History and Economics, by any chance?'

'Exactly. Then you did know?'

'No, but I've been putting two and two together. I'll even go so far as to tell you who Prospero is.'

'Be careful, you're likely to slip up here,' Hyde warned him good-naturedly.

'No, I'm not! It all fits. Antoinette is hot stuff on history – she must be to write a pile of books like that and get them published by a decent publishing house. But it's not her only line of country. She writes those spicy historical romances to pay her grocery bills, but she's got the brains and knowledge to do more, in a field closely associated with history: namely, politics and economics!'

'Where does all this get us, then?' asked Ruth.

'Simply this: know thine enemy. Antoinette Sheen rates high on the list of suspects for murder. I'd been led to expect a feather-brained sex-bomb, but the truth is we're dealing with a cool, astute, and highly intelligent woman.'

'Who writes political articles for a highbrow weekly under the pen-name of Prospero?' Hyde suggested.

'No, I don't imagine it's quite like that. Naturally, I'm only guessing, but I shouldn't be surprised to learn that Prospero is Professor Dalesford's pseudonym.'

'Dalesford?'

'Yes. You see, nobody is going to pay serious attention to articles like that if it's known they're being written by a woman novelist, the author of lurid romances. So Dalesford – who strikes me as a vain fool – takes the glory, while Antoinette does the donkey-work. I don't know who collects the cash – they probably share it between them.'

Hyde stood up to stretch his legs and started to fill his pipe. 'Now that's inspired guesswork, Holt, because as it happens you've hit the nail on the head! Certain information we've been able to obtain confirms everything you've said. Dalesford *is* Prospero. And I have further news: the Yard's calligraphy experts say it's ninety per cent certain that the person who wrote that poison-pen note in green ink in the *New Feature* was Julie Benson.'

Holt nodded. 'That fits. Who but his own secretary would know that the Professor doesn't actually write the stuff himself? Julie wants to point the finger of suspicion at Antoinette, whom she hates like poison for having taken Vance from her . . .'

Ruth's tone of voice had a slight touch of frost about it when she filled the pause that followed, but she spoke seriously and gained attention. 'It could just be that Julie does know something, don't you think? Maybe she's got a few facts tucked up her sleeve which she's not yet told. Isn't it just possible that it's Julie Benson who's speaking the truth?'

The Inspector cleared his throat and exchanged a guilty look with Holt. 'Ruth's right, as usual. It's perfectly possible,' he acknowledged. 'I shall have to tackle Miss Benson again.

For one thing, she's got to answer for sending anonymous accusations through the post.'

'I'm afraid you're going to have to have Antoinette on the carpet, too, Inspector,' Holt said, taking the envelope out of his pocket. 'She claims this letter was sent to her yesterday, with Vance Scranton's signet ring inside it. The ring is probably genuine – Julie or Vance's parents can confirm that – but I have my doubts about the typewritten letter and the way she says it came to her.'

Hyde took the ring eagerly and examined it. 'Now we may be getting somewhere at last! Did you look at it carefully, Holt?'

'No, I've had no time.'

Hyde handed it back. 'Well, what do you make of the insignia on it?'

Holt turned it this way and that, viewing it from every angle. 'It's pretty simple, isn't it? Just Vance Scranton's initials, with the V planted over the S.'

'Right! I can see that now. But on the Christopher postcard . . . Here, take a look for yourself.' He took from his wallet a photostat copy of the card which had been sent to Vance. 'This is what our cypher department have been able to produce.'

Ruth's face lit up as she and Holt bent over the photostat. The message that had once clearly read 'HAVING A WONDERFUL TIME. REGARDS FROM CHRISTOPHER' was now distorted by a series of capital letters appearing between the innocent words, and the Vance Scranton symbol was self-evident. The complete message read:

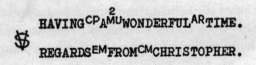

103

'Was this a code message written in special ink?' Ruth asked, warmth and excitement flooding back into her voice.

Hyde nodded. 'We had the cards treated. This code came to light on the first card, the one that was sent directly to Vance just before he died. But there was no concealed message on the second card.'

'The one Jimmy Wade produced?'

'Yes. One might be forgiven for wondering if the second is a fake.'

'Black mark for Jimmy the Undertaker,' said Ruth. 'Doesn't the V and the S at the beginning of each group look like a dollar sign?'

'That's exactly what misled me,' Hyde agreed. 'But now that we have the ring it's perfectly clear what the V crossed by an S means. And the boy's involvement in this strange business appears to be proven beyond doubt.'

'But what does the code mean?' Ruth wanted to know.

'Our experts haven't come up with the answer to that yet. The trouble is, these three and four-letter blocks are so simple they could mean any one of a thousand things. Give our eggheads a really knotty description of the latest nuclear rocket written in cyrillic script by a foreign spy and they'll have the answer for you inside half an hour.'

Ruth's enthusiasm was so obviously dashed by Hyde's words that he felt compelled to add a spot of encouragement. 'In one direction we've taken a step forward, though. Those snapshots you got from the back of Curly's mini-bus look like amounting to something.'

'I thought they were too blurred,' she said.

'Not a bit of it. We had them enlarged to a considerable size and sent some copies to Interpol. The two men in the van were burnt to cinders, as you know, so your photographs were all we had to identify them by. Interpol came back with a theory – which hasn't yet been confirmed, mind – that the two men were petty French criminals.'

'French?' she said with surprise.

'Yes. Petty criminals wanted on a charge of operating an illegal printing press in Paris. But before you jump to the conclusion that this means counterfeit bank notes, listen to the rest of the puzzle. They weren't printers of forged money, apparently – all they seem to have printed were old French newspapers!'

'How old were the newspapers supposed to be?' Holt enquired.

'Anything from eighty to ninety-five years. Odd, isn't it? Why reprint exact replicas of Parisian newspapers of the 1870s and 1880s?'

Holt paused. 'I require notice of that question.'

The Inspector smiled. 'Fair enough. When you come up with some more of your inspired guesswork on this little conundrum I'll be delighted to hear from you.'

Holt nodded. 'It'll give me something to think about while I'm waiting for Professor Dalesford to douse the lights at the College tonight.'

Chapter Eight

The chimes of midnight floated across the moonlit Downs and reached Philip Holt's ears as he stood waiting in the deep shadow of the copse. Despite his warm clothing he shivered slightly. Nearly an hour had gone by since the last boisterous shouts from students on their way to bed had echoed over the ground and the last lights of the College had been extinguished. He had forced himself to wait before making his entry, although all was quiet; there would be no possible explanation if he were caught snooping around Scholars' Row at this hour of the night.

He had no clear idea what he was looking for, nor quite why he preferred to make his search in elaborate secrecy when Inspector Hyde could easily have arranged for him to visit Vance Scranton's study by daylight. It was partly a strong intuitive feeling that had made him want to return, and partly the impression that Dalesford had hustled him through the room with suspicious abruptness. Holt did not take kindly to being hustled.

He peered at his watch and judged it time to go. Checking his pockets once again to make sure that nothing such as keys or loose change could jangle and make his presence known, he stole from the shadows of the elms and moved noiselessly on rubber-soled shoes across the close-cropped lawn. The moon seemed unusually bright. It obviated the need of a torch, but he was glad he had taken the precaution of blackening his face and wearing dark clothing; it made him feel less conspicuous.

The first shock came when he found the door to Scholars' Row was locked. This was not on the programme. Until the time of the murder, he knew, it had been usual for it to be left open.

There was nothing for it but to break in by a window. He was not sure of his ability to pick out Vance's study from outside, but here the brilliant moonlight helped him. It shone at an oblique angle into the row of ground-floor rooms and at his second inspection he was able to single out a picture on the wall which he remembered noticing during his brief morning visit. It was a good copy in oils of Leyster's *The Jester*, the original of which hung in the Rijks Museum. Holt guessed that this was another example of Antoinette's work.

He unwrapped a penknife and a strong piece of perspex from his handkerchief, and forced the window-catch without much difficulty. It was fortunate that the outer shutters had not been closed, he thought grimly, as he hoisted himself over the sill and dropped silently to the carpeted floor. For a moment he was tempted to close the shutters and switch on the light; they were of solid wood and would probably let no glimmer through. But he soon abandoned the idea, realising that, however well the shutters might protect him from discovery from the outside, he could easily be betrayed by a crack of light under the study door.

* * *

For a moment or two he stood in the centre of the room, letting his eyes grow accustomed to the shadows and strange moonlit shapes, almost sniffing like a wary dog, probing with all his senses. In this room a murder had been committed . . . Who had stood there, gun in hand, as a body holding two glasses and a bottle of port had slipped to the floor? . . . Had it been a blue-eyed blonde, a cantankerous Professor, a bird-like undertaker. Had it been a beautiful and brainy authoress? Or Vance Scranton himself? Or had it, in fact, been none of these?

No flash of inspiration, no weird telepathic communication reached him. No face swam with clarity into his mind, not even a conviction as to the murderer's sex. One thing only was certain: whoever it was, man or woman, had been a supremely confident person, a cool, calculating thinker possessed of iron nerves and an above-average brain.

He took out his pocket torch and dimmed its beam with his handkerchief. Then, moving with the utmost caution, he began to examine the room.

He concentrated first on the desk. It was here that he had hoped to find something of importance. To his annoyance he found all the drawers empty; Dalesford had evidently taken it upon himself to put Vance's papers under lock and key.

Scrutinising the walls, he found nothing unusual. He took the picture from its hook and looked at the back of the canvas. He had been right, it had been painted by Antoinette and she had scrawled a message in black ink to accompany her gift. 'To Van, from Antoinette, in the hope that one day you will learn to laugh like this.' The inscription was dated in the summer of that year; about the time, Holt reckoned, when their affair would have been coming to an end. She had not succeeded in getting him to laugh like Leyster's gay fool, and they had parted. As friends? . . . Or as bitter enemies?

There were no other pictures or ornaments on the walls, apart from a calendar significantly halted at the date on which the body had been found. Methodically he moved about the room, inspecting the various items of furniture and personal possessions but learning nothing new.

There were a vast number of books – too many to be accommodated solely by the bookshelves – and the surplus volumes were stacked in piles on the floor wherever there was room. The choice of subjects was varied: there were scholarly tomes on history, politics, economics; works of general interest, much ultra-modern fiction; large quantities of magazines, most of them French, a number of Antoinette's novels, and a series of handsomely illustrated volumes on Art. The fields of interest were indeed widely-spread, but there was nothing strikingly out of place. Holt kneeled and took Antoinette's novels from the shelf to glance at their fly-leaves. Flippant, affectionate messages were written on each, but again nothing untoward caught his eye. Next he pulled out one of the heavy Art books – it happened to be devoted to Claude Monet – and opened it at random. A torn scrap of yellowing paper fluttered to the floor. As there was nothing written on it he assumed it had been a place-marker and crushed it in his palm.

It was then that he became aware of faint footsteps. In a flash he had jammed the book back into place and darted to the window.

Above the thumping of his heart he heard a heavy key being fitted into a massive lock – undoubtedly the entrance door to Scholars' Row. Holding his breath he listened to the door at the end of the corridor creaking open. Then, as footsteps sounded in an approaching crescendo, he leapt over the sill, fastened the window behind him, and dropped silently onto the grass below.

An oblique blade of moonlight divided the outside wall into light and shade; where he crouched was deepest black whilst a few inches above his head, at the level of the window sill, everything was illuminated by cold silver light. A dryness began to pervade his mouth as he waited, tensely, straining his ears for significant sounds. He identified the opening of the study door . . . and an instant later the midnight visitor had crossed the room without switching on the light, thrown open the window, and was reaching out both arms for the wooden shutters.

Holt pressed his body against the wall directly beneath the window, not daring to risk more than a side-glance upwards. There was a mild complaint of metal as the heavy shutters swung on iron hinges in need of oil, and in a matter of seconds the window was effectively sealed off. Even when the study light was switched on with an audible click, no chink escaped through the solid wood.

Catching his breath Holt half rose and pressed his ear to the shutter, and after a moment he was rewarded. Quite distinctly he could hear something heavy being moved about inside, followed by a slithering sound as though some clumsy object, like a body or an awkwardly filled sack, were being dragged across the floor. The invisible operation took three minutes at the most. Then he heard the light being switched off.

Quickly he dropped to the ground again and hugged the wall. But instead of the shutters being re-opened there was a scraping of metal and the unmistakable sound of an iron bolt being shot home, followed by something which sounded like the snap of a padlock. A moment later Holt heard the light being flicked on once more, as though the intruder wanted to give the room a last-minute look over, then it was clicked off again and the study door closed.

Holt jerked to his feet and ran along the outer wall to the entrance of Scholars' Row. He was convinced that he had reached it before his quarry. He halted in the shadow of some bushes and strained his ears once more for the sound of footsteps and a sliding sack. Nothing came. For what seemed an eternity he waited . . .

Suddenly a car choked into life some distance away. Holt wheeled and ran in the direction of the sound, but a tall building, which he knew to be the gym, blocked his way. He rounded the corner and realised he had not been quick enough. There was the smell of a car's exhaust in the night air, and a fractional glimpse of red tail-lights disappearing down the hill towards the village. Of the car itself only one impression had been clear. Holt knew, beyond a shadow of a doubt, that the motor which had sprung into life and sped through an unmistakable series of gear changes into top, belonged to only one brand of car in the world. It had been a Volkswagen.

At last he permitted himself to breathe normally and set off towards the dark lane where he had parked his hired Cortina. It would be interesting, he decided, to find out how many of the people connected with the Vance Scranton case possessed a Volkswagen.

So far he knew of only one.

It was tempting to jump to conclusions – but Inspector Hyde had frequently cautioned him against this cardinal sin. One must keep an open mind until a fact was proved beyond all shadow of doubt.

It would be equally interesting to casually ask one or two people for the time. He would just ask them the time; it would be as simple as that. They would either not possess a watch and consequently cease to excite his immediate interest, or they would glance at the watches on their wrists . . .

The person – male or female – who had reached out from the darkened room and closed the heavy wooden shutters above Philip Holt's head had displayed quite clearly in the brilliant moonlight an unusual characteristic: that of wearing a gold wristwatch on the *inside* of the wrist.

Chapter Nine

'On our short list of suspects, or shall we call them dubious persons,' Inspector Hyde was saying, 'we still have only one Volkswagen owner, and so far no one who wears his or her watch on the inside of the wrist.' He poured some more coffee into Holt's cup. 'You're quite sure about Professor Dalesford?'

Holt grunted an affirmative, his mouth full of toast. He was taking a late breakfast in his hotel room. He was dressed, for after allowing himself only a few hours of sleep he had already made one trip that morning. 'Dalesford seems to be in the clear. When I saw him up at the College this morning I made an excuse to ask him the time. He produced a whacking great pocket watch – half-hunters, I believe they call them, don't they? Julie Benson's in the clear too. She's got a tiny platinum model, worn in the normal way on the outside of her wrist.'

'I see. How is she today? Fully recovered from yesterday's fainting fit?'

'It seems so. She's even agreed to have lunch with me.'

'Oh? Where?'

'Here in Eastbourne, at a place called The Golden Peacock.

She didn't seem very keen on my choice of restaurant – said it's terribly expensive – but I thought it might be interesting to take a look around the place where that French student says he saw Vance Scranton.'

'Quite so,' Hyde murmured. 'And over lunch you'll show her the signet ring and evaluate her reactions, I shouldn't wonder. I wish I could be there, hidden under the table or something! This ring could be devilish important. Curly thought it important or he'd never have mentioned it, Christopher referred to it with invisible ink on a postcard; Miss Sheen decided to hand it over to you.' The Inspector shifted in his chair and addressed Ruth, who was standing at the window, apparently admiring the view of the sea. 'You're quite sure Antoinette doesn't wear a largish gold watch on the inside of her wrist, Ruth?'

'Dead certain,' was the reply. Whilst Holt had been at the College she had visited the salmon-pink bungalow. Sure that Antoinette would recognise her, Ruth had decided not to attempt any disguise. She had simply knocked on the door, announced that she was Philip Holt's secretary, and asked if she could use the telephone. She told Antoinette that Philip had sent her into East Dean to collect the Mustang from the garage, but as it was still having paint sprayed on its damaged mudguard she would not be able to drive it back as planned. Antoinette had proved unexpectedly obliging and insisted on driving Ruth back to Eastbourne herself in her green Mini Minor. With Antoinette's hands resting on the steering wheel for the best part of fifteen minutes it had not been difficult for Ruth to see that she wore no wristwatch at all.

'That doesn't prove much, unfortunately,' Hyde pointed out when Ruth had finished her explanation. 'It doesn't mean she never wears a watch at all.'

'No, but she's still got a glorious sun tan!' Ruth said enviously. If she normally wears a watch there'd almost certainly be a tell-tale patch of white on her wrist.'

Hyde was impressed by her perception. So was Holt, but he made no comment.

Hyde began to pace the room. 'Holt, there's one aspect of your midnight adventure that I don't quite understand. This arm that reached out above your head and closed the shutters – surely you could tell if it was male or female? I mean, the clothing, for one thing – and surely women's watches are generally much smaller than men's?'

'Yes, usually,' Ruth put in, 'but some girls are wearing man-sized watches, you know. It's a fashion gimmick.'

'It all happened so quickly I'm not prepared to be too adamant,' Holt admitted. 'The watch had a gold metal strap and the face was rather on the small side for a regular man's watch, but rather larger than the majority of women wear. As for the clothing . . . well, it seemed to be some kind of knitted garment like a long-sleeved pullover or cardigan; it was the sort of thing both sexes wear nowadays. No, the only two things which might lead us somewhere were that bit of newspaper that fell out of the Art book—'

'I'm anxious to see what the labs make of that. I'll have it sent up to Town straightaway,' Hyde assured him.

'—and the absolutely undeniable sound of a Volkswagen engine. Two slender threads of totally unconnected information in return for an uncomfortable night's work. When Dalesford let me into Vance's study this morning I couldn't see that a single thing had been touched. I can only assume that whatever was lugged about in that bumping sack either didn't belong to the room in the first place or else had been replaced before I got there today.'

115

'Whoever it was had a key to the Scholars' Row entrance door. Dalesford and Julie Benson are the most obvious, of course, but on the other hand . . . How about the shutters – were they still bolted?'

'Yes. The Professor explained it as a necessary security precaution, until the room is re-occupied.'

Hyde nodded thoughtfully. 'M'm . . . that seems reasonable enough on the face of it, I suppose – except for the fact that they were still open at a time when the rest of the College had presumably been checked and locked up for the night. Either Dalesford knows who closed those shutters and is covering up, or—'

'Or maybe the man who was supposed to bolt them simply forgot to do it!' said Ruth. 'Dalesford would never know the difference, so long as he found them shut when he went to the study in the morning.'

'Yes, absolutely,' agreed Hyde. 'It could be as simple as that . . . I'll have a word with the caretaker about it. Meanwhile, we're left with the gold watch worn on the inside of the wrist, and someone who owns or drives a Volkswagen . . . Let's tot up the score again, as far as we know it: Antoinette possesses a Mini Minor and no watch; Professor Dalesford has a half-hunter and no car – he's rather bitter about it, as he is about many things. Julie Benson runs a Vespa and wears a small platinum watch in the normal way. Nobody seems to remember what sort of watch Vance Scranton wore. He used to drive a Triumph Spitfire, but he seems to have sold it some weeks ago. Which leaves us with Jimmy Wade, whose taste in watches is, for the moment, unknown—'

'But whose taste in cars is definitely known,' Ruth butted in, turning from the window. 'He's just driven up to the hotel this very minute.'

116

'In his Volkswagen?' Hyde asked quietly.

'Yes.'

Holt pushed his breakfast tray to one side and joined Ruth at the window. 'As you once pointed out, it's an atrocious shade of blue.'

Hyde asked, 'Is he alone?'

A stout man got out of the passenger seat, bade farewell to Wade, and hurried off.

'No. He appears to have given a lift to Abe Jenkins.'

'Are they coming in?'

'Wade is. Jenkins has departed.'

The Inspector stood up and made for the door. 'Then I think I'll make myself scarce. Nobody knows I'm down here yet, so it must be you he's calling on.'

Just before he closed the door Hyde put his head round the corner and said, 'Don't forget to ask Mr Wade what time it is . . .'

Holt's luncheon with Julie Benson at The Golden Peacock went better than he had expected. Until he could tactfully steer the conversation round to matters of import he had not really known what to talk about. Julie very soon provided the answer.

'Is it true that you're a famous fashion photographer, Mr Holt?' she asked eagerly.

Holt sipped his Noilly Prat and smiled. 'I do some fashion work now and then, as well as feature-essays, commercial stuff, and just about anything that'll turn an honest penny. But my principle activity is portraits.'

'It must be lovely to be in the fashion trade. I've often thought I'd like to be a model.'

Inwardly Holt sighed. Practically every slim blonde in

Great Britain between the ages of thirteen and thirty seemed to want to become a model. He let Julie chatter on, and fed her an occasional bit of professional gossip to keep her happy. Only once did the conversation veer towards Vance Scranton, but she was obviously loath to discuss him, beyond expressing the hope that he might really still be alive. Abe Jenkins' newspaper article seemed to have been responsible for this hope – not her brother-in-law's claim to have seen Vance in the Underground. Wade's pretext for calling at the hotel – he was in the area on business, he had said – was to confide to Holt that he had not mentioned the incident to Julie. It was kinder not to raise the girl's hopes too soon, he felt.

It was towards the end of an excellent lunch, when she gave the appearance of being completely relaxed and at ease with him, that Holt began to apply the pressure.

'Tell me, Julie, if the world of fashion calls, won't Professor Dalesford be desolate to lose such an efficient secretary?'

She gave a tiny chuckle. 'Oh, he'd easily manage without me. There really isn't all that much to do up there anyway. I sometimes think he only keeps a secretary for prestige.'

The remark was quite shrewd, Holt thought.

'I should have thought there'd have been a lot of typing to do,' he said. 'His lecture material, courses of study, and his Prospero articles . . .'

There was a pause and he thought he detected a slight flush of uneasiness on the girl's face.

'Oh, those. Well . . .'

Holt said smoothly, 'Or does Miss Sheen deliver them ready typed, to save you the bother?'

'Miss Sheen? I . . . I don't quite see what Miss Sheen has to do with it . . .'

'Julie, I'll be quite frank with you. I happen to know that

she writes the Professor's articles for him. And, of course, you know that. I also happen to think that you were counting on this fact reaching the light of day sooner or later, when you wrote that accusation in green ink on the *New Feature* and sent it to the Savoy.'

'Mr Holt, I really don't know what you're talking about!'

'Nonsense! Scotland Yard has taken specimens of your handwriting and compared them with the words written under the Prospero article. But it wasn't the Professor you were aiming at, was it? – although you don't particularly like him. It was Antoinette you had your knife into. Why? Plain jealousy, because she stole Vance from you? Or do you really know something – are you concealing some facts which the police ought to know?'

The girl had turned very pale and now sat stiffly in her chair, toying with her coffee spoon. Holt was astonished at the change which had come over her. Quite clearly he read in her eyes a debate: whether or not to deny that she had written the Prospero note. He saw her reject this tactic and take up the challenge of his frontal attack. The fluffy little blonde had become a hard, calculating, self-possessed young woman. 'You disappoint me, Mr Holt. I did hope you might prove to be different from all the others.'

'Different? In what way?'

'I'd hoped your line of work and your experience might have made you immune to the sex tricks of a creature like Antoinette Sheen. But apparently not. You men are all the same! That woman has only to wiggle her hips and blink her false eyelashes and every male within miles goes completely ga-ga. She's hypnotised you! You can't see straight any more, you can't see her for what she really is!'

'And what's that, may I ask?'

119

'A monster! A ruthless, perverse, hypocritical nymphoma-
niac . . . a Hydra . . . a whore . . .'

Hólt let Julie empty her vocabulary, inwardly marvelling
at the youngster's range of adjectives and the extent of her
spite. The outburst revealed far more about the girl herself
than the woman she was reviling. Eventually Julie calmed
down and began listing the number of men with whom
Antoinette was said to have had affairs. It was quite a list.
Holt tried, with difficulty, to get a word in edgeways.

'I must tell you, Miss Benson, she hasn't seduced me yet.'

'She will! Just give her time!' Julie stared round the restau-
rant as if seeking tangible victims of Antoinette's sex appeal.
A gleam of triumph lit up her eyes. 'Look over there! Do
you see those two men standing by the cash desk? The one
with the fair hair is French, his name's Henri Legere. He's
the current paramour. As usual, he's nearly a decade younger
than she is.'

Holt recognised Legere, the young man who thought he
had seen Vance. 'Can you catch his eye?' he asked quickly.
'I rather want to talk to him.'

'He's already seen us. He's coming over.'

'And who's the distinguished looking fellow he was talking
to – the one who's just about to leave?'

'That's Ashley Milton. He owns this place.'

'M'm . . . I wish I'd had a chance to ask him who his
tailor is,' Holt murmured appreciatively.

Henri Legere reached their table, bowed low, and offered
his hand to Holt. '*Bonjour*, Monsieur Holt.'

The two men shook hands in the formal Continental style.

To Julie he offered only half a bow and a guarded smile.

'Good morning, Monsieur Legere,' said Holt. 'Have you
seen anyone interesting lately?'

'No, I regret to say I have not. I would surely have contacted you had there been any further news.'

'I see. There's something I meant to ask you yesterday when we talked about your friend Vance Scranton. When the two of you were together, did you you speak in English or in French?'

Legere looked puzzled. 'I don't think I quite understand . . . English, of course. Vance was an American, I do not think he knew more than five words of my native tongue. If he did he certainly could not pronounce them.'

Both men laughed and, persuading Henri to take a vacant chair at their table, Holt signalled a waiter for more coffee.

When it was brought Holt dipped a hand into his jacket pocket and without a word of warning produced Vance Scranton's signet ring. His gaze flickered from Henri to Julie and back again as he placed the ring on a plate in the centre of the table.

The two young people gasped.

Holt said evenly, 'Can either of you tell me whose ring this is?'

'It belonged to Vance,' said Legere promptly. As he reached over to pick up the ring his shirt cuff slipped back to reveal a man's watch of silver and steel on a black leather strap.

'How did it get into your hands?' Julie demanded.

'I'm afraid I can't answer that, for the time being, at any rate,' Holt replied.

She laid a hand impulsively on his sleeve. 'Mr Holt, can I have it? Please. Let me have the ring as a keepsake. I'd like to have something that belonged to him; I've got nothing to remember him by. He'd have wanted me to have it, I'm sure . . .'

Holt pounced upon her words. 'A moment ago you were

quite prepared to believe that Vance is alive. Now you talk of him in the past tense as though he were dead.'

'Oh no, I mean . . . It's just that . . . Oh dear, you're getting me all confused . . . Oh, look!' she said with sudden relief. 'There's Jimmy!'

Jimmy Wade was entering the restaurant, his face wreathed in a mixture of smiles which managed to convey delight at seeing them and enxiety that he might be intruding. He bustled over to their table.

'I trust you'll forgive me if I'm disturbing you,' he began. Then, addressing Julie, 'As you told me you were lunching with Mr Holt I thought I might drop by and pick you up. If your Vespa is still out of action, dear, I expect you'd like a lift up to the College?'

Julie nodded, a trifle uncertainly.

Henri Legere said, jokingly, 'She could always sit on the rear of my bicycle.'

'You ride a bicycle, do you?' Holt said casually. 'How do you like riding "on the wrong side of the road"?'

'It is terrible! But it is even worse with a car.'

'Oh, do you run a car as well?'

'No, but occasionally Mr Wade allows me to borrow his. He is very generous and lends it to just anybody who asks.'

Holt's brain raced in top gear. Jimmy Wade had passed the watch test before lunch; the reference to the car offered an unexpected opportunity. He seized it and went on gently probing. 'It's a very generous man who lends his car, Mr Wade. Had I known you were here last night I might have thrown myself on your mercy – my own chariot's under repair.'

'I'm afraid you'd have been unlucky, great as the pleasure would have been,' Wade responded, his india-rubber face signalling thwarted good intentions. 'My car had already been borrowed.'

Holt's heart leapt. 'Really?' he began, but to his immense annoyance the line of enquiry was terminated abruptly by Legere, whose action in replacing the signet ring on the plate instantly caught Wade's full attention.

'Good gracious me!' he twittered, swooping on it with one of his incredibly swift, bird-like movements. 'Forgive me for saying so, but isn't this Vance's ring?'

'You recognise it?' Holt said.

'I do indeed. Julie dear, do you remember that time when you brought Vance to visit us at Honor Oak and I pulled his leg about having the dollar sign on his ring?'

She managed a nod and a thin smile. 'I remember.'

Wade chuckled. 'He didn't take kindly to my mild witticism, did he?'

'By all accounts he wasn't blessed with a very great sense of humour,' observed Holt.

Julie flushed with annoyance at the criticism. She stood up and said it was time for her to report back on duty at the College.

Jimmy Wade made a rush towards the coat-stand, beating Legere by a short head, whilst Holt pocketed the ring and went to the cash desk to pay his bill. The three men exchanged pleasantries about the size of this bill – The Golden Peacock was by no means cheap – and then strolled back to the table together.

To Holt's surprise, Julie had been joined by a stranger. It was the tall, distinguished looking man in the well-cut suit whom they had seen talking to Legere earlier on.

Julie introduced him. 'Ashley, this is Mr Philip Holt.'

Ashley Milton offered a slender hand. 'Ah, the famous

123

society photographer.' He spoke in a weary drawl. 'It's an honour to have you eat at my humble restaurant, Mr Holt. I trust you fared well?'

'We had an excellent meal, thank you,' Holt answered shortly. He found the man's manner irritating; it was faintly patronising.

Jimmy Wade finished his task of helping Julie into her coat and was now trying to catch Milton's eye. The latter seemed in no hurry to greet either Wade or the Frenchman, and a petulant expression crossed his lengthy features when Wade finally managed to address him.

'If you'll forgive my mentioning it, Milton old chap, you haven't returned my spare car keys yet, you know.'

'Oh – how beastly careless of me!' Milton fished languidly in the trouser pocket of his beautifully tailored suit and produced a broad flat car key on a small chain. Holt could read the emblem of the car's brand name quite clearly. Cut into the key's form were the letters 'V W'.

Milton then turned to Holt. In an exaggerated movement he stretched out his left arm and crooked it in order to look at a gold watch on the inside of his wrist.

He said in his bored vocal slouch, 'Holt, you don't by any chance happen to have a few moments to spare, I suppose?'

'I think I can manage that,' Holt answered steadily.

Chapter Ten

Later that afternoon Holt conferred with Inspector Hyde in his hotel room.

'I haven't met Ashley Milton,' Hyde said. 'What's he like?'

'Conceited. Clever,' Holt answered. 'With great difficulty I restrained myself from punching his nose. He has a maddening habit of talking down to you.'

'Sounds rather like Vance Scranton would have become in another twenty years,' Ruth said. 'Did they know one another?'

Holt nodded. 'All too well, so it seems. That's what Milton wanted to see me about. It appears he had a very good motive for wanting to kill the lad, and he thought it would be a good idea to clear himself with me and explain that, despite provocation, he didn't commit the murder.'

'Go on, Holt.'

'Milton says that young Scranton was blackmailing him.'

'Does he indeed?' Hyde sank his chin on to his chest and sucked at his pipe. 'It sounds ugly – but credible. Anything in writing, by any chance?'

'Yes, some letters. Ashley Milton wrote them when he was a young man. There was a rather mucky affair with a very young girl.'

'A minor?' Hyde asked.

'Yes. She was fifteen. Somehow or other Vance got hold of these indiscreet letters and put the bite on Milton.'

'For how much – did he tell you?'

'Nearly two thousand pounds.'

The Inspector pursed his lips in a silent whistle. 'No wonder he's scared of being suspected of murder! There's a real motive there . . .'

'But it seems to fit together, doesn't it? That was Milton in Vance's study last night, and it's fair to assume that he was looking for the blackmail letters. Did he offer any proof?'

'That he was being blackmailed, do you mean? Or that he didn't murder Vance?'

'Did he offer any proof of either?'

'Well, he showed me the cheque stubs of the sums he's been paying Vance over the past two years or so. As for his alibi, he says he was tinkering about on his boat on the night of the killing.'

'That wasn't the sort of night one would choose to tinker about with one's boat—'

'He didn't say he went out to sea in it.'

'Just as well for him – there was thick fog! What type of craft is it?'

Holt shrugged his shoulders. 'I don't know much about them myself, but I think "luxury motor yacht" would be about the right description. It's the sort of thing you see anchored in the harbour at Monte Carlo. Milton showed me a colour photograph hanging on the wall of his lounge – sumptuous place he has, above The Golden Peacock.'

'We'll have some discreet enquiries made into the private life of Ashley Milton!' Hyde promised. 'We'll find out more about his luxury yacht, and we'll also check what his sources of income are, apart from The Golden Peacock. From what you've told me, it seems he's living it up rather grandly on the proceeds of one restaurant, especially if the Scranton boy was dipping into the till from time to time.'

'Yes, I see what you mean. But, although Milton seems to have had a motive for shooting Vance, we're not absolutely certain that it was Vance who was killed, are we? If Vance is still alive, Milton could well be telling the truth.'

'I suppose Milton couldn't have killed the wrong man by mistake, could he?' Ruth suggested. 'I mean, could he have thought it was Vance who was in the study?'

The two men thought this over.

'It's a distinct possibility, Ruth,' said Hyde seriously. 'If the victim had his back to the murderer and the shot was fired as he turned round . . .'

'But we must keep an open mind, eh, Inspector – until we've got definite proof?' said Ruth with a delightfully cheeky grin.

'Quite so,' said Hyde with a smile.

Holt was pressing his fingertips to his temples in worried concentration. 'One thing doesn't tally. If Milton was looking for blackmail letters last night, and if it *was* a sack I heard being dragged across the floor . . . well, they must have been incredibly heavy letters!'

'Perhaps he put them in suitcases,' said Ruth brightly, 'intending to search through them at his leisure.'

'If they'd been suitcases he'd have carried them in the normal manner,' Holt pointed out.

'Then how about letters in boxes, or slipped between the pages of books—'

'*Books!*' Holt jumped to his feet and hugged her. 'I think you've hit it, Ruth! That's exactly the sound a pile of books

127

would make . . . heavy books, dragged in a sack to prevent them slipping out of the holder's grasp! By Jove, I wonder where this leads to! Now, supposing it was the books themselves that Milton wanted to examine . . .' The telephone rang and Holt waved impatiently to Ruth to answer it. 'If it's Abe Jenkins I'm not available,' he said crisply, going over to the window and staring out to sea.

It was some seconds before he realised that there was a deathly silence in the room. He turned and saw that Hyde was staring at Ruth.

'It's for you,' she said in a strangled tone. 'A man's voice . . . He says he's Vance Scranton!'

'I don't believe it!' Holt exclaimed. In one stride he was beside Ruth and had seized the phone from her hand. He put his palm over the mouthpiece and looked quickly at Hyde. 'What if it's another hoax, like Lewisham?'

'Force him to prove his identity,' Hyde urged softly.

Holt nodded and released the mouthpiece. 'Philip Holt here.'

'Fine. This is Vance Scranton.' It was a young, strong voice with a marked American accent.

'Robert Scranton, did you say?' said Holt, playing for time.

'No, that's my father. This is Vance on the phone. The prodigal son, you know?'

'No, I'm not sure that I do know,' Holt replied carefully. 'The last time somebody claiming to be Vance Scranton spoke on the telephone, it was a trick and a man was murdered shortly afterwards.'

'Oh, sure – you mean Curly. Say, didn't he look terrible with that black wig and the lipstick and all?'

Holt's heart missed a beat. The wig had got into the press

reports of the murder, but there had been no mention of the lipstick question-mark on Curly's skull.

'Did you kill him, Scranton?'

'Holt, I'm in no mood for answering questions. I'm in a jam and I need your help.'

'Where are you? Where are you phoning from?'

'Sorry, I can't tell you that. I can't tell you anything at all unless you do a little job for me. Then you can hear the whole sad story. Is it a deal?'

'What do you want me to do?'

'You've got my ring, haven't you? My signet ring?'

'How the devil did you know that?'

'No questions, or the deal's off. Now listen carefully . . . If you deliver that ring to a safe place, as soon as I know it's there I'll meet you and give you all the answers to the Scranton Quiz Programme.'

'Where do I deliver the ring?'

'To old Harry Dalesford.' Vance gave a laugh. 'Yeah, the Professor himself. Only he mustn't know about it, see? Find some excuse to call on him and drop that ring into the fancy clay jar he keeps on his desk – he stuffs a load of pens and pencils in it as a rule . . . You got that? . . . Don't try and double-cross me, Holt, or I'll find out for sure and then I just won't turn up for our date.'

'Where and when is that date to be, Scranton?'

'Tomorrow night, around midnight, on the beach.'

'Which beach? Eastbourne's a big area.'

'Under the Pier. Got it, Holt . . . Under the Pier. Midnight tomorrow.'

There was a click and the line went dead.

Hyde was the first to break the silence. 'Was it the real thing?'

'The line was bad, but I think so. He knows I've got the ring!'

Holt went on to recount the part of the conversation which they had not been able to hear. Ruth was entranced with this latest development, but Hyde said nothing.

'What do you want me to do, Inspector?' Holt asked presently. 'Shall I go along with his plan, hoping to God that he keeps his word? Or are you going to sound the general alarm and have him arrested?'

The Inspector took some time before replying. It was a difficult decision to make. At last he said, 'In order to arrest him I've first got to have my hands on him. That's easier said than done. But if he gives himself up of his own accord . . . Holt, I suggest you go through all the motions of falling in with his plan. Do just what he asked – but with this one difference: I shall have a small army of police in plain-clothes – fishermen, tourists, courting couples, and so on – posted in the shadows of the Pier, ready to pick him up if he does keep his end of the bargain. If he fails to appear, then I'll issue a warrant for his arrest and sound the alarm.'

'I wonder who told him you'd got the ring,' Ruth said. 'The lady who gave it to you, by any chance?'

Holt shrugged his shoulders. 'Possibly. Antoinette isn't the only suspect, though. It could be any one of the people I met at lunch today.'

'Let's take another look at that ring,' said Hyde. 'Maybe there's more in it than meets the eye.'

Holt delved into his jacket pocket. 'That's funny – I distinctly remember . . .' With a perturbed expression he began to feel in his other pockets.

'Did you transfer it to your overcoat?' asked Ruth.

'Or your wallet?' the Inspector suggested.

Holt foraged in both these places with mounting anxiety and no success. There was a strained silence whilst he turned every pocket inside out. Finally the inescapable conviction that the ring was missing could no longer be denied. A thief had been at work.

Who? Henri Legere or Jimmy Wade as they joined him at the cash desk and strolled back with him to his table? Julie, under cover of the fuss Wade made as he helped her on with her coat? She had pleaded with Holt to let her have the ring as a keepsake. Or was the pickpocket Ashley Milton himself, forewarned by Julie of the ring's existence, and clever enough to get Holt on his own in the relaxed surroundings of his private apartment?

As Holt tried to reconstruct the scene and account for each suspect's movements, he realised with dismay that it could be any one of them.

The Inspector put through several calls to Scotland Yard and the three of them talked in his hotel room till late in the evening. One thing was crystal clear: the opportunity to pin Vance Scranton down to a particular time and a particular place was too good to miss. The loss of the ring could not be allowed to prevent the rendezvous under the Pier. It was agreed that Hyde should have a copy made, as accurately as they could remember it, and Holt would make some excuse to visit Professor Dalesford in the morning.

They discussed the curious choice of the Professor's pencil-jar as a receptacle, and agreed that any one of four people – Dalesford, Julie, Antoinette, or Legere – would be in a position to pick the ring up easily.

When the telephone rang Holt answered, in case it should

131

be Vance. But to his surprise it was Vance's parents. The call was short and Holt provided an account of it immediately he had hung up.

'That was the Scrantons. They decided to come down here and they're staying at the Grand. It seems they've had a letter forwarded to them. It was addressed to Vance at the College and Dalesford opened it by mistake.

'What was in the letter?' Hyde asked.

Holt made a wry grimace. 'Belated birthday greetings. From Christopher.'

The Inspector sprang to his feet. 'That confounded ghost again! Has Scranton brought the letter with him?'

Holt nodded. 'Mrs Scranton asked me to go round first thing in the morning – says they're too tired to see me tonight. She didn't sound as friendly as usual. I could be wrong, but I thought I detected a note of impatience in her voice. They're probably wondering when my investigations are going to show some results.'

'You'd have risen very considerably in Mrs Scranton's estimation if you'd told her you'd just conversed with her son on the telephone,' the Inspector said with the faintest hint of a twinkle in his eye.

Holt smiled. 'Yes, I would, wouldn't I?'

'What are you two playing at?' Ruth protested. 'Think of that poor mother, half out of her mind with worry and doubt—'

'Yes – so overwrought, in fact, that the moment I tell her I've spoken to Vance she'll rush off and do something foolish and upset the applecart completely!' Holt pointed out.

Hyde grunted agreement with this point of view.

Holt went on, 'This is a very delicate matter we're trying to bring off, this rendezvous with Vance. It's like setting a

132

time-bomb – if we let the parents tamper with the fuse the whole thing may blow up prematurely . . . Don't you agree, Inspector?'

'I do indeed. First things first: contact Vance – and *then* it will be time to break the news to the parents that their boy is alive, and in all probability a double-murderer!'

It was a bright, blustery day with strange-shaped masses of grey cloud scudding across the sky as Holt drove to Deanfriston with Mr and Mrs Scranton in his newly-repaired Mustang. They had expressed a wish to meet some of their son's friends, which had conveniently provided Holt with the desired excuse to visit the College.

The Christopher letter – Number Three in the strange series of communications – was in his pocket. It was frustrating not to know whether it was blank like Number Two, or if it contained a code message like the first one. But they would know by late afternoon, since Hyde had taken the precaution of ordering an expert down from the Yard, complete with materials.

Also in Holt's pocket was a copy of the stolen signet ring. Hyde had put on a turn of speed and got things done during the night. A special messenger had delivered the duplicate ring by breakfast-time. Hyde had also detailed a couple of investigators to delve into Ashley Milton's private life, and was himself making a personal check on the luxury yacht moored a few miles away at Newhaven. Ruth was spending the morning on some investigations of her own at Birling Gap. And with any luck at all, by midnight at the latest they would meet up with the elusive Vance Scranton himself. Wheels were beginning to turn at last!

The Mustang rounded the crest of a hill and the College

133

came into view. Dipping towards the village below, Holt caught sight of a group of riders on horseback. Antoinette had been on his mind and he slowed down to see if she was amongst them. But, rather to his disappointment, she was not. It consisted of young men, obviously students from the College. One rider recognised him and cantered towards the car, his fair hair blowing in the wind. It was Henri Legere.

Legere called out a cheerful greeting as he came up.

'*Bonjour*, Monsieur Legere,' Holt replied. 'Let me introduce you to Mr and Mrs Scranton.'

The handsome young Frenchman bowed low in the saddle and beamed at the Americans.

'I promised they'd meet some of Vance's friends,' Holt said, 'but I didn't know we'd be so fortunate as to bump into you *en route*. Tell me: when on earth do you find time to do any studying?'

Legere emitted a rich peal of laughter. 'It must seem that I am very lazy, Monsieur Holt. In fact I am taking a complete rest after some exhausting examinations.'

'I see. Then perhaps you'd have time to call on Mr and Mrs Scranton during their stay down here and talk about Vance? They're longing to chat with someone who was at the College with him.'

'But naturally, I should be delighted.'

'Good, that's settled then!'

Holt was about to let in the clutch when Legere leaned towards him and said quietly, 'You have a moment, Monsieur Holt? I have something important to say to you.'

It was a little awkward, but Holt excused himself to his passengers. Legere dismounted and led his horse to a convenient spot some few yards away.

'Do you remember my mentioning to you, the first time

I met you, that I share my rooms in Eastbourne with a Scotsman named Graham Brown?'

'Yes, I think I do. You said he was away, visiting his parents, I believe?'

'That is right. At least, that is what I thought. But I have received no news from him for over ten days and now I am worried. I thought perhaps he might have become ill so I telephoned to his father in Scotland.' Legere paused dramatically and glanced towards the Mustang parked at the roadside. 'Monsieur Holt, I am very worried. Graham did not go to Scotland. At least, he did not arrive there. His father was under the impression that he was here at the College.'

Holt frowned. 'It does sound rather odd, I must say. Have you notified the police?'

'No, I thought I would wait until I see you again. But I expect Mr and Mrs Brown will get in touch with the police if they think it is necessary.'

'Yes, I expect they will.'

Legere began to climb into the saddle.

'By the way,' said Holt, 'what's Graham Brown like? Physically, I mean. Tall – short – fair – dark?'

Legere considered for a moment. 'How shall I say? . . . He has brown hair, he is of medium height . . . nothing very special about him. To look at he was a bit like Vance. In fact, I would say they were very similar. Well, I must go or I shall not be able to catch up the others. *Au revoir*, Monsieur Holt.'

Holt stood watching thoughtfully as Legere rode away. He was a handsome man, full of Gallic charm, and he sat his horse well. It was quite possibly true, as Julie had declared, that the young Frenchman was Antoinette's current lover.

135

With a twinge of envy Holt put the thought out of his mind and strode back to the car.

It was a disappointment to find that Professor Dalesford was not in his office when they arrived.

Julie Benson, looking somewhat flustered, began stabbing buttons on her internal call-box in a nervous attempt to trace the Professor's whereabouts. She did not invite them into Dalesford's room but kept the three of them waiting in a small anteroom where she evidently did her work. After a series of fruitless telephone calls she jumped up, announced that she was going to look herself, and ran from the room.

'She seems in an awful tizzy,' Mr Scranton commented, scratching his close-cropped head in a puzzled manner.

His wife shot him an amused glance. 'Robert sometimes you're very obtuse! Don't you realise what an ordeal it is for a girl to meet the parents of the boy she's engaged to – or rather, was?'

'You mean she's scared of us?' said Scranton with good-natured bewilderment.

'Unless it's Mr Holt who's sending her into such a tizzy,' Mrs Scranton added coyly. 'I can well imagine the disastrous effect he has on young female hearts.'

Holt appeared not to have heard her comment. He was engrossed in peering through the striated-glass panel into the Professor's office. He straightened up, turned the handle, and said as he entered the room, 'Either the Professor is a remarkably untidy man or else . . . Yes, rather as I thought: he's had a visitor.'

The first thing that had caught his eye was the fancy clay pencil-jar, smashed into three pieces like a split coconut. The rest of the room looked as though a gang of

136

teenage hoodlums had been to work on it. The Scrantons gasped, and a moment later they heard a shriek from Julie Benson.

Holt turned round sharply and said, 'Please spare us the customary fainting fit, Miss Benson – there really isn't time! Tell me how this could have happened. Haven't you been outside in the anteroom all morning?'

Julie looked deathly pale. She gulped and shook her head. 'No. It must have happened while I was . . . The Professor always allows me a coffee break . . . I must have been gone longer than usual.'

'How long?'

'Nearly . . . nearly half an hour.'

'Didn't you look into his office when you got back?'

'No, I didn't.' She gestured helplessly towards the internal call-box. 'I buzzed him to tell him I was back, and when he didn't answer I just got on with the pile of letters he'd given me. It never entered my head that . . . Oh, Mr Holt, where is he? What's happened? What were they looking for, these hooligans?'

'Are you sure you don't know, Miss Benson?' Holt said harshly.

She shook her head, looking miserable. Her eyes began to flood with tears.

Scranton stepped gallantly into the breach. 'Mr Holt, can't you see the poor kid's upset? It wasn't her fault, she wasn't here when all this happened. A blind man can see that Miss Benson didn't have any need to tear the Professor's room apart if she wanted to find something.'

The American's solid common-sense calmed Holt. The signet ring had not been specifically mentioned, but what he had in a general way pointed out was completely logical. If

Julie *was* Vance's accomplice in the scheme to regain the ring she would hardly have wrecked the room before Holt's arrival at the College. In fact, she would have been more likely to present him with the opportunity to deposit it by showing him straight into the Professor's room. He felt a little ashamed of his anger and diverted his energies to finding Dalesford. With Julie's help at the internal phone, some of the students who were not in the lecture halls were summoned and search parties were organised.

It was Holt who finally found him.

Dalesford, apparently dazed and in pain, was lying face down in the rose garden, partly hidden by some tall rose bushes still in bloom. His hands were tied behind his back with the thin leather strap torn from his binoculars. His spectacles lay in fragments on the gravel path near by.

Holt lifted Dalesford's head and wiped away some of the mud with his handkerchief.

The Professor moaned and opened his eyes, without recognition. 'I haven't . . . got it, I tell you . . . Please leave me alone . . . I don't know anything about . . . the ring.'

'Dalesford!' Holt hissed, shaking the limp figure gently and speaking in a low voice. He was anxious to gain the Professor's attention before any of the search parties should find them. 'I'm a friend, Dalesford – I'm Philip Holt – don't you recognise me?'

The Professor gave a low groan and said something about his broken spectacles.

'Who was it?' Holt questioned him, urgently. 'What did they want?'

'I don't understand . . . a ring . . . I know nothing about it . . .'

'What were you doing out here in the first place?'

'I . . . had a free period . . . between classes . . . Oh, I feel dreadful . . .'

'I thought that must be why you had the binoculars with you. Here – let me untie your hands. How did it happen?'

'Something . . . in the bushes . . . hit me from behind . . . terrible pain . . . I must have passed out . . . When I came to, they were searching me . . . in my pockets . . .'

'Who was searching you? Tell me – what did they look like?'

'I don't know . . . They smashed my spectacles. I can't see a thing without them . . . They twisted my arm behind my back – the pain was terrible, I can't stand pain . . . They were looking for a ring, that's all I know. I must have passed out again. Next time I came to I was lying in the mud. I heard horses, and then I must have—'

'You heard horses? Are you sure?'

'Yes. Not near. Quite far away. But I had my ear to the ground, I heard hoof-beats distinctly . . . Oh dear, I think I'm going to be sick!'

Dalesford rose to his feet and tottered towards a hedge. A moment later he was seen by one of the search party and students began to converge from all directions. There had just been sufficient time for Holt to make a reasonably thorough examination of the ground in and around the rose garden; a search that, despite soft earth, had failed to reveal a single impression of a horse's hoof.

Holt stood at the window in the small functional office belonging to the Secretary of the College and watched the clouds race across the sky. He was waiting for his call to Eastbourne to come through, having deposited the Scrantons with Julie so that he could make his call in complete privacy.

He had to make up his mind what he was going to tell

139

Hyde. Had it been sheer coincidence, meeting Henri Legere on horseback like that? If it had not been coincidence why had there been no hoof-marks near the rose garden? How valid was the Professor's impression of the sound of horses? On a windy day sound could travel far and, even if it had been Legere's group which he had heard, they might easily have been a long way off. And why would Legere want the ring anyway; indeed, how could he have found out where it was to be left? Legere could well he perfectly innocent. He had certainly made no attempt to conceal himself when Holt's car had topped the brow of the hill and the file of riders had come into view. But if it was, in fact, the Frenchman who had been responsible for the incident, it was clear that he could not have been the pickpocket at the restaurant. Only one thing now stood out more clearly than before: the signet ring was an object of great desirability in the eyes of several people.

Almost as though he had been able to read Holt's train of thought, Inspector Hyde's first words when the call came through referred to the ring. But the information was the last thing in the world that Holt had expected.

'Before you tell me your news, let me get a word in edgeways,' the Inspector began. 'The ring's been returned! We've got it back.'

'Good God! I can't believe it!'

'It's true. It's been handed in.'

'By whom, for God's sake?'

'By Jimmy Wade. He brought it this morning.'

'*Jimmy Wade!* I might have guessed! He's got a pair of hands like a conjuror!'

'Not so fast,' Hyde cautioned. 'He says he was merely bringing the ring for Milton. It seems one of Milton's waiters was cleaning under the table where you sat yesterday and found it there.'

'Rubbish!' Holt snorted. 'I certainly never dropped it. And even if I had, how would Milton have known that—'

'He says the waiter is a very observant fellow and noticed you showing the ring to Julie Benson and the others. He therefore assumed it was yours.'

Holt sighed. 'I don't know who's the bigger liar, Milton or Wade. What the devil are they playing at?'

'We may know sooner than you think. At least we've cleared up one aspect of this baffling case. We know who was actually murdered in Vance's study.'

'Ah! May I make a guess?'

'Waste of time. The dead boy's parents identified his body this morning. They came down by fast train from—'

'From Scotland,' Holt cut in. 'Their name is Brown. Vance Scranton killed his fellow student, Graham Brown, and nearly succeeded in passing off the body as his own – God knows why, though! Am I right?'

'How do you do it, Holt? Inspired guesswork again?'

'No. I met Henri Legere riding on the Downs when I was on my way to the College. He put the idea into my head.' Holt gave an account of the meeting, and went on to describe the dramatic events which had followed.

Hyde listened intently, only allowing himself an occasional startled exclamation.

'Are you coming out here, Inspector?' Holt asked when he reached the end of his story.

'Yes. I ought to see Dalesford, that's obvious; and I think I'd better have a talk with this Frenchman. There are a lot of odd coincidences that he can start explaining.'

'True enough. But you can't get away from the fact that

it was he who took steps in the first place to contact Graham Brown's parents.'

Hyde gave a disbelieving grunt. 'It would have come to light sooner or later anyway. He was just trying to earn an easy credit. You'll think a lot less kindly of Henri Legere when you hear what Ruth was able to dig up at Birling Gap this morning.'

'Has she been to see Antoinette again?'

'No. Antoinette's neighbour.'

'But she hasn't got a neighbour! Antoinette lives in the middle of a field. The nearest house is at least two hundred yards away!'

'That's the neighbour,' said Hyde dryly. 'I'll leave Ruth to tell you the details. Did you get the Christopher letter from Scranton?'

'Yes, I'll give it to you when you get here.'

'You won't be there to give it to me. I've got a special job for you and Ruth. Is there anyone at the College who's absolutely reliable?'

Holt thought for a moment. 'Yes, I think so – the Secretary. I'm phoning from his office now.'

'Good. Leave the letter with him and I'll pick it up.'

'Fair enough. Now, what's this job you've got for us? Don't make it a long one – I've got a date with a murderer at midnight, don't forget.'

'I hadn't forgotten. Listen – I've been out to take a look at Ashley Milton's yacht at Newhaven. It's called the *Sunset* – a beautiful vessel, you could sail round the world in it. It's festooned with radar and radio masts and depth-sounding equipment, far more than is usual for a private boat in these parts. Some shore-hands I got talking to say its engines are unusually powerful too.'

'It sounds a luxurious toy for a man who's been paying out hundreds of pounds in blackmail,' Holt remarked.

'Quite so. We're probing into Milton's finances. That may prove very illuminating.'

'Did you get on board the *Sunset*?'

'That's just it; I couldn't.'

'Why not?'

'The crew would have recognised me. There are four men in all, and at least two of them are old lags.'

Holt whistled. 'That doesn't sound in keeping with the stylish Ashley Milton, does it? I suppose you want Ruth and me to clamber aboard and snoop around?'

'Not clamber, dear chap – just slip. It would be better not to let the crew know of your intentions. The ones I saw are rather a rough lot, I'm afraid.'

Chapter Eleven

'I'm sorry about Antoinette, really I am,' said Ruth in a small voice as Holt drove with dangerous speed towards Newhaven. She glanced at him nervously. His face was set in very hard, almost cruel lines.

'Come off it, Ruth. You never did like her—'

'I won't pretend I did. But I also don't happen to like horrible old men acting as Peeping Toms. I actually saw him leaning out of the window with his telescope, which is why I decided it might be worth while making his acquaintance. Nasty lecherous old man – fancy having nothing better to do in life than spy from two hundred yards away on the activities of your neighbours!'

'It's a popular national pastime,' said Holt dryly.

'I think it's detestable!'

'It's proved very handy for us.'

Ruth sighed. 'Yes, I suppose we ought to look at it in that light. Not only did the old man see Henri Legere leave Antoinette's bungalow on horseback on the morning of the accident, but he "happened" to be watching with his spyglass one day and saw a young blonde climb through Antoinette's bedroom window. That could tie up with what she said about an amateur burglary.'

'A young blonde? Could it be Julie Benson?'

'Yes, but looking for what? Nothing was stolen.'

'The ring, perhaps.'

'That's just guesswork.'

'Inspired guesswork, as Hyde would say. Lesser mortals call it intelligent deduction. Anyway, Legere's in the hot seat, now, with a devil of a lot of explaining to do. My car brakes, for a start.'

'Of course, it hasn't been proved that he cut them.'

'If he didn't, then it was Antoinette! We definitely saw somebody on horseback. If it wasn't Antoinette then it was Legere acting on her instructions. He wasn't up at the College, he told me so himself.'

'No, but Julie was,' Ruth said unexpectedly.

'Say that again.'

'Julie was at the College on Wednesday morning, wasn't she?'

Holt looked at her in surprise. 'Do you realise what you're implying? That Antoinette might have an entirely clean pair of hands!'

Ruth shrugged her shoulders. 'It's possible, isn't it? Just because she seems to go in for love affairs with younger men, that doesn't necessarily mean that she's privy to all their secret activities. Whatever racket Vance or Legere might be mixed up in, Antoinette may know nothing about it. If there is a direct line linking Julie and Legere, and perhaps Ashley Milton as well, then maybe Antoinette is bypassed altogether.'

'My word!' Holt laughed. 'You *are* being charitable all of a sudden.'

'I'm simply trying to be objective and not too catty.'

'Then I think you're trying too hard. How do you explain Antoinette's curious action in handing over the ring, along with that obviously faked letter?'

Ruth shook her head. 'I can't explain it – except that it reminds me of that party game where you all sit in a row and try to get rid of the hot potato before the music stops. That ring is obviously very significant and she certainly didn't waste any time in passing it on.'

'Milton didn't keep the ring long, either.'

'Milton? I thought it was Jimmy Wade who returned it to the police?'

'It was, but he said—'

'He said! Nothing will ever make me trust a man as smooth as Smiling Jimmy . . . My goodness!' she added in a sarcastic tone, gripping her safety belt, 'she holds the corners well, doesn't she?' Holt was going through the series of curves which embraced the flat mouth of the river Ouse as though it were a straight road. 'That's Newhaven in sight across there – start slowing down or we'll overshoot the runway!'

Holt grinned and braked gently. As he coasted into the port of Newhaven they again went over the details of their plan of action.

As things turned out, there was no need for Ruth to hire a dinghy. They had agreed that she would take a rowing boat out to the vicinity of Milton's yacht, lose an oar, and fall in the water whilst struggling to retrieve it. The *Sunset* was riding at anchor some way out in the harbour; at a convenient distance, moored to the quayside, stood a small cabin cruiser ideal for their purpose.

Casually, Ruth strolled over the plank on to the deck of the deserted cabin cruiser, pretended to trip over a coil of rope, and fell with a shriek and a loud splash into the freezing water . . . There, carefully losing all sense of direction, she struck out wildly for the *Sunset* and allowed herself to be rescued by willing deckhands who threw down a rope ladder and hauled her out of the water. It had involved a small risk, but Holt had calculated that no matter what sort of men the *Sunset*'s deckhands were, no seaman would refuse to help a woman struggling for her life in icy water near his ship.

Such an unexpected touch of drama on a dull November afternoon was enough to take the minds of all crew-members from their desultory work. All four men clustered round Ruth and shepherded her to a warm cabin below decks. Meanwhile Holt took a dinghy and rowed swiftly out to the *Sunset*'s side. He found a convenient rope and climbed aboard.

Down the starboard side of the upper deck he crept, until he was within earshot of Ruth's raised voice, and there he learned what he needed to know – that all the crew had crowded into the cabin and was plying her with steaming tea, blankets, brandy, and excited conversation. For as long as she could hold their interest he had the boat to himself.

Keeping alert for the sound of her cabin door being opened, Holt began his task. He wasted no time on the trim, well-equipped upper decks, nor on the lavish fittings of bar and saloon below, but made straight for the cabins amidships.

By a stroke of good luck he found Milton's private cabin almost immediately. A row of elegant tropical suits made by a French tailor had Milton's name in them. Holt went through the pockets, but except for some Paris Metro ticket stubs he found nothing. Next he tackled the various cup-boards built into the bulkhead, but these also yielded no more than several articles of good quality clothing.

He was beginning to get anxious. Time had ticked away since Ruth had been hauled aboard – precious minutes in which he had been able to discover nothing. Despairingly he pulled at drawers in the small fitted table, but they were locked and he dared not force them open. The delicate balance between success and failure hung on his leaving absolutely no trace of his visit. He gave a last glance round the cabin, then nipped out into the passageway and silently closed the door behind him.

He was debating which cabin to tackle next when he was startled by a high-pitched buzzing. It came from a cabin further up the corridor, and he hid behind a bulkhead as footsteps clattered down an iron companion ladder from the deck overhead and approached down the gangway.

A seaman, muttering curses in French, lumbered past a few feet away. With a blow of his hand Holt could have felled him, but this was no moment for heroics.

The man entered the radio room, and a second or two later the buzzing ceased. The seaman's voice came clearly through the half-open door, and it was at once obvious that a conversation by radio-telephone was taking place. The words exchanged were in French, but it went very fast and seemed to be mostly in slang so that Holt could make little sense of it. One thing emerged with undoubted clarity, however: a distinct sense of urgency and impending disaster! Two names were mentioned, which made Holt's blood run faster – Christopher, and a French name which sounded like Dunant.

The seaman at the receiving end swore violently and

slammed a metal object – possibly a microphone – into place. The radio was switched off and then came the sound of a pen or pencil scratching over paper and the noise of a sheet being ripped from a pad. Holt flattened himself into the shadows as the door burst open and the Frenchman hurried out.

When the footsteps clattering up the companion ladder ceased, Holt darted into the radio room.

What he saw nearly took his breath away . . .

He knew very little about radio technology, but it was apparent that the mass of radio equipment in the tiny cabin was first-rate and quite extensive. He had no time to gaze at the array of dials, plugs, knobs, and wires on the complicated set. His eyes swept over the table and he found what he was looking for – a scribbling-block near the microphone and a ball-point pen alongside. Holding the pad at an oblique angle to the light, he could scarcely restrain a grunt of satisfaction. The ball-point pen used by a man in a savage frame of mind had made a sharp tracing of the message he had scribbled down.

There was no time to decipher it. Holt tore the top sheet from the pad and, not wishing to risk damage to the impression by folding it, he slipped it under his shirt.

A quick inspection of the rest of the room confirmed that these were careful men, too thorough to leave information lying about for unwelcome visitors.

He left the door open behind him, as the seaman had done, and stole out to the upper deck just in time to see Ruth being escorted off the boat.

He waited whilst two of the men rowed her the short distance to the quayside, and watched her go into a café which announced by a sign outside that it housed a public telephone. She seemed in control of the situation, but Holt guessed that after the receipt of the urgent message the men had decided to hustle her off the *Sunset* as quickly as possible.

Was Christopher expected, he wondered? And who was Dunant? Holt was tempted to remain on board in the hope of finding out, but it was a faint hope and he had other problems to attend to. There was Ruth's safety to think of, and the message on the paper under his shirt, and the rendez-vous with Vance at midnight.

He made his way to the stern, noted with relief that his dinghy was still moored alongside, and slid down the rope without making a sound.

For a long moment before taking the oars he sat completely still, straining for some indication of the whereabouts of the two remaining deckhands. Suddenly an agitated quarrel in French broke out; it came from the forward wheelhouse. There was nothing for it but to risk being seen and trust to luck that they were too involved in their argument to notice him as he pulled away.

It was the longest thirty yards Holt had ever rowed, but his luck was in and he reached the safety of the moored cabin-cruiser and was soon on the quayside.

Hearing the sound of a car, he turned, and was just in time to see Ruth climb into a taxi outside the café and disappear from sight with a grateful wave to her rescuers. The men made no attempt to have her followed, but made their way leisurely back to the *Sunset*.

Holt breathed a sigh of relief. She had carried out her dangerous and physically uncomfortable part of the scheme without exciting suspicion. As Inspector Hyde was fond of saying, Ruth was quite a girl!

Holt took the paper from under his shirt. Held in a certain light it was fairly legible, but unfortunately it did not make much sense to him because most of the words used were in a kind of French *argot*. 'Tell Christopher . . . something . . . something . . . Dunant . . . something . . .'

What was needed, he decided, was someone who spoke fluent French, including the *argot* of the streets, not found in a dictionary of correct grammar . . . Who? . . . There was Henri Legere, of course, but he was scarcely a suitable choice . . . No, Hyde would soon find a source of translation; the best plan was to return to the hotel immediately.

But, on the other hand, there *was* someone else . . . someone whose salmon-pink bungalow lay on the direct route back to Eastbourne. Holt told himself, with a slight tingling of the blood, that he really had no alternative.

When he rang the door bell there was the sound of a window being opened round a corner of the bungalow.

'Who is it?' came Antoinette's attractive voice. 'I hope it's someone nice.'

'Why, does it make a difference?' Holt countered.

'It does indeed. I'm in my bath.' She gave an embarrassed laugh and added, 'Do I detect the friendly tones of Philip Holt, by any chance?'

'You do, Miss Sheen.'

'Ah, that *is* someone nice. I won't be a moment.'

After a brief interval Antoinette opened the front door and it was at once apparent to Holt how she had managed to be so quick. She wore only a white thigh-length bathrobe and the water was still gleaming on her golden-brown skin. She did not open the door fully, for which Holt was thankful, bearing in mind her Peeping Tom Neighbour with the telescope.

151

Francis Durbridge

He edged past her, disturbingly aware of the fragrance of her body, and she led the way into the studio.

'Please excuse the attire,' she said. 'I thought it bad manners to keep you waiting on a windy doorstep.'

The tall, graceful figure bent towards the fire to add more logs, the brief bathrobe proving hopelessly inadequate for the activity. Glancing up at him and making a vague effort to pull it more closely around her she added with a smile, 'if it worries you, I'll go and put some more clothes on.'

'I think I'll manage to survive.'

She remained where she was, kneeling by the fire and looking up at him, then she asked quietly, 'You don't trust me, do you, Philip?'

Holt said, 'Let's just say there are times when it pays to be cautious.'

Antoinette smiled and rose to her feet. 'Like now?' she said softly.

'I'm afraid this is a business call, Antoinette. Perhaps one day I may make a social one.'

'Is that a promise?' She was moving closer to him. 'When this Vance Scranton affair is cleared up perhaps . . . ?'

'There's . . . nothing I should like more.' He managed an unsteady smile.

'I really think you mean that.' She was devastatingly close. 'For a man hell-bent on saying "No" you have a charming way of saying it . . .'

It was by no means certain what might have happened next; fortunately for Holt he was saved by the bell. The telephone rang.

Antoinette stiffened. 'I suppose I'd better answer it.' She crossed the room and picked up the receiver. 'Hello . . . *Ah, salut, Henri! Ça va?*'

152

Holt realised with a sudden stab of irritation that it must be Henri Legere. He forced himself to listen with wooden indifference, taking professional note of Antoinette's excellent accent and fluent French. The conversation seemed to be concerned with a theatre date at Bexhill that evening. Bexhill was a few miles the other side of Eastbourne.

When she hung up she pulled the bathrobe closer about her and headed for her bedroom door, calling over her shoulder, 'I'd better get dressed. That was Henri Legere. I expect the gossips have told you he's my current boyfriend. Not a very serious one,' she added.

'I had heard,' said Holt dryly.

'I believe you've met Henri. What did you think of him?'

'I don't really know enough about him to form an opinion,' Holt replied noncommittally.

Antoinette laughed. 'Neither do I. I expect that sounds odd, but he's a bit of an iceberg. At least two-thirds of him are under water. I still don't have a clue as to what makes him tick.'

Holt raised his eyebrows at this remark. It echoed in an uncanny fashion something that Ruth had said earlier that day. Was Antoinette in the clear? Did she really know nothing about the private lives of the young men whose physical charms appealed to her? Common-sense ruled this out as unlikely, yet it was an established fact that many a woman had lived with a man for years without realising she was married to a thief or murderer.

Holt drew the piece of paper from the *Sunset* out of his shirt, glad that Antoinette could not see him.

'You speak excellent French,' he called out to her. 'Do you know the *argot* of the streets as well?'

'I ought to,' came a muffled reply. She was obviously pulling on a sweater. 'I studied for three years at the Sorbonne.'

'Did you, by Jove! Lucky girl! I can cope with correct French, but their slang has me beat. I heard an odd phrase at the cinema the other day.' He glanced at the paper and, omitting the names Christopher and Dunant, read out the French words. 'What the devil does that mean?'

She replied without hesitation. 'Oh, that's a racy way of saying that things are getting too hot for someone and that he or she will have to go underground for a while, till the pressure is off. What film was this?'

'Oh, it's running in London,' Holt lied glibly. 'I forget the title. It was a pretty exciting film.'

Antoinette came back into the studio dressed in a thick fisherman's jersey and blue jeans. She made a deprecating gesture at herself. 'My working clothes. I'm on a painting jag again. What do you think of my Rembrandt?' She moved to the easel which was draped by a cloth.

'What became of the Vermeer?' Holt asked.

'Oh, I got tired of it,' she said carelessly.

'What a pity. May I see it?'

'No, I'm afraid not, I threw it away. The bread looked stale. This is the one I'm interested in now.'

She pulled the cloth from the canvas to reveal the half completed painting. It was a copy of one of Rembrandt's portraits of his son Titus.

Holt studied it carefully, then said, 'I should imagine it's going to be terrific! Tell me: why do you go in for copying all the time? Why not try something of your own, something original?'

'I will, one day. You have to walk before you can run. First I must learn how to draw, how to mix colour, how to lay it on. All students learn by copying, if they're serious about art.'

'I see . . . Meantime,' he said jokingly, 'you could make a

pretty penny by passing off your work as original Old Masters and selling them to some unsuspecting Texan oil king. Did you know one of the Titus portraits fetched two and a quarter million dollars recently?'

'Yes – and poor old Rembrandt got paid fifty *gulden* for it at the time. That's justice for you!'

Holt nodded. 'It's a strange world, the world of art. There are some crazy prices about. I think it has something to do with status symbols.'

Antoinette favoured him with her most enchanting smile. 'It's funny you should say that. I remember Vance saying something very similar. He said what's the use of being a Persian sheikh and owning half a dozen oil wells if you haven't got an Old Master to hang on the walls of your desert palace? No Old Master – no status amongst your fellow sheikhs, apparently.'

Holt laughed and it was on the tip of his tongue to take her into his confidence and tell her that Vance was alive. But, with difficulty, he restrained the impulse, forcing himself to remember that from Delilah and Salome to the present day, women had used their beauty to dazzle men and befuddle their judgement at crucial moments. Was the betwitching Antoinette doing just that? Was she a superb actress, capable of pretending she did not know that Vance was alive, Graham Brown dead, and two people nearly killed when the hydraulic brake tubes of Holt's Mustang were severed only a mile or two from her bungalow?

Without warning she said, 'When are you going to come to the point, Philip?'

He was momentarily taken aback. She really was nobody's fool. He pretended not to have followed her train of thought, whilst he gathered his wits.

'The point of what?'

'This visit. You said it wasn't a social call. What's on your mind?'

'Oh – well . . . I wanted to ask you a few questions.'

'Fire away, then!'

'Do you know a man named Ashley Milton?'

'Yes, I do.'

'Is he a friend of yours?'

'Not really. He's very knowledgeable, cultured, and so on, he knows a great deal about music and painting – but as a man he's an utter wash-out!' She grinned. 'You know me: I like a man to be a man – and if possible a hunk of a man!'

Holt stuck to his course. 'One thing puzzles me about Milton. He's merely the proprietor of a restaurant – admittedly a very good one – but he seems to be enormously wealthy.'

'Oh, he is. Oodles and oodles of it.'

'Then where does it all come from?'

'I've no idea. Inherited, I suppose,' she said casually.

'Another thing that puzzles me is his choice of friends. Henri Legere for one.'

'Now that's simple. Ashley Milton's passionately fond of anything to do with France. He speaks the language perfectly.'

Holt nodded. 'Another friend of Milton's appears to be Jimmy Wade.'

She wrinkled her brow. 'Jimmy Wade – do I know him?'

'He's an undertaker by profession – or a funeral director, if you like that term better. He's Julie Benson's brother-in-law.'

'Oh, you mean that little pink-faced creature who hops around after her like a magpie? I've seen him but I never knew his name. No, I'm afraid I don't know anything about him. *He's* not exactly what you'd call a hunk of a man, is he?'

Holt was forced to laugh.

There was a pause, then Antoinette stood squarely in front of him and spoke in a coaxing tone. 'Philip, I don't like that look on your face . . . It bodes no good. "Here comes the nasty bit," it says . . . Come on, better get it off your chest!'

'Very well.' He offered her a cigarette, which she refused, and he lit one himself, inhaling deeply before going on. 'It concerns Vance's signet ring. I don't think you were telling me the exact truth about that, were you?'

For the first time her eyes refused to meet his. She made no reply.

'The ring itself is genuine,' he went on, 'but not your story of how it came into your possession. You lied about that letter, didn't you?'

She gave a long sigh and sank into a chair. She kept her head down and her hands clasped flatly between her knees, and this time she spoke in a dull monotone. 'Yes, I lied to you. I wrote the note myself. No one sent me the ring – I had it all the time.'

'How long had you had it, and who gave it to you?'

'Vance gave it to me, just before he was murdered.'

'Oh. Then why make up a cock-and-bull story about it, Antoinette? Wouldn't it have been simpler just to hand the ring over, if you'd decided not to keep it?'

She sat quite still and he thought she was not going to answer. When she eventually did so her voice was scarcely audible. 'I'm not very proud of this, Philip. You'll probably decide to cross to the other side of the street next time you see me. I was afraid; I was just scared to the roots about what might happen.'

'But what did you think would happen? Why were you so afraid?'

'I thought the police would automatically assume that I took the ring from the dead man's finger. I couldn't prove that he'd given it to me, not when he was dead. I got frightened and I made up that note.'

'Well, I don't think any of us are immune from fear, it's nothing to be ashamed of. But there's one flaw in your story.'

'Really?' She stared at him.

'Yes. Why give me the ring at all? Why didn't you just keep it and say nothing?'

To his surprise she nodded slowly. 'Yes, that stands out a mile, doesn't it? And the trouble is, I don't have a satisfactory answer. I don't really know why I gave you the ring, except that I had a strange compulsion to get rid of it. It sounds unconvincing, I know – but I can't help it, it's the truth . . . You see, it was an odd kind of gift from Vance in the first place – he was a selfish young man and giving presents wasn't really his line of country. I don't know why, but I had a queer feeling that he . . . *pressed* that ring on me, almost as if it could . . . Well, it sounds silly, but almost as if it could do me some harm. There was a . . . a malicious gleam in his eyes. I've already told you he was a strange boy with some dark, twisted threads running through his makeup.'

Abruptly she stood up. Her supreme self-confidence was cracking at last. Tears were trembling on her lashes and her voice was harsh as she turned on him. 'I ought to be trumpeting praises for my dead lover – treasuring his ring as a tear-jerking little keepsake! Instead of which I run him down and can't wait to get shot of the damn thing! So there you have it – the Artist's Portrait of Herself! . . . And now that you've studied the portrait, Mr Holt, I'd be very glad if you'd go!'

She did not bid him goodbye, but ran into her bedroom and slammed the door.

Shaken, and leaving behind him the sounds of muffled sobbing, Holt let himself out into the darkening afternoon.

As he drove away, a blue Volkswagen appeared in the rear-view mirror. He applied his brakes quickly; the Volkswagen had come from the Deanfriston direction and had not crossed the main Newhaven-Eastbourne road in time for its driver to have seen him.

He left the Mustang and ran back along the road, keeping under cover of a hedge, until he could see the bungalow clearly. The Volkswagen drove up, Jimmy Wade got out and advanced to the front door with a quick, bobbing step.

The hall light came on and the front door opened. Holt watched Wade make a neat little bow and enter the bungalow, and one minute later the studio curtains were drawn firmly across the large french windows.

Holt ground his teeth. So much for the man whose name she did not even know, he thought savagely! Though he doubted whether she had had time to get back into her bath for a repeat performance.

'Where's Ruth? Why isn't she here? I hope to God nothing's happened to her, Inspector!'

Holt sounded overwrought as he burst into Hyde's hotel room, full of fears for Ruth's safety and blaming himself unjustifiably for not having followed her taxi himself.

Hyde was reassuring. Ruth had telephoned during Holt's absence. The taxi-driver had had her a little worried, she said, so she had decided to take the London train and throw any suspicious person right off the scent.

'That sounds just like Ruth,' Holt agreed.

'True enough. She's nothing if not thorough.'

'Yes, and she got a thorough soaking at Newhaven! If she

159

should catch a chill . . .' Holt looked really worried. 'What about that taxi-driver? Are you sure she's not in any danger? If anything happens to Ruth as a result of this, I'll never . . .'

'Ruth will be all right, Holt! There's no need to worry . . . Now tell me what you were able to find out on board the *Sunset*.'

Holt gave an account of the afternoon's developments, omitting only one or two details which were not entirely relevant to the Scranton case. He passed the radio message to Hyde, who immediately set about making telephone calls.

'The name Dunant rings no bells for you?' Holt asked him presently.

'None at all. But it's a fair bet that he'll be known on the other side of the Channel.'

Then the Inspector leaned back in his chair and began to fill his pipe. After a moment he glanced up at Holt. 'You're looking uncommonly black about the gills, my dear chap.'

'I hate making a fool of myself!' Holt said tetchily. 'Especially over women.'

'You mean about Ruth just now? Nonsense! You had a perfect right to be concerned about her. I'd have thought very poorly of you if you hadn't.'

'When did she say her train will be in?'

'Not much before midnight. But I've arranged for her to be met at the station. She'll be all right.'

'Good! . . . But it's not over Ruth that I nearly made a fool of myself,' he confessed.

'Ah! . . . Antoinette?'

'Yes.'

'Oh, don't worry; your visit wasn't entirely wasted.' You got the translation and as soon as my call from Interpol comes through we shall probably know what this is all about.'

He read the message again. '"Tell Christopher that Dunant is going underground for a while because the *flics* are making things too hot for him."'

'How about the third Christopher letter? Is it negative?'

'Yes. Fuller from the Yard tested it this afternoon. I'm rather afraid someone's trying to pull the wool over our eyes. Only the first message contained the invisible code, and what that code means still has me foxed. But I do begin to see a vague pattern to the affair as a whole. I expect you do too?'

'A pattern with a distinctly French motif?' Holt suggested.

'Exactly! Firstly, there were those two acquaintances of Curly's who tried to force you off the Brighton cliffs. They were two petty criminals from France, wanted on a charge of operating an illegal printing press in Paris. Their speciality was old French newspapers . . . Next we have Henri Legere. I questioned him this afternoon, but I don't feel I got anywhere. All I could prove was that he has a peculiar talent for being in the wrong place at the wrong time . . . Then we have Ashley Milton – a Francophile with too much unexplained money, who has his suits made in Paris, owns a luxury motor yacht crewed by Frenchmen and old lags, and receives cryptic messages in Parisian argot . . . I shan't be at all surprised if Interpol tells us that Monsieur Dunant conducts his affairs, whatever they may be, from Paris too.'

'And yet, oddly enough, the Christopher postcards and the letter have all come from a sedate English watering spa – Harrogate.'

'A simple method known as a "post-box" could explain that. Someone at the Paris end posts a sealed envelope or package to a middleman in Harrogate. The package contains letters or postcards, already addressed, and the middleman simply stamps them and sends them off. Possibly he's completely in the dark about the whole business – he'd be merely carrying out his instructions.'

'Then do you think this fellow Dunant may be Christopher himself?'

Hyde shook his head. 'Today's radio message passed on urgent instructions *from* Dunant *to* Christopher, so all the signs point to Christopher being on this side of the Channel. And not so far away from the *Sunset*, I'd say.'

'Are you going to arrest Milton?'

'On what charge? There's no cast-iron proof that he's done anything wrong as yet. Using Wade's car, searching Vance's study at midnight, possibly borrowing and returning a ring, owning an expensive boat with a questionable taste in deck-hands . . . I admit, a lot of suspicious facts are piling up, but there's not an ounce of solid proof!'

'But surely you'll haul him in for questioning?'

The Inspector debated this. Then he said, 'I may . . . and I may not. I have an idea that it might be wiser to lull him into a feeling of security. Let him think we're not interested in him. That way we can work undisturbed. Every time I pull someone in for questioning during a murder case people expect a dramatic turn of events. That wretched newspaper fellow, Abe Jenkins, was nosing around the College again this afternoon. He's the worst of the lot, and heaven knows what balderdash he'll print in his next piece.'

'Milton's obviously up to his neck in this affair, though.'

'Quite so. I'll have him tailed, that much I promise you. He went up to Town this morning. As soon as I hear he's back in Eastbourne I'll have him shadowed. I'm keeping a twenty-four hour watch on the *Sunset* as well. You see, Holt, I don't want to act too hastily. It might send a lot of rabbits bolting back to their warrens with fright.' The Inspector glanced at his watch. 'Only a few hours to go. Everything hangs in the balance as to whether the chief rabbit, Vance Scranton, comes out of *his* warren at midnight.'

'You've got your men posted?' Holt stood up.

'A small army of them, and some plain-clothes police-women too. Luck's on our side, There's a fog rolling in from the sea; it'll help keep them out of sight.'

'It will help Vance too,' Holt remarked.

'Quite so. But either he comes or he doesn't. If he does, we'll have the answers to the whole baffling business, I hope. If he doesn't, then I'll set the hounds of hell on his tail! Either way, we can't overlook the fact that the Crown intends to charge him with the murders of Curly and Graham Brown.'

'M'm . . . Holt scraped his thumbnail thoughtfully against his front teeth. 'I wonder if Graham Brown was another of Antoinette's lovers? You saw his parents – did they mention her?'

'No, I don't think her name came up. Why – what made you say that?'

'I'm trying to spot just where she fits in. It's obvious that she's got her fingers in the pie somewhere, but just what her precise role is—'

The telephone rang and Hyde seized the receiver. 'Hyde speaking . . . Yes, put him through.' He shot an excited look at Holt and murmured, 'Paris *bureau* of Interpol.'

Holt made no attempt to follow the conversation. It was brief and from Hyde's end consisted chiefly of startled mono-syllables. When he hung up there was a faint gleam in his eyes. 'I think we have the answer to your query about Miss Sheen's role in this business. Late this afternoon Interpol succeeded in laying their hands on a man named Jules Dunant. They've been after him for quite some time. He passes himself off as a business man in the retail newspaper trade – in Paris.'

'And his other line of business?'

'A highly profitable painting racket – forgeries of Old Masters . . .'

Chapter Twelve

Fog was rolling in from the sea. It seemed to penetrate the hotel walls, striking chill into the very furniture of Holt's room.

The last quarter of an hour before midnight sounded from a nearby church tower. He stood up, buttoned his jacket, tied a thick scarf round his neck, and was just pulling on his duffle coat when the telephone rang. He picked up the receiver quickly, thinking it would be Hyde from a call-box near the Pier.

'Is that you, Inspector?'

'No, it isn't!' snapped a familiar American voice. 'The Inspector's down on the beach floundering around with all those other Goddamned cops you put on my tail!'

'Scranton!'

'Yeah, that's right – this is Vance! Now see here, what kind of a fool do you take me for? I warned you I wouldn't show up if you brought the police into this.'

Holt thought rapidly. He was convinced that Vance was bluffing, otherwise why bother to phone? 'But you'll still meet me?' he ventured.

'Yeah? What makes you so sure?'

'Because you want the ring, and I've still got it. There was a bit of confusion up at the College this morning.'

'Sure, I heard all about that.' Vance gave a little laugh. 'Poor old Harry Dalesford got coshed.'

'Who told you that?'

'Oh, no! Sorry, pal, I'm not that naïve! Okay, so you've got the ring. I'll give you fifteen minutes to bring it out to me. If you're not here by then I'll know you're wasting time rounding up the police again. Have you got the message loud and clear this time? No coppers, or it's no dice.'

'Very well. I give my word. Where do I meet you?'

'Take the Pevensey Road out of Eastbourne. It's long and straight, I can see you coming. I'll be parked on the seaward side, with my sidelights on. Dip your headlights four times, so's I know it's you.'

'All right. It would help if I knew what kind of car to look for.'

'A blue Volkswagen. A nice little guy lent it to me. Be seeing you, Holt – and don't forget that ring!' A second later he had cleared the line.

A blue Volkswagen, lent by a nice little guy . . .

Holt looked at his watch. It was ten to twelve. Despite having given his word he debated for a moment whether to drive to the Pier and tell Hyde of the last-minute change in plan. But was this wise? Vance obviously had an accomplice or he could not have found out about the fracas at the College. If Holt failed to drive out alone on the road to Pevensey, this accomplice, whoever it might be, could perhaps warn Vance in time. He had no choice.

Checking that the ring was in his pocket, he unlocked his suitcase and took out the pistol which he had police permission to carry. He made sure that his torch was secure in his pocket, then locked his door behind him and ran downstairs to the hotel lobby, where a sleepy night porter tried to way-lay him.

'There's a Mr Abe Jenkins waiting for you in the bar, sir.'

'Tell him I'm out – at the cinema or something!' Holt shouted as he ran past the man and out to his car.

The fog was irregular, occasionally non-existent and at times dense, and he had to crawl through some of the streets, but in a few minutes he had nosed his way through the town and out on to the Pevensey road. Presently it straightened out, and by keeping his eyes glued to the line of cat's-eyes down the centre he was able to put his foot down a trifle and so relieve some of the tension that was tightening inside his body like the strings of a violin.

Vance Scranton at last! For ten days they had hunted this elusive Will-o'-the-wisp, not even sure if he were dead or alive. Now Holt was about to meet him face to face . . .

Macabre tree-shapes and isolated gloomy farmhouses flitted past; from time to time he could hear the sea breaking on the shore to his right, and every now and then came the mournful bleat of a foghorn. Minutes ticked away and he began to wonder if he had missed the blue Volkswagen. Then suddenly twin spots of red and the vague outline of a car loomed out of the mist on the far side of the road.

Holt braked and dipped his lights four times, then pulled in at the left-hand kerbstone.

Was it the car he was looking for? He lowered his window and peered out. Dirty, yellowish vapour shifted and swirled between him and the parked vehicle. It was impossible to be certain. He took out his revolver and slipped off the safety catch, listening intently for the slightest sound. None came.

He switched off his lights, and backed a few yards, swinging the Mustang's nose to the right so that when he switched on his headlights they would point directly across the road at the parked car. Then he stepped warily onto the road, gripping his gun in one hand, the other arm stretched towards the dashboard. He pulled the knob for full headlights . . .

'Put out those lights or I'll shoot!' a voice screamed from the mist.

Holt flung himself sideways into a ditch as a spatter of shots rang out, smashing into the Mustang's lamps with a hideous noise of splintering glass and metal. As he lay breathlessly on the damp ground he attempted to place the voice. He had heard it before, though it was definitely not Vance Scranton's.

'Come out here where I can see you, you dirty blackmailer!' the voice yelled hysterically, rising in pitch.

Holt recognised it now. It was Ashley Milton. Cupping his hands and still lying prone he shouted, 'Milton, will you put that damn fire-iron away! This is Philip Holt! Do you understand? I'm alone – Scranton isn't here!'

There was a curious whimpering sound, followed by an uneven crunch of footsteps on the road. '*Who?*' It was more an escape of breath than a word. 'Who did you say?'

'Philip Holt.' He got to his feet and switched on his torch. It played like the beam from a cinema projector on the screen of yellow fog. 'For God's sake put that gun away – you've smashed up my car in a fine old way.'

'Oh, my God . . . I didn't mean . . . Oh, heavens, what a mess!'

The tall form of Ashley Milton appeared out of the mist. He was wearing a dark overcoat with velvet lapels and an incongruous bowler hat. Holt shone his torch in the man's face. All trace of his habitual elegance and condescending manner were gone. He looked old and haggard and shaken to the core.

'I thought you were Vance Scranton,' he muttered, waving the gun uselessly as though it were an empty can of beer. 'I've never used one of these things before . . . I . . . I . . .'

'Did you intend to kill him?'

'No . . . God, no! . . . I don't know what I intended, I'm nearly out of my mind . . . He rang me this evening in London – told me he wanted some more money. He insisted I came down to the coast immediately. I didn't know what to do. Then I thought of trying to frighten him with a gun, make him abandon his incessant demands. I thought I might even force him to hand me back those hateful letters. I must have been completely crazy – you can't scare people like him so easily . . .' He took out a white silk handkerchief and wiped his face. Then he asked dully, 'How did you find me here? I suppose you had me followed?'

'I wasn't following you, Milton. I had a date with Vance too.'

'Say that again – *you* were going to meet him here?'

'Yes. Arranging for you to be here at the same time, and then failing to turn up himself would appear to be a typical example of his sadistic mind.'

'The twisted little bastard!' Milton spat out with venom. 'Why did he want to meet you?'

'I was supposed to hand over his signet ring.'

'His signet ring?'

'Yes. The one I seem to have dropped under the table in your restaurant yesterday.'

Milton shook his head in a bewildered fashion. 'I'm afraid I don't know what you're talking about, my dear fellow. Did you drop a ring at The Golden Peacock?'

Holt stared at him, watching his breath coming in short bursts and vaporising in the cold, damp air.

'You returned it yourself, to Inspector Hyde. Or at least, you gave it to Jimmy Wade and asked him to hand it over.'

Milton's eyebrows were arched in something like their customary mockery. 'Really? It sounds most intriguing. When is all this supposed to have happened?'

'This morning.'

'But I went up to Town very early this morning.'

'Yes, and Wade tells us he was at The Golden Peacock pretty early too.'

'Come to think of it, I dare say he was.' Milton looked down his nose. 'The mother of one of my waiters has just died. Wade probably wanted the funeral business.'

'But you didn't see him?'

'No, I didn't.'

'What did you have to go up to London for?' Holt asked pointedly.

'H'm? . . . Why did I go to Town? Oh, just business, tedious business. But do go on, Mr Holt, this is fascinating. What is supposed to have happened next? Wade's a ducky little liar isn't he? Just tells as much of the truth as investigation will bear, and then slips in a thumping great lie.'

Holt was sincerely puzzled. 'You say you didn't give him the ring, then?'

'How on earth could I have done so? I've never seen the wretched thing!' Milton looked down at the Mustang's headlights. 'Well, you won't get very far on a night like this without any headlights. You'd better travel back in my old jalopy. I'm awfully sorry about bashing up your gorgeous limousine, Mr Holt. Of course I'll pay for the damage.'

Milton led the way to his car and Holt shone his torch

over it at close quarters. It was a Saab, not unlike a Volks-wagen in contour; its colour, on inspection, proved to be a blue much darker than the choice of Jimmy Wade.

'Perhaps you'd care to drive?' Milton suggested. 'To tell you the truth, I'm still feeling a trifle shaky.' He indicated the gun which he was now forcing into his overcoat pocket. 'I'd no idea these things made such a rumpus.'

'The first time you've used one, eh?' Holt said, settling behind the wheel and acquainting himself with the Saab's dashboard. 'Where did you get it from?'

'M'm? . . . What did you say?'

'I asked you where you got that gun from. They don't hand them out free with packets of Corn Flakes, you know.'

'Ah, yes, I see what you mean . . . Well – as you correctly surmise – I'm afraid I don't have a licence.' He laughed feebly. 'I wouldn't be too sure that the owner has one either. I pinched it from a rather scruffy member of my crew. You remember, I own a boat out at Newhaven. She's really rather smart – you must come aboard some time.'

'I should enjoy that,' Holt said stonily, switching on the ignition.

The thoughts in his brain were whirling like leaves in an autumn storm, but he recalled Hyde's words: 'Lull him into a feeling of security. Let him think we're not interested in him.' So, poker-faced, and muttering only an occasional comment about the swirling fog, he concentrated on the return drive to Eastbourne.

They had been cruising slowly along for four or five minutes when Milton suddenly bounced forward from his reclining position and let out a cry. *'What in God's name is that!'*

To their left a ball of orange flame had ballooned into the

171

night, and a violent explosion followed. The Saab seemed to shiver like a frightened horse.

Holt swung off the road and braked sharply. 'Looks like a boat on fire,' he said breathlessly, struggling to focus through the shifting pattern of fog.

'That's not out at sea!' Milton said emphatically. 'You can see the silhouette of a Martello Tower behind the flames. That fire's on land!'

A moment later Holt was forced to agree with him. In the garish light of the leaping flames he caught a fragmentary impression of the solid outline of a tower, a relic of the days when the South Coast had prepared itself against Napoleon's threat of invasion. Milton had already scrambled out of the Saab and Holt followed. A second later the blood froze in his veins as a hideous scream of agony rent the air.

'Come on!' Milton shouted, producing his torch. 'Mind your footing, it's marsh ground round here.'

Holt switched on his own torch and followed Milton over the uneven marshy terrain. The distance to the conflagration was greater than Holt had realised, and the going was slow. Both he and Milton stumbled several times. As they struggled on across the marsh they became aware of the distant howl of a police siren and the clanging of a fire-engine's bell.

Milton slipped, and grabbed at a rotting fence-post to stop himself from falling. He was panting for breath and had lost his bowler. Gesticulating towards the leaping flames he shouted, 'Do you know what that is, burning out there, Holt? Look, man, you can see the outline clearly!'

Holt came level with him and through a gap in the fog caught a glimpse of the tell-tale silhouette of a Volkswagen, though its colour was not apparent. On a sudden shift in the breeze came the sickening smell of burning flesh.

Along the track which the Volkswagen had obviously taken, the headlamps of a police car stabbed the night at a reckless speed. The fire-engines followed closely. Black, golden-helmeted figures moved grotesquely in the light of the flames, moving swiftly in disciplined action as commands were shouted, and a moment later great gouts of white foam burst with blistering force on to the nearly gutted frame of the car. The air was acrid with an appalling stench of smoke, chemicals, burning metal, and charred flesh.

Eventually the flames sputtered and sank, and with police floodlamps bathing the scene in chrome-yellow light two men in silver asbestos suiting advanced on the remains of the wreckage.

'They're mad to try it,' Milton declared in anguish. 'If there was anyone in that holocaust . . .'

Holt felt his sleeve being tugged. A fat man with a press camera appeared out of the fog.

'Any comment, Mr Holt?' the newspaper reporter demanded brightly.

With a stab of fury Holt recognised Abe Jenkins. 'Yes! How the devil did *you* happen to be on the spot so quickly?'

'I followed you out of your hotel. You can't shake me off as easily as that, you know. I lost your trail in the fog, but then I heard fire-engines and I made for the fire. Who's in that Volkswagen?'

'How should I know?'

'Then how about making a guess?'

'No comment – sorry!' said Holt curtly.

'Come off it! Surely the famous amateur sleuth, Philip Holt—'

Milton grabbed Jenkins roughly by the elbow. '*I'll* risk a guess, my man. Come with me . . .'

Half-pulled, half-stumbling, Jenkins followed at Milton's heels to the edge of the semi-circle of police officers and firemen round the smoking wreck. The two men in asbestos suits were staggering clear with the remains of what had once been a human being. Milton forced his way through a gap in the group and knelt at the side of the body as it was laid on a tarpaulin.

After a moment Milton looked up and searched amongst the onlookers for Holt. 'You never knew him, did you?'

There was a pause, then Holt said, 'You're sure – quite sure – that it's Vance?'

'There's little doubt, I think,' Milton answered.

A familiar voice coming from the front of the semi-circle made Holt jump. 'No, there's no doubt at all!' the voice proclaimed. 'Poor devil,' it added quietly, to no one in particular.

The voice belonged to Jimmy Wade, and Holt, subduing his surprise at encountering the undertaker, hastened to his side.

'And I thought Julie was using my car . . .' the little man was muttering to himself.

'You lent Miss Benson your Volkswagen?' Holt enquired. 'And you're sure that's your car that's been burnt?'

Wade stared at Holt and nodded sadly. 'Yes, those are my number-plates – or what's left of them.'

Whilst Abe Jenkins blundered around taking flash pictures of the carnage Wade continued to gaze with dismay at the smouldering heap. Holt was about to ask Wade where Julie was when Inspector Hyde appeared and hurried to join them.

'Are you all right?' he asked anxiously.

'Yes, Inspector. But for Pete's sake make sure there was no one else in that car!'

174

'There was no one else,' Hyde said. 'We've checked thoroughly.' He turned to Wade. 'Would you mind telling me what brought you to this area tonight, Mr Wade?'

Wade managed a quick smile. 'Yes, we – er – just bumped into all the commotion and . . . well, we were curious to see what it was all about.'

'We?' Holt rapped at him. 'You have someone with you, sir?'

'Yes. A lady. Miss Sheen.'

For a split second the Inspector betrayed his astonishment. Then he said with restraint, '*You* were with Miss Sheen?'

'That's right.' Wade stared through the smoke and fog and the confusing mêlée of firemen and police. 'Where on earth has she got to? She was here a moment ago.'

Quietly Hyde answered him. 'She's over by the hedge there, being sick. The sight of that charred body was too much for her. But you haven't answered my question, Mr Wade. How did you happen to be in this area?'

'We were driving back from the theatre in Bexhill, in Miss Sheen's car.'

Holt intervened. 'I thought Henri Legere was taking her to the theatre?'

'Yes, he was. That is to say, he intended to.' Wade beamed automatically at the two men. 'Unfortunately he had to cry off, for some reason or other, and I happened to be with Miss Sheen at the time that he telephoned her, so I . . . took the liberty of offering my humble services for the evening.'

'So you just happened to be with Miss Sheen at the time, did you, Mr Wade,' remarked Holt dryly.

'Yes, I did!' retorted the small man, with an unexpected flash of defiance.

'I didn't know you two knew each other.'

'There seems to be quite a lot of things you don't know, Mr Holt,' said Wade, drawing back his shoulders and thrusting out his chin. 'Otherwise you'd have solved this dreadful case by now.'

Inspector Hyde made a wry face which bordered on the verge of a smile, but Holt refused to catch his eye.

The Inspector addressed Wade. 'Perhaps you'd be so good as to come down to the station and make a statement about all this extra knowledge that you're hinting at, Mr Wade.'

'Come down to the station? You mean – now?'

'Yes – now.'

Wade shrugged his shoulders. 'Very well, Inspector, if you think it's absolutely necessary.'

Milton was at their side. 'Inspector, I should like to make a statement too, if I may?'

'I *was* going to invite you, sir,' said Hyde quietly. 'Shall we go?'

Dawn was breaking by the time Inspector Hyde decided to call a temporary halt to the interrogations. The three suspects who had undergone his exhaustive questioning were allowed to return to their homes on the strict understanding that they did not leave the district.

Holt said wearily, 'Aren't you taking rather a big risk with regard to Milton?' He stared at his own sleepless, unshaven face in the grimy window before opening it to let some much needed fresh air into the room.

'Why Milton more than Wade or Miss Sheen?' Hyde asked.

'Because he strikes me as being much the most potentially dangerous of the bunch.'

'I dare say. But they were all suspiciously near the scene of the fire within a few minutes of its having happened. All

176

deny having had anything to do with the murder, and for the time being we've no evidence to prove the contrary. It would be very illuminating to know if Vance really did ring Milton and arrange to meet him here. But, whatever the truth is, we can't accuse Milton of having blown up Vance in that Volkswagen – he was sitting next to you in the Saab when it happened.'

Holt shook his head like a swimmer coming out of the water. 'Milton has a finger in the pie somewhere, I feel it in my bones!'

'Unfortunately, intuitive feelings aren't sufficient grounds for an arrest.' The Inspector sighed. 'Short of a charge of murder – which I'm not yet prepared to make – the law demands that I set him free. But, as I promised you last night, I shall have him very carefully watched.'

'Wade and the girlfriend too?' Holt asked, adding caustically, '"That sophisticated painter-woman", as Wade once called her!'

Hyde nodded. 'They *are* an odd pair, aren't they? I don't much care for his explanation of their friendship, true or otherwise.'

'You mean that story that they've been seeing one another in an attempt to solve the Scranton mystery by themselves?'

'Yes. We don't want a lot of amateurs meddling in this affair!'

Holt cleared his throat and grinned.

'Oh, I wouldn't call *you* an amateur, Holt,' the Inspector laughed, catching the implication. 'No, we're very glad indeed of your help on this case. But people like Wade and Miss Sheen are a different matter. It could be dangerous, for one thing – these crooks aren't using the kid glove technique.'

'On the other hand,' said Holt reasonably, 'they might just

come up with some startling information. But what beats me is why Wade should suddenly take it upon himself to turn detective.'

'He said it was driving him mad, watching Julie become a nervous wreck on account of Vance's disappearance. That's why he decided to start his own investigation, he says. I don't think there's much doubt that the man is in love with her. He more or less admitted it.'

'So he's in love with his sister-in-law . . . I doubt whether she cares two hoots for him. But it still seems amazing that a meek little chap like Wade should suddenly become so enterprising. And equally odd that he should choose an exotic woman like Antoinette for a partner.'

'M'm . . .' Hyde mused. 'You never can tell . . . Perhaps it's the other way round; it may be her idea. She could be the instigator of the scheme, and Wade just following doggedly in her footsteps.'

'That sounds more like it!'

'Either way, I don't care for it. But their story does stick together, after a fashion. They did go to the theatre at Bexhill and they were on the perfectly normal route home. The only weak point in the story is the time lapse between the end of the play and their appearance after midnight at the fire. Even allowing for their stopping for a drink on the way – and I shall check on that this morning, of course – they should have passed through Eastbourne earlier than they did.'

Holt raised an eyebrow thoughtfully. 'Wait a moment! Supposing the whole thing is a blind, a smoke-screen to divert our attention from his true activities? Acccording to Milton, Wade must be the pickpocket who stole the ring at The Golden Peacock. Milton flatly denies having given it to Wade to pass on to you.'

'One of them is a point-blank liar!'

'Yes, but which one? And did you notice Wade's reaction when he saw his own car burning?'

Hyde frowned and thrust out his lower lip, trying to recollect the scene. 'He looked pretty dismayed, so far as I remember – but that's only natural.'

'His version was that Julie had asked him for the loan of his Volkswagen. I should have thought Wade would have been scared to death when he saw the burning wreck that she might still be inside it! Instead of that, he seemed to assume quite casually that she hadn't used the car at all.'

'Logic is on your side, I agree. But it doesn't follow that he was telling the truth about lending the car. It's possible that Vance contacted him direct.'

'Yes. Vance's words were "A nice little guy lent it to me."'

Hyde rubbed his stubbled chin and stood up. He looked at his watch. 'I suggest we get a shave and a spot of breakfast. By then it will be time to disturb the beauty sleep of Julie Benson.'

Holt yawned. 'What about Mr and Mrs Scranton? Don't the parents have a prior right to know their son's really dead, beyond all doubt this time?'

'Of course they do. I'll go up to the Grand and break the news myself as soon as we've finished with Julie.'

'What items are written on her slate?'

'*Item One*: You showed her the ring at the restaurant and almost immediately afterwards Vance knew you had it. Who told him? *Item Two*: You were ordered to drop the ring in a jar on Dalesford's desk. What more convenient place for Julie to collect it and pass it on to Vance? *Item Three*: There was a rumpus at the College and you failed to deliver the ring, and again Vance got to know. *Item Four*: Wade says

Julie asked for the loan of the Volkswagen; Vance was the one who used it.'

'It's high time we questioned that young lady.'

The two men were half-way through their breakfast in the police canteen when a telephone message told Hyde that someone had already disturbed Julie Benson's beauty sleep. Apparently acting on the news which only the impetuous Jimmy Wade could have brought her, the young girl had tried to take her own life by an overdose of sleeping pills.

There could be no doubt about the authenticity of the suicide note which lay beside her bed; Scotland Yard had analysed her handwriting a week earlier.

Now that Vance is really dead, life no longer holds any meaning for me.

The note was addressed to Christopher.

Chapter Thirteen

Three people were pacing the quadrangle of Deanfriston College as the sun gradually penetrated the dispersing mist.

Only Ruth looked fresh, well-groomed, and wide awake. She had returned from her roundabout journey late the previous night and gone straight to bed, unaware of the drama that was taking place on the Pevensey Marshes. After daybreak, however, she had lost no time in running Holt and the Inspector to earth and learning of the latest developments.

'Will Julie pull through, do you think?' she asked.

'The doctors give her a fifty-fifty chance,' Hyde answered.

'She's the one person who can tell us who Christopher is.'

'I'm afraid we can't wait for Miss Benson to tell us.' Hyde was emphatic. 'Even if she survives she may lie in a coma for days. Also, there's no guarantee that she'll do all the talking we'd like, even if she does regain consciousness.'

'But do we have to broadcast that fact?' Holt asked quietly.

The Inspector halted and gave him a level glance. 'As a matter of fact, the same thought had been running through my head. Keep her under lock and key and spread the word that she's recovering rapidly and will soon tell all.'

'No, that's too dangerous,' Holt objected. 'Remember what

happened to Curly. I've no great love for Julie Benson, but her life won't be worth a row of beans once it gets out that we expect her to turn Queen's Evidence.'

'Couldn't the Inspector put a guard on her?' Ruth suggested.

'No, it's too big a risk,' Holt assured her. 'When Christopher is finally brought to trial, the Crown will want all the evidence it can get, and Julie must be alive to give it. As I see it, there are two alternatives open to us. If we announce that Julie's dead, what effect do you think that would have, Inspector?'

Hyde paced the quadrangle again, ignoring the occasional groups of passing students who stared curiously at him and then turned away to gossip energetically about the latest rumours. Work seemed to have come to a standstill at the College now that Professor Dalesford had been attacked and his secretary attempted suicide.

Eventually Hyde returned to his companions' side. 'Trying to fake Julie's death could be rather tricky. We'd have to go through the motions of having an autopsy, we'd have to arrange for the body to be removed from the College, and there'd have to be some form of funeral or cremation service – all under the curious eyes of the College, not to speak of Christopher and his friends. I doubt if we could get away with it. And if it leaked out that we were trying to bamboozle the public I could expect to find my name at the bottom of the pension list within twenty-four hours!'

'I fully agree,' said Holt. 'From the practical point of view, things could go wrong. But I meant what would be the likely effect on Christopher and Company?'

'Considerable relief, I should think,' the Inspector replied. 'They might feel so secure as to do something foolish and play straight into our hands. On the other hand, with Vance dead and this Jules Dunant arrested it's just possible they'll all dive for a hole in the ground and stay there for months to come.'

'Which is just what we don't want!' urged Holt. 'That brings me to the alternative. We let it be known that Julie is alive, but at the same time we let word leak out that she's already begun to confess. Abe Jenkins is still hanging around the area, and for once he could be of use to us. He'd have it in the headlines before you could say "Sensation!" "Suicide Girl Talks." "Arrests Expected Hourly." – that sort of thing . . . Now what effect would that have, would you say?'

Ruth was delighted by the prospect. 'It would be like the small boy at the Guy Fawkes' party who threw a lighted squib into the whole collection of fireworks!'

Inspector Hyde's normally unemotional features seemed to catch some of Ruth's animation. 'It's certainly worth a trial! We'd have to plan it carefully. I'd need at least four hours to set the trap. The whole idea could prove disastrous if any one of them slipped through our fingers.'

'But do you think the guilty ones will bolt as soon as they hear that Julie is talking?' Holt persisted.

'I'm prepared to take that gamble. Just give me enough time to get my men posted, and a short-wave radio hook-up from various observation posts to a central headquarters, then you can toss your lighted squib into the box of fireworks, and we'll see who runs first.'

'And what will you do when they start running?' Ruth asked.

'Follow them.'

Shortly after Hyde had left the College and returned to Eastbourne, where he had the unhappy task of telling Mr and Mrs Scranton what had happened to their son, two new members joined the nursing team who were keeping an unbroken vigil at Julie Benson's bedside.

A team of road workers drove up to a spot on the East Dean road within sight of Antoinette's bungalow and set up a workmen's hut. The short-wave radio set inside it enabled this team to keep in direct touch with Inspector Hyde's Command Post.

The baker's delivery van which was keeping a close watch on Jimmy Wade's activities at the lodgings he had taken in nearby Ocklynge was also equipped with short-wave radio.

The unobtrusive man who had been shadowing Ashley Milton since his interrogation at police headquarters was reinforced by a middle-aged couple who seemed content to spend all their time sitting near the bandstand. This position commanded a good view of The Golden Peacock, and they even repaired to the restaurant itself and enjoyed some excellent coffee. Communications were more difficult for this couple – they had to rely on public call-boxes – but their reports were nevertheless prompt and efficient.

The shadowing of Henri Legere seemed at first an insoluble problem, but he obligingly solved it himself by turning up at The Golden Peacock during the course of the morning and, a bare half-hour later, driving off in Milton's Saab in the direction of Newhaven. There, the plain-clothes men disguised as dockhands, whose job it was to keep the *Sunset* under observation, reported that Legere had boarded the luxury vessel carrying a considerable amount of personal luggage.

With all the suspects under surveillance, Hyde was ready to toss the burning squib . . .

His first move was to summon Abe Jenkins and one or two other crime reporters to an informal press conference.

Jenkins came hurrying from the Grand Hotel, where he had been trying to extract some exclusive copy from Mr and Mrs Scranton as they packed, preparatory to leaving for London and America. Mrs Scranton was nearing a nervous breakdown and Robert Scranton had been rather abrupt. Though resigned to learning the worst about his son, he was scarcely enthusiastic at having his bereavement plastered all over the sensational press.

This hostile reception had left Jenkins with a bitter tongue. 'What sort of parents are they, I'd like to know!' he commented in a loud voice as the small conference gathered. 'They aren't even waiting for the funeral before they scuttle back to America.'

'Abe,' said a rival journalist, 'you're just sore because they wouldn't give you some juicy copy. If you'd learned to handle people with a bit more tact you might have found out that the boy's remains are being flown to the Scranton place in Minnesota. What on earth is there to keep them hanging on here – happy memories of burning cars, or just the sight of your lovely face?'

Inspector Hyde rose to subdue a ripple of amusement, and then read out a prepared statement giving the official version of the events on the Pevensey marshes and the subsequent attempt by Julie Benson to take her own life.

Questions followed, thick and fast. Some of them had to be deftly avoided; some could be answered without endangering the plan.

'Are you quite certain it was Vance Scranton in the burning car?'

'Yes.'

'Did he die of burns or suffocation?'

'A combination of both, we think. The results of the

185

autopsy will be announced shortly, just as soon as we have them.'

'Why was he killed?'

Another voice added, 'Yes, and why did he fake his own death ten days ago, and substitute that Scottish student's body for his own? What's it all about, Inspector?'

'I'm afraid we haven't got all the answers yet,' Hyde replied. 'Miss Benson broke down during her testimony and the doctors have ordered complete rest before we may question her again. But what we have learnt is that Vance Scranton was an important member of an international organisation gambling for very high stakes. It's my personal guess – and this is most definitely off the record, gentlemen – that for reasons of his own he decided to quit. Whether he wanted to branch out on his own or whether he simply wanted to get out and go straight, I don't know. At any rate, he must have decided that the simplest and safest way of severing connections was to counterfeit his own death. I repeat that this is strictly off the record and largely what a friend of mine calls "inspired guesswork".'

'You say these people were gambling for high stakes. Can you be a bit more explicit?'

'I'm afraid not. In the interests of security, and until certain persons have been apprehended, the police are not in a position to divulge this fact.'

'Because you don't actually know the answer?' said Abe Jenkins, a veneer of joviality coating a vicious barb.

'We know it, Mr Jenkins, have no fear.'

'I heard a rumour that Miss Benson hasn't recovered from her overdose of sleeping tablets,' Jenkins probed.

Hyde looked affronted. 'Are you trying to say that she is dead and that the authorities are concealing the fact?'

Jenkins gave a knowing smile. 'Don't look so shocked, Inspector. It wouldn't be the first time you tried to pull the wool over our eyes.'

Hyde's manner was curt and anger glinted in his eyes. 'Miss Benson is alive. You may talk to her doctors and nurses any time you wish, and you may look through a screen and satisfy yourself that she is breathing. Are there any more questions?'

'Yes.' A reporter from a respected county paper stood up. 'There's some concern among the public at the apparent inactivity of police investigations. Since the first murder at Deanfriston College more than ten days have passed and four people possibly connected with the case have been killed. When can some arrests be expected?'

The Inspector stood up, signalling the closure of the conference. A taut silence filled the room. With not the slightest attempt at melodrama he looked at his watch and said casually, 'Within a very short space of time, gentlemen.'

The room emptied as a wild rush for available telephones took place. Hyde knew it would be only a matter of hours before the evening newspapers blazoned the news of imminent police action. The radio and television news services would report it even sooner. The squib had been well and truly ignited.

Hyde hurried off to his Command Post and there he found Holt and a very worried looking Sergeant waiting for him in the room adjoining the main radio room.

'What is it, Sergeant? You look as if the heavens are about to cave in.'

'I think they are, sir.' The Sergeant handed him a typewritten report. 'This is the post mortem on Vance Scranton's body. The second paragraph is the one that made me sit up!'

'Me too,' murmured Holt.

Hyde sank into a chair and studied the document with a set face. On reaching the second paragraph he uttered a single colourful exclamation, then read in complete silence to the end.

The room was still heavy with silence when the door burst open and Ruth swept in. One quick glance at the faces of the three men told her there had been a major development.

'Something's happened!' she proclaimed at once. 'What have I been missing?'

'We now know for sure how Vance was killed,' Holt answered. 'It definitely wasn't an accidental fire.'

'Tell me.' Ruth took off her coat and threw it over a chair.

'Well, as you know, Vance agreed to meet me on the road to Pevensey. He thought I had the ring. Somehow, Milton – whom we thought was still in London – must have got word of this meeting. Anyway, Milton got to the rendezvous first . . .'

'But why should he do that?' Ruth asked, really puzzled. 'He couldn't have wanted the ring – he'd already found it and given it to the police.'

'Via Jimmy Wade,' Hyde reminded her. 'Don't forget we've not proved that story yet.'

'It couldn't have been the ring Milton was after, Ruth,' Holt explained. 'You see, if he knew about my appointment with Vance he must also have known I was the one who was supposed to have the ring. He didn't try to get it from me – so I think we can assume that what he wanted was Vance in person.'

'According to this report,' Hyde said stiffly, 'Milton must have got there first and shot Vance—'

'*Shot* him!' Ruth looked stunned.

'Yes, there's no doubt about it. It's in the post mortem. He was shot.'

'This is what we think must have happened,' said Holt. 'Milton had an accomplice with him. I imagine the accomplice drove off, with the body, in the Volkswagen which Vance had borrowed, and Milton stayed put, waiting for me.'

'But why?' queried Ruth.

'I was to be Milton's alibi. When I came on the scene he gave a very convincing performance of a man with nervous hysteria – he let rip with a hail of bullets at my headlights. That was to make sure that I'd abandon my car and make the return journey in his Saab. Meanwhile, the accomplice set fire to the Volkswagen and then screamed out. It was the scream that fooled me! I thought it was someone dying in agony from the flames. I was wrong; Vance was already dead. They set fire to the car in the belief that the body would be so charred, so thoroughly burned, that we'd never suspect the real cause of death.'

'Milton had the nerve of Old Nick!' Hyde said incredulously. 'Instead of trying to ignore the fire he insisted on leading the way over the marshes and then identifying the body. I'd never have thought a man could commit murder and then have the gall to take a detective by the hand and show him the body!'

'It's astounding,' said Holt. 'The only slip-up was the gun. That may provide a definite link with the murder.'

'How?' asked Ruth.

'He'd already shot Vance – that was one bullet fired. And we've also got some bullets from the Mustang, fired from the same gun. They've been sent to the Ballistics department and if they tally with the one found in Vance's body, it'll be Milton's undoing.'

'Then what are we waiting for?' Ruth exclaimed. 'Can't you arrest Milton on the spot?'

'I just want confirmation from the Ballistics people, that's all. Then we'll have a watertight case.'

'We're waiting to hear from them now, Miss,' the Sergeant added.

As the afternoon wore on the atmosphere at the Command Post grew more and more tense. Holt and the Inspector looked tired and strained. Even the habitually cheerful Ruth began to look a little jaded.

Then at last one of the radio-telephone sets in the adjoining room sprang to life.

'It's Station Three calling, sir!' someone shouted through the half-open door.

Hyde pushed back his chair and bolted to the set. A switch was flicked and he was handed a microphone.

'Hyde here. Go ahead, Three.'

'The party we're interested in has just left her bungalow and is driving away in a green Mini Minor, direction Eastbourne.'

'Get on her tail immediately! Report the moment she stops anywhere!' Hyde replaced the microphone on its hook, looking perturbed. 'What worries me is the fact that we've no radio contact with the roadworkers' van that's tailing her. They've got a stationary set that works all right in the road-menders' hut, but it's no use in a moving vehicle. They'll have to rely on call-boxes.'

A few minutes later the Inspector's worries were dissolved in a startling manner.

Station Four, shadowing Jimmy Wade, reported that he had dashed out of his lodgings in Ocklynge and into a green Mini Minor which had driven up outside and stopped for only a few seconds. Station Four's bakery van was equipped with two-way R/T, so both Wade and Antoinette were safely under control. As the reports came in, detailing the route they were taking, it became obvious where their destination lay.

Twenty minutes later all doubt was removed.

Hyde barked commands to the technicians in the radio room. 'Alert Station Five! Tell them to keep a sharp look-out for the arrival of a green Mini Minor, and to contact Station Four which will arrive on her tail!'

Ruth whispered to Holt, 'Which is Station Five?'

'My guess is Newhaven,' came the reply.

'Guess correct,' Hyde said over his shoulder. He ordered maps of the English Channel and pored over them.

'Are you going to let those two board the *Sunset*?' Ruth asked in astonishment.

'If that's their plan, yes.'

'And you'll let them sail?'

'Again, yes, if that seems to be their plan.'

'But that's slipping the country! Can they do that?'

'It isn't a criminal offence if their passports are in order. I want to see where they'll go.'

Ruth loooked at her watch. 'How are you going to manage that? It'll soon be dark.'

Hyde smiled reassuringly. 'We'll manage – with the help of radar.'

A telephonist called out, 'Ballistics on the wire for you, Inspector!'

Hyde hurried to take the call. When he returned a minute later a grim nod told Holt and Ruth all they needed to know. 'The same calibre! – Sergeant, I want two squad cars, fully-manned and armed, immediately! We're picking up Milton. He carries a gun and can use it effectively!'

As he bustled from the room he patted Ruth's shoulder. 'Sorry, Ruth, this one's not for unarmed civilians. You stay behind and hold the fort. We'll be back within a quarter of an hour.'

Ruth looked more jaded than ever.

In the squad car *en route* to The Golden Peacock Hyde said pensively, 'In a way I'm almost sorry I've got to arrest Milton. I've no choice, of course, it's my duty to pick him up. But I'd have preferred to have him wandering around free, just to see where he'd lead us.'

'Never mind,' said Holt. 'At least we've got three of them tucked away on the *Sunset*. I wonder which is Christopher?'

Hyde shrugged his shoulders. 'Let's ask Ashley Milton.'

Unfortunately Mr Milton was not at home.

Nobody knew, at first, how it had happened. The plain-clothes couple on duty near the bandstand swore that he had not left the restaurant by the front entrance; the man watching the back door was equally certain. A thorough search of Milton's private apartment revealed nothing other than some hints pointing to a hasty departure.

It was not until many vital minutes had elapsed that some muffled moans from the Ladies' Lavatory attracted the search party's attention.

The door was locked and they had to break in by force. There they discovered a scarlet-faced elderly woman, bound and gagged and minus her jacket and skirt. When the mortified lady had been released and supplied with temporary covering only a very unobservant person would have failed to notice how exceptionally tall she was, for a woman.

Just about as tall as Ashley Milton.

Chapter Fourteen

The twin-engined blue and white Beechcraft lifted smoothly off the runway at Orly and climbed towards low clouds. As Holt unfastened his seat-belt and glanced back, rain spattered over the passengers' windows and obscured his brief view of the lights of Paris.

'That visit was short and sweet,' he said dryly to Inspector Hyde, who sat opposite him in the small but comfortable aircraft. 'There was I, all set to enjoy a stag weekend in the sinful city without a bossy secretary nagging at my elbow, and then you insist on leaving almost as soon as we've arrived.'

'You can blame Ashley Milton for that.' Hyde rubbed his palm across sleep-starved eyes. 'There's nothing I would have enjoyed more than a good meal and an evening at the Lido myself. Instead of that, we've had a sandwich and just about worked the clock round.'

'Damn Mr Milton! Who would have thought such a languid creature could have shown such a turn of speed?'

The Inspector nodded grimly.

Milton had indeed surprised them. By the time his escape from the restaurant in the guise of a tall and somewhat angular female had been discovered he had reached the private flying-field near Polegate and taken off in a chartered plane held at instant readiness for just such an emergency. He had thus, in a matter of minutes, succeeded in bypassing the clamp-down on all air and sea transport leaving the country which Scotland Yard had ordered.

Interpol had picked up the trail when the plane had been spotted parked near a hangar on a field near Le Havre. The *Sunset* had left Newhaven and was steering a course almost due south, so it seemed likely that Le Havre was the meeting place and Hyde had made arrangements for a reception committee when the *Sunset* should arrive there.

Then a storm in the Channel had sprung up. The first inkling that they were reading the minds of the enemy falsely came in the shape of a telephone call from the French *Sûreté* in Paris. Jules Dunant's apartment, no great distance from the eighteenth *Arrondissement* where the illegal printing press had been discovered, had been broken into and set on fire. A short while later news was flashed that the *Sunset*, under cover of darkness and the sudden storm, had made a ninety-degree change of course and was steaming due west at full speed.

In an atmosphere of acute concern and nervous tension Holt had studied maps of the Channel and Northern France with Hyde and other police officers.

'Where the devil are they heading for? Cherbourg? The Channel Isles? St Malo? Or are they just running before the storm until the wind drops and they can turn back for Le Havre?' Hyde was nonplussed.

Holt had then offered a suggestion. 'Supposing that was just a blind? From Newhaven, Le Havre and Dieppe are the standard ports to steam for – it's too obvious. I'd say that they're making for somewhere else, and that Ashley Milton's in Paris. I shouldn't be surprised if he had some unfinished business with Dunant to attend to before joining up with the *Sunset*. If we're lucky, we might pick up his trail in Paris. How quickly could we be there?'

They had flown within the hour in a police chartered Beechcraft and, on meeting the Inspector's opposite numbers of the *Sûreté*, had rushed immediately to Dunant's apartment.

No one had actually expected to find Milton there, nor did they think he would have been kind enough to leave a visiting-card, but in a way he had done so, for the attempt to burn all evidence of the Christopher organisation in Dunant's flat echoed the attempt to burn Vance's body.

Enough evidence was salvaged, in addition to that which the French police had previously amassed, to make the general pattern a lot clearer.

Jules Dunant, the French officials explained, was a frustrated artist. His lack of recognition in the Parisian world of art had made him turn in bitterness to the lucrative field of forgery. Although his activities had been suspected for some time, the *Sûreté* had deliberately held back, trying to discover his outlets. It was no crime to paint copies of Old Masters; the matter became criminal only when the copies were passed off as originals and sold to gullible clients for huge sums. This was where the link across the Channel, namely Deanfriston, came in.

Dunant had posed as manager of a large retail newsagent's. Considerable quantities of French newspapers and magazines were despatched each week, some being sent abroad, and this had been Dunant's source of export. The forged paintings had been smuggled out of the country, one at a time, at irregular intervals, concealed in the bulky parcels.

Holt had spotted the connection directly. 'Now I understand why Vance had so many French periodicals in his study, although Legere told me he couldn't speak a word of French!'

The explanation of the private printing press reproducing newspapers eighty years old was also forthcoming. Jules Dunant's speciality was the period of the French Impressionists when most of the painters of that prolific school had been at the height of their powers. The alleged masterpieces were 'found' in attics and at remote jumble sales, and in order to make the fakes look more authentic they were generally 'discovered' wrapped in tattered, yellowing newspapers more than half a century old. It was a clever touch; an old frame was a useful adjunct, but the use of contemporary newspapers, suitably dusty and specially treated to give the appearance of age, showed the finesse of real genius and must often have clinched a deal.

The significance of the signet ring and the exact identity of the head of the Christopher organisation had not yet been cleared up, but several minor pieces of the mystery now fitted into place. It had been Vance's weighty books on the History of Art which Milton had dragged away at midnight in a sack, probably for fear that incriminating notes might have been made in the margins. At first Holt wondered how he had failed to notice their absence on the following morning, then he realised that it would have been easy for Milton to fill the empty spaces on the shelves with volumes from the various piles lying about the room, and the switch would not have been obvious. The slip of paper which had fallen from the pages of the book on Claude Monet had stemmed from Dunant's printing press.

The invisible-ink code on the Christopher postcard now explained itself. CP, MU(2), AR, EM, CM simply informed Vance Scranton that he could expect delivery of a Camille Pissarro, two Maurice Utrillos, an Auguste Renoir, an Edouard Manet, and a Claude Monet.

'The total value of that little lot – assuming one treated

them as genuine – being roughly how much, Monsieur?' Hyde had asked one of the French experts.

'Ah . . . it is impossible to say, *Inspecteur*. Perhaps one might take as a guide the price which that lovely Monet fetched in June 1965: half a million dollars.'

Holt whistled. 'Enough to pay for the *Sunset*, eh, Inspector?'

The Beechcraft banked and made for a gap in the clouds. Below them the Channel was a savage dark green flecked with streaks of white. The small aircraft bumped uncomfortably as it descended, and through driving rain the vast port of Cherbourg began to take shape.

'Do you think they're here?' Holt asked tensely.

'It's a fair guess. They were last sighted off Pointe de Barfleur,' the Inspector replied. 'If I'm wrong we'll try the Channel Isles and St Malo. Fasten your seat-belt, Holt, we're just about to land.'

Hyde lowered his binoculars and turned away from the window of the French Customs Office. The innocent-looking *Sunset* was riding at anchor in the harbour below.

The police, advised in advance by telephone from Paris, had alerted Customs and Port Authorities and a circle of quick-witted, flexible men now sat round the table, eagerly discussing a plan of action.

'The situation is far from simple,' Hyde was saying. 'I have a British warrant for Ashley Milton's arrest on a charge of murder, but Milton is no longer on British soil and I don't even know if he's on board the *Sunset* yet.'

Holt's suggestion was that they should wait in the Customs Office – out of sight, but with an excellent view of the boat – and keep it under observation until he arrived.

Hyde shook his head. 'In this appalling rain we might miss him altogether, and there's a chance he may already be on board. I want the whole bunch of them, the entire Christopher organisation from the top man down to the lowest deckhand – with some of their forged masterpieces as well, if possible.'

'You want rather a lot, *Inspecteur*,' pointed out the senior French Commissar.

'Oh, I'm aware of that,' Hyde conceded. 'But I've got a plan, and I think I can get what I want by the use of patience and caution. If we go marching on to the *Sunset* in broad daylight armed with my arrest warrant they'll see us coming. They'd have time to destroy whatever evidence they may have on board.'

Holt was the quickest to follow Hyde's line of thought. 'Are you suggesting we smuggle ourselves aboard and hope to catch them red-handed?'

'More or less. But I don't propose that we try and sneak over the side like a couple of stowaways. We must choose something simpler, something more open.'

'Disguise yourselves as a couple of seamen,' a Frenchman suggested.

'Neither of us could attempt the rolling gait of a sailor and get away with it, the crew would spot us as impostors within a minute!' Hyde said. 'No, I have a better idea. We'll pose as officials of the French *Douane*.'

'French Customs officers! Splendid!' Holt was enthusiastic and the plan met with general approval.

Uniforms were soon provided and a genuine official named Jean Thouard was selected to pave the way.

He was followed along the quayside by two smartly-dressed assistants; a young one with chestnut hair, short beard, and

198

heavy spectacles, and an older man who appeared to be suffering from a severe cold, for most of his face was buried in a voluminous handkerchief. They kept their heads well down against the driving rain and all three boarded the *Sunset* with little ceremony. They felt the eyes of the crew searing into them and heard a certain amount of grumbling and cursing in both languages, but when Thouard requested permission to search for contraband goods no hint of resistance was met.

Hyde was the first to catch sight of Milton as he stepped out of the chart room to greet them. Happily, the Inspector was blowing his nose with the huge handkerchief and his body blocked the view of Holt which Milton might otherwise have had.

Customs Officer Thouard stepped forward and momentarily engaged Milton's attention immediately. Annoyance crossed Milton's face, but he responded in fluent French and graciously gave them the freedom of the boat. He did not accompany them himself, but assured Thouard that they would be welcome to join him for a drink in the saloon when they had completed their mission. They would find nothing naughty, he promised them.

It was an airy performance with Milton as cool as a cucumber. He was evidently a man whose nerves thrived on moments of danger; he could scarcely have welcomed an official inspection at that time.

Holt and the Inspector made themselves inconspicuous on the afterdeck. In answer to Holt's raised eyebrows Hyde shook his head and whispered, 'Not yet. Let them all gather in the saloon. We'll mess it up if we tackle them one by one . . . Come on!'

They descended a companion ladder and carried out a search of the crew's quarters and the engine room, without success, then made their way to the passengers' cabins. In the first one they found a woman's comb and hairpins near the wash-basin and faint traces of lipstick on the hand-towel – it was obviously Antoinette Sheen's.

Before they had a chance to look further they heard Thouard complaining that the adjoining cabin was locked, and when Holt stepped out into the passageway he recognised the locked cabin as being Milton's.

'He will have to open it!' said Thouard sharply. 'I will go and demand the key.'

Violence flared on the instant of the Frenchman's departure. One of the British deckhands came clumping towards them. He passed Hyde, then without warning swung around again and snatched his cap, growling nastily, 'I thought I wasn't mistaken! Bless me, if it isn't my old friend—'

Holt's fist felled the man like a slaughterer's hammer.

The Inspector acted almost as quickly. In a moment he had ripped out the leather laces from the man's boots and tied his wrists behind his back. With equal expertise he stuffed a handkerchief in the ex-convict's mouth and bound it with his own tie.

'Quick – in here!' Holt cried, indicating Antoinette's cabin.

They dragged the heavy body and bundled it unceremoniously into an empty clothes closet. Holt pocketed the key.

'If he's told his pals he thought he recognised you, then Thouard's in danger. I'm going up!'

'Two will be better than one,' Hyde said, sprinting after him.

On deck they made their way cautiously, moving from cover to cover in a silence broken only by the swish of rain and the sudden blast of a powerful liner's siren. While running feet thundered down the starboard deck and descended to the engine room Holt lay motionless behind a pile of lifebelts. The liner sounded her siren again and his gaze was attracted by the rain-blurred outline of a huge ship at the harbour mouth. The silhouette was familiar and for a second he was puzzled, then the three famous funnels told him that it was the *Queen Mary*; she called frequently at Cherbourg on her way to or from Southampton. He remembered that her draught was too big for her to dock at the quayside; a lighter used for transporting passengers and luggage from dockside to liner was already beating up to the mighty vessel. A thought flashed into his mind . . . this was how Milton and the others planned to make their escape!

In the same instant Holt noticed the Inspector tugging at the wet cords of a tarpaulin covering a lifeboat slung on davits at the ship's side. Hyde beckoned to him. From the lifeboat came a gentle tapping and a low moan. Both men wrenched at the cords with numb fingers, and struggled to pull the tarpaulin aside.

There, staring up at them with large, compelling eyes, lay the trussed and gagged body of Antoinette Sheen.

Holt unfastened the gag from her mouth. She choked and coughed for a second or two, then said quietly, 'You look idiotic in that beard! . . . For heaven's sake untie my ankles, Philip! I've got cramp. You'll find Wade tied up in the other lifeboat.'

Hyde ran to the other side of the deck and began to haul the second tarpaulin free. A dishevelled and woebegone Jimmy Wade clambered stiffly to the deck.

'Time to blow the alarm, Inspector?' Holt called.

'I think so!' Hyde pulled a whistle from his pocket. Three blasts would summon help immediately.

But the whistle did not quite reach his lips before a

staggering blow on the shoulder sent it flying from his hand. Twisting round, they found themselves surrounded by Milton, Legere, and three members of the crew armed with rifles.

'You should have blown it a little earlier, I think,' Milton said with steely calm. 'Take them to the saloon.'

There they found Thouard with an ugly bruise on his forehead and his arms behind him tied to the shaft of his chair. The chair, like the rest of the furniture, was screwed to the deck.

'*Je m'excuse*,' he apologised. 'I was not careful enough.'

'Nor were we,' acknowledged Holt quietly.

Held at gunpoint Hyde and Holt were searched and relieved of their pistols.

One of the English deckhands eyed the Inspector with huge enjoyment as he kept them all covered with his rifle. 'Makes a change, don't it, Inspector?' he chortled. 'The larse time it was me and Curly what was up for bein' in unlawful possession of—'

'Who murdered Curly, Fats?' Hyde barked. 'He was a pal of yours, wasn't he? Who killed him?'

The man known as Fats gave an oily grin. 'Now that would be tellin', wouldn't it?'

Wade coughed nervously and straightened his tie. 'If you'll permit me to say so, Inspector, it's a waste of time trying to extract anything from that horrible fellow, or his companion. Miss Sheen and I offered them money but they refused to be helpful.'

Hyde gave Wade and Antoinette a puzzled stare. 'Obviously this is not the moment for recriminations, but what the dickens are you two doing on this boat?'

'The same as you – playing cops and robbers!' said Antoinette, continuing to rub the circulation back into her ankles and wrists. Even under these unfavourable circumstances she managed to look poised and attractive in the blue jeans and thick sweater.

Wade managed the mere ghost of one of his former smiles. 'In a manner of speaking we rather foolishly tried to take a leaf out of your book. Julie had mentioned Milton's yacht, and as I was convinced that he was behind all this mystery I thought we might be able to find some kind of evidence and pin the blame fairly and squarely on him. It was rather a shock to find Legere on board.'

'I can imagine,' said Holt meaningfully, with a sidelong glance at Antoinette.

She laughed derisively. 'I certainly picked a dud there, I have to admit! In fact, I seem to have quite a talent for doing just that. The man's a swine and I was an idiot not to see it. Naturally, he wouldn't let us off the *Sunset* once we were on board . . . I always did dream of being abducted aboard some rich old sugar-daddy's luxury yacht,' she added wistfully, 'but I didn't bargain for being trussed up like a turkey and thrown into a lifeboat.'

'How long had you been in there?' Hyde asked.

'They tied us up as soon as we sighted the French coast.'

'Did they hurt you much, Antoinette?' Holt asked her anxiously.

She shrugged her shoulders and glanced at Wade for confirmation. 'I'm afraid Henri is not exactly the gentle type.'

A sound came from the entrance to the saloon. Legere was standing there. 'The English prisoners are about to have a visitor,' he reported.

'Who would that be?' Hyde demanded.

'A man named Christopher . . . He's just puffing and panting his way over the ship's side now.'

The tension of expectancy rose almost to snapping point as the sound of Milton's voice, intermingled with another, filtered through to the saloon.

'*It can't be!*' Wade gasped and jumped from his chair but he was cuffed back by a member of the crew. Wildly he glanced from Holt to the Inspector.

Hyde nodded gravely, and Philip Holt said slowly, 'I'm afraid it is. I've been wondering about the possibility for some time.'

Chapter Fifteen

Robert Scranton's gangly form filled the doorway as he took off his hat and brushed some of the rain from his coat. He was having trouble with his breathing and although his keen eyes took in the situation with one shrewd glance it was some moments before he could actually speak. When he did so his tone was quiet.

'Say, that's quite a gathering you have here, Ashley. Is this the normal uniform of the British police when overseas?'

Milton entered the saloon behind him. 'They indulged in a little fancy dress – that's how they managed to get on board.'

'Very ingenious. Well, let's not waste any time. Start the engines and get under way. I'll take the wheel.'

Milton gave commands to his crew and hurried on deck in Scranton's wake. One of the French deckhands stayed on guard with a rifle, the other two hurried to their duties, and within a minute the throb of the diesel engines vibrated through the ship's hull. The limited view through the saloon portholes of dockside cranes and buildings began to change; they were pulling away from the quayside.

Holt passed the Inspector a wordless message. He pointed

unobtrusively to his wristwatch, then spread wide the fingers of one hand and raised his eyebrows questioningly.

Hyde nodded and muttered, 'Yes, about five, I should think.'

'*Silence!*' roared the French guard, brandishing his rifle.

Antoinette looked at the man coolly and remarked in a casual voice, 'What an *ugly* man, don't you think, Philip?'

The guard jerked his rifle at her and threw out a stream of abuse.

'Does he speak any English?' Holt asked.

She shook her head. 'No, I don't think so, but he has a vile command of his own tongue. He promises to shoot the next one who opens his mouth. Says it's all the same to him whether we die now or out at sea.'

The yacht gathered speed and began rolling and pitching as they met choppy cross-currents flowing in from the mouth of the harbour.

Milton put his head round the door to make sure everything was under control.

Wade shouted at him, 'What do you intend doing with us, Milton?'

'What do you expect, my dear fellow?' Milton was on top of his form, enjoying danger like a hound sniffing the scent of a chase. 'We shall either put you all to sea in one of the lifeboats when we're far enough out, or we shall deposit you on some uninhabited rock off the Brittany coast. You won't be found for weeks, I dare say. You'll survive, but only just. The *Sunset* is a very powerful craft, you know – we'll be hundreds of miles away by then . . . *Good God, what was that!*'

Above the beat of the engines had come a whooshing sound and a huge splash, and the crack of a gun brought them all to their feet. Holt was quick, but Milton even quicker. Holt hurled himself at the guard and sent the rifle flying; Milton jumped backwards out of the saloon, slammed the sliding door and locked it.

'Hit the deck, everyone!' Holt yelled. He grabbed the rifle and swung the butt hard in the face of the groping French deckhand. The man collapsed like a sack. Antoinette was already at work releasing the Customs Officer. Rifle fire spattered outside as Hyde struggled vainly with the locked door.

'Holt! Blow this thing open with the rifle! We've got to get clear of this place before Scranton turns his men loose on the lot of us!'

Holt fired three times at the lock and there was a tearing of smashed wood and metal, but despite their combined efforts the sliding mechanism seemed jammed. Another heavy warning shot whooshed and exploded over the *Sunset's* bows; the boat lurched to starboard, knocking them all off balance.

Wade was the first to scramble to his feet. He picked up the rifle by its muzzle, muttered a polite 'I wonder if I may?' to Holt, and took a vigorous swing at one of the portholes. At the first blow the glass cracked, at the second it splintered, leaving a jagged gash.

'Room for a little one, I think,' said Wade succinctly, and began squirming his way through.

'See if you can get to the engine room!' Holt shouted. 'Pull any lever that says STOP!'

In the confusion that followed it never became clear whether Wade actually did pull a lever, whether he cowed an engine-hand at the point of the rifle into doing so, or whether the engine-hand acted on Scranton's instructions from the bridge. At any rate, Scranton must have seen that the game was up. The *Sunset* began to lose way and by the time Holt had battered his way through the porthole two pursuing boats of the Harbour Police – one of them mounted on hydrofoils and capable of speeds over fifty knots, the other equipped with some impressive looking armaments at bow and stern – had come alongside and heavily armed naval police were ordering the *Sunset* crew to surrender.

Holt ran to the wheelhouse and discovered Robert Scranton's gaunt body slumped at the helm. He bent to examine him as Hyde and Antoinette came running up.

'Is he dead?'

'I believe so. But I don't think he stopped a bullet. I think it was his heart – the excitement was too much for him.'

Antoinette asked, 'Would someone mind telling me how he came to be here in Cherbourg?'

As if in answer the *Queen Mary* gave a tremendous blast on her siren.

Hyde said as the echoes died, 'He obviously just disembarked from the *Queen Mary*.'

'He made it known that he and his wife were flying back to the States,' Holt added, 'but he must have slipped away from the airport at the last moment.'

'So much for Christopher!' Hyde said with satisfaction. 'Milton is handcuffed to Legere, and Legere is handcuffed to the ship's rail. And if that isn't security enough, guess who's guarding them both with a rifle?'

'Jimmy Wade?' guessed Antoinette with a cascade of laughter in which the others joined.

'None other! That little chap's full of spirit. He looks quite disappointed that it's all over . . . Well, shall we go and say "hello" to our friends from the *Douane*?'

'I thought they were never going to get here,' admitted Holt. 'That was the longest five minutes I've ever experienced.'

'True enough. But actually they kept pretty much to schedule. The Commissar said it wouldn't take them more than five minutes to reach us if they saw the *Sunset* pull away from the quay.'

'Anyway, I was glad to get out of that saloon alive.'

'So were we all.' Antoinette tucked her arm through Holt's as they stepped out into the rain. 'But I wasn't scared. I knew I could rely on you – you're a real hunk of a man!'

The traffic speeding up the Champs Elysées speared the night with diamond brilliance, and the great City was getting into its stride, intent on offering pleasure. In tune with the City a couple strolled towards the garden of the Tuileries and found a bench beneath the trees.

'. . . Inspector Hyde has more charm than I gave him credit for,' Antoinette was saying. 'Fancy letting me fly to Paris in his Beechcraft!'

Holt smiled at her. 'We had to come here anyway. The Paris jails are the safest for types like Milton and his crew. Besides, there were a lot of loose ends to be tied up after yesterday's little fracas at Cherbourg. But don't let's talk about that, Antoinette . . . Have I told you how attractive you look in that new dress?'

'You have, several times . . . But you can tell me again.'

'Wouldn't you like to be a model, Antoinette?'

She shook her head.

'But I thought every girl in Great Britain between the ages of thirteen and—'

'No – not me.'

Her eyes looked into his and the theme of murder and

fraud which had first brought them together seemed very far away . . . Her tawny hair, the colour of trees in autumn, fell across his chest and she moved closer to him.

'I don't recall your looking quite so attractive ever before, unless it was . . .'

The fragrance of her perfume had recalled a memory . . . of a tall brown-skinned girl . . . in a short white bathrobe . . . in a salmon-pink bungalow . . . in the green English countryside . . .

When their lips parted after a long embrace her voice was just a whisper. 'Philip . . . are you quite sure you still want to "do the Town"?'

'I'm beginning to go off the idea,' he murmured. 'Perhaps we should be getting back to the hotel . . .'

When they reached the hotel foyer they were greeted by Inspector Hyde. He glanced briefly at Antoinette and placed a hand on Holt's shoulder.

'I've just phoned through to Eastbourne,' he said. 'I thought you should know – Ruth's ill!'

Chapter Sixteen

Ruth smiled to herself as she read the card that had come with the flowers.

To Ruth – a Very Efficient Private Eye. Get well soon. Philip.

A very efficient Private Eye! He had long regarded her as just a very efficient secretary, so she looked upon it as a small promotion.

She propped the card against the bowl of fruit at her bedside – that was a gift from Inspector Hyde. Now he really was a sweetie! Fancy bothering to telephone her from Paris in the middle of all that excitement.

After events had taken Hyde and her boss out of the country Ruth had returned to the hotel, somewhat despondent, feeling the first symptoms of a heavy cold. She had spent a disturbed night, kept awake by a headache and the violent storm at sea, picturing a tossing *Sunset* with its strange assortment of characters on board. Lying in bed the following day had been frustrating. Surrounded by magazines and a depressing array of inhalants, cough pastilles, and cold cures, she had pondered over the Scranton case in detail, wondering what could now be taking place across the Channel on French soil.

It had not been until Monday evening, when Hyde had telephoned from Paris, that she had been put briefly in the picture, and the next morning the two men had flown back to Eastbourne. Even then she had seen them only momentarily before they dashed off to visit Julie Benson, but they had promised to look in again that afternoon and tell her the full story.

This prospect made her feel slightly better. She leaned back against the pillows and began to flick through the pages of a magazine.

Presently there was a tap on the door. Ruth drew a box of man-sized paper handkerchiefs towards her and answered with a sneeze.

Holt came in first. 'Hello, Ruth! How are you feeling?'

'Oh, not too bad. I told you, it's only a cold – nothing to worry about.'

'Well, mind you take care of yourself,' warned Hyde, following Holt into the room. 'Don't go taking any more risks. You're a very valuable young lady!'

'Oh, thank you, Inspector! But so is the questionable Julie Benson, I'm afraid. How is she?'

'She's much better. And she's decided to talk! Yes, we've found out quite a lot from Julie Benson.'

Ruth held her enthusiasm in check just long enough to allow her visitors to be comfortably seated, then she said eagerly, 'Well, come on – tell me what's been happening!'

Hyde summed up briefly. 'Milton and Legere are safely under lock and key; they have a lot to answer for. Antoinette is absolutely innocent. Julie's a silly little girl who was in love with Vance and let it cloud her judgement. Wade's in love with Julie and got himself involved because he was trying to help her.'

There was a pause.

'Is that all?' said Ruth in exasperation. 'There must be more to it than that. Tell me the rest!'

'What exactly do you want to know?'

'Everything! Start right at the beginning, Philip, and let's hear what you've found out.'

Holt did as she asked and, with Hyde's help, the story gradually unfolded.

'Robert Scranton was an ordinary business man dealing in washing machines. One day he was asked if he'd like to buy a valuable old painting. Scranton was no art expert himself – but his son was. Vance realised it was a forgery but he also recognised the quality of the work, and he and his father decided to look into it further.'

'And then what happened?' Ruth asked.

'They traced the painting to Dunant in Paris and began to deal in fakes in a big way. That was how it all started.'

'Scranton had a right-hand man in England,' Hyde explained. 'That was Ashley Milton, and his job was to control the financial side of things and keep an eye on Vance.'

'Those cheque stubs he showed me—' Holt put in. 'They didn't represent blackmail money at all, they were the sums he'd been paying Dunant; through Vance, of course.'

'Anyway,' Hyde continued, 'business boomed and Milton bought a yacht; they used it to cruise round the world at intervals, looking for potential markets for the paintings. The organisation gradually expanded and eventually Scranton disappeared behind the code name of Christopher.'

'But whatever made Vance kill that student at the College?' asked Ruth, her interest mounting.

'For some reason or other Vance wanted to quit,' Holt told her. 'But Milton wouldn't hear of it and he cabled Scranton in America. As soon as Vance knew his father was coming over to England he decided that the only way to get out of his clutches was to fake his own death.'

'Go on . . .'

'So he invited Graham Brown to his study on the night of the concert – when he knew Scholars' Row would be deserted – and saw to it that Graham got there first. All Vance had to do was walk in and shoot him, fake the evidence, and then simply disappear.'

'I'm with you so far,' Ruth nodded, suppressing a sneeze. 'What next?'

'Julie Benson was still very much in love with Vance and she promised to keep his secret and help him all she could. Milton suspected what had happened and put the pressure on Vance, via Julie. He threatened to hound him to the ends of the earth unless he returned the ring.'

'Yes, but why all the fuss about the ring – did you find out about that?'

'Yes.' Hyde took up the explanation. 'Scranton had two rings made. One was kept by Dunant in Paris, and the other by Vance in England. They used the rings to make special impressions on various documents and parcels, as a means of identification and to convey certain information. So you see, the ring assumed a vital significance, and that's why everyone seemed to be trying to lay their hands on it.'

Ruth herself fitted another piece into the mental jigsaw puzzle. 'In fact, Vance couldn't buy his freedom because he didn't have the ring; he'd already given it to Antoinette . . . And Julie broke into her bungalow in an attempt to get it back, but she couldn't find it!'

'Exactly!' Holt confirmed. 'When I showed it to Julie in the restaurant she promptly reported the fact to Vance, and they thought up the idea of getting me to put it in the Professor's pencil-jar.'

'Who beat up Dalesford then? Was it Legere?'

'Yes. He overheard the plan; he happened to be in the next telephone cubicle when she was phoning from The Golden Peacock.'

'But none of them realised,' Hyde pointed out dramatically, 'that in the meantime Milton had stolen the ring from Mr Holt!'

'Oh, so it *was* Milton who stole it!' Ruth looked doubtful. 'In that case why give it to the police?'

'Well, as soon as he heard about Dunant's impending arrest he got scared and thought the wisest thing to do was to get rid of it again quickly. He got Jimmy Wade to take it to the Inspector and managed to throw suspicion onto him in the process.'

'Then what was that ridiculous little man up to?' Ruth said hotly. 'If he was so concerned about Julie, how come he didn't tell her the police had the ring? The girl was running round in circles trying to help Vance to get it!'

'I think Mr Wade was more sinned against than sinning,' the Inspector said leniently. 'He didn't realise what was going on. He knew Julie was terribly upset over Vance's death – or disappearance – and he was trying to be kind to her, but he didn't really know the half of it. I don't think she took him into her confidence very much.'

Ruth was silent whilst she worked it out, but she soon had the picture clear in her mind. 'Vance knew nothing about the police having the ring and was still desperately trying to get hold of it, is that it?'

'Absolutely! And Milton took advantage of the situation. He'd already decided that Vance would have to be eliminated; things were getting out of control.'

'Milton arranged – through Julie, of course – to meet Vance at Pevensey. Vance agreed because he fully expected to be in possession of the ring by then and he was hoping to bring the whole thing to a conclusion. But Milton turned up before I did – and you know what happened.' Holt stood up and casually sampled a grape from the fruit bowl.

'You said Milton had an accomplice with him when he shot Vance,' Ruth reminded him. 'Who was that?'

'It was Legere,' he said, busy dealing with the pips. 'He'd had to . . . break his date with Antoinette in order to . . . help Milton with the plan. So it was quite true what Jimmy Wade told us about stepping in and taking her to the theatre . . . M'm, these are pretty good, Ruth.'

Ruth smiled and indicated the fruit, inviting both visitors to help themselves.

'Well, perhaps just one,' Hyde said, leaning forward and gingerly plucking a grape from its stem.

'Go on – take a few,' Ruth urged.

'Oh, well . . . if you insist.'

'We really mustn't eat all your grapes, Ruth,' Holt said unconvincingly, scooping up a handful and munching them as he went on with the, story.

'What about Curly?' Ruth enquired. 'How does he come into it?'

'Curly,' said Hyde, 'first met Legere at the races. It was Curly whose help was enlisted to find a crew to man the *Sunset* – hence the old lags on board.'

'I still don't see why he should have been killed.'

'Yes – well . . . You tell her about that, Holt.'

216

'You see, Ruth,' Holt said quietly, 'Robert Scranton made one big mistake. When he arrived in London and heard Vance was dead he thought it was true. He'd no reason to disbelieve it at that stage. He and Mrs Scranton were genuinely upset – inscensed, in fact – and they asked me to help track down his killer.'

'Go on, Philip . . .'

'Later on, when Mrs Scranton had actually seen her son near the Savoy and they'd had a chance to talk to Milton down in Eastbourne, Scranton learned the truth and realised that you and I were a threat to the organisation and that our investigations must be stopped at all costs. The attempt to force us over the Brighton cliffs failed, so when Robert Scranton received a phone call from his son—'

Ruth said, 'If Vance wanted to get away from his father why did he phone him?'

'He wanted money – quickly – so he let Scranton think he had the ring and promised to do a deal.'

'Oh, I see.'

'Well, when the father got his call he saw a golden opportunity to fix us for good and all. He asked us both along to Lewisham, intending to kill us as soon as we got to the house. The plan misfired because Scranton felt ill.'

'And yet he gave us the money to take to his son . . . Why?' Ruth looked completely bewildered.

'He gave us the money because he had an accomplice waiting there, and he reckoned that even if he didn't go himself this accomplice would take care of us, as well as get the ring from Vance.'

'But he didn't even try, did he?'

'No. You see, that accomplice was Curly, and he was dead by the time we arrived.'

217

'*Curly!*'

'He'd been scared to hell over the Brighton job, and it was easy for Scranton to threaten him into doing what he wanted. When Vance got there, there was a quarrel and a nasty skirmish. Curly'd had a big win at the races, and Vance decided not to wait for his father to show up. He took Curly's cash and made off. We appeared on the scene shortly afterwards.'

'Oh . . . now it all begins to fall into place,' Ruth agreed. 'But it beats me how you *know* all this! Robert Scranton's dead – Vance is dead – Curly's dead . . .'

'You're forgetting Julie Benson,' said Hyde. 'She was in touch with Vance all along. And we've also got Milton and Legere in the bag. Between them we've got pretty well all sides of the picture.'

'Then do you think I could ask you one or two questions?' she asked with a disarming smile.

'You've been asking questions non-stop ever since we came in!' Holt declared, throwing back his head and laughing good-humouredly as he dipped into the fruit bowl again.

'Ruth's really enjoying herself,' chuckled the Inspector. 'Come on, Ruth – let's have it!'

'I don't understand why Vance gave the ring to Antoinette when he was planning to disappear. If he'd simply put it on Graham Brown's finger it would have avoided all the commotion.'

'He did that because he thought it would be bound to lead the police to Antoinette sooner or later. And once they'd reached her they'd connect her wonderful talent for copying with the Christopher set-up. You see, it was a sort of double revenge – against his father because he wouldn't let him quit, and against Antoinette because she'd rejected him. As people have been constantly pointing out, Vance wasn't possessed of a very charming nature.'

'And Antoinette? Was she trying to clear herself? Is that why she got friendly with Jimmy Wade and played detectives?'

'Partly. And because she felt sorry for the little man. She also told me she wanted to pull off something spectacular in the hope that she might gain esteem in my eyes.'

'Mr Holt was apparently next on her list of conquests,' Hyde said with a twinkle in his eye.

Ruth did not voice her thoughts on the subject. Instead she enquired about the Christopher postcards.

'They all came from Milton,' Holt said. 'The first one was genuine, sent quite legitimately in Christopher's name, before Vance's disappearance. The second one, and the letter, were intended to divert suspicion from the right quarters and confuse the police.'

Eventually Holt and the Inspector said they must be getting along.

'Hurry up and get better, Ruth,' Hyde said. 'You've shown outstanding courage and no little enterprise in this whole affair. I'll see that the Commissioner gets to hear about it.'

As he closed the door behind him and the two men paused for a moment in the corridor outside, Ruth overheard Hyde say, 'You've got a remarkable secretary there, Holt. I don't think you fully appreciate her. She's really quite a girl!'

'Yes, I was just beginning to get that idea myself,' Holt replied. 'Hyde – you're right! Ruth *is* quite a girl! I think maybe I should raise her salary.'

'You do that. And I should get her some more grapes whilst you're about it, old boy.'

As their laughter receded down the corridor Ruth gave a huge grin. From 'Secretary' to 'Private Eye' – and now a rise in salary . . . Perhaps she was making some progress after all . . .

She reached out towards the fruit bowl and started to peel an orange.

The Ventriloquist's Doll

Paul Temple was in his study finishing off a chapter of the new novel he was writing, when Steve, his wife, opened the door.

'You've got a visitor, Paul,' she announced. 'And he looks very distracted about something. I told him you were working, but he said it was most urgent.'

'Who is he?' asked Temple.

'Ivor Mount, the famous ventriloquist.'

Temple looked surprised.

'What does he want to see me about?' he asked.

'He's lost Marmaduke Bailey.'

'The doll that's insured for £10,000!' exclaimed Temple. 'All right, ask him to come in, will you Steve?'

When Ivor Mount came in, he seemed very agitated indeed. He was a short, dark man in the late forties, with bushy hair turning grey at the temples. He still held his broad-brimmed black hat, which he twisted nervously in his fingers.

'I don't know which way to turn, Mr Temple, and that's a fact,' he began. 'I can't do anything without Marmaduke.'

'You've been to the police, of course,' said Temple.

'Oh yes, but they haven't been able to do very much so

far. I wonder if they realise how much Marmaduke means to me.'

'When did this happen?' enquired Temple.

'Yesterday, on the train to Fordbridge. I was playing there in pantomime. I went to the restaurant-car for lunch, leaving Marmaduke in his box in my compartment. When I came back, the box had gone.'

'Was there anyone else in the compartment?

'No one at that particular time.'

'Did you have the train searched?'

'Not till I got to Fordbridge. It stopped, at Townleigh first, and a lot of people got out there. I'm certain one of them must have had the box.'

'Had you missed it by then?'

'Yes, but the train was packed with youngsters coming back from their holidays, so there was some confusion, and it wasn't easy to get along the corridors.'

Paul Temple nodded.

'They'd be boys from the Four Elms School,' he said. 'It's near Townleigh. Go on, Mr Mount.'

'Well, the railway people called in the police, of course, and they are making enquiries, but so far nothing has turned up. I have tried to keep it out of the papers, but I expect it will be in this evening's editions.'

'Couldn't you carry on with another doll?' asked Temple.

'I could, after a fashion. But the managements of the theatres wouldn't accept it. They stipulate Marmaduke specifically in all my contracts. You've got to help me, Mr Temple. The insurance company is offering £500 reward, and I'd give twice as much to get Marmaduke back.'

Temple could not help feeling sorry for the little man, though he did not altogether relish the idea of breaking off his writing to take on what seemed to be a fairly straight-forward case of theft.

'All right, I'll do what I can for you, Mr Mount,' he promised at length. 'If you care to look in sometime tomorrow, there may be some developments.'

When the ventriloquist had left, Temple telephoned New Scotland Yard and spoke to Inspector Vosper.

'Vosper, could you do me a favour? Find out from your local police station at Townleigh if any boy happens to be missing from Four Elms School.'

Vosper rang back ten minutes later.

'How did you get on to this, Temple?' he asked. 'There *is* a boy missing. His name is Clive Wayman, of 15 Dorset Road, East Kensington. His mother swears he caught the train all right, but he hasn't turned up at the school. Have you got a line on him at all?'

'Nothing definite as yet, Vosper,' replied Temple, taking a rapid note of the address on his writing pad. 'I may have some news a bit later on.'

He took a taxi to the address in East Kensington, and found Mrs Wayman looking very worried.

'Clive's been getting quite a handful lately,' she told Temple. 'I haven't been able to do much with him these holidays. He's obsessed with the idea of being an impersonator on the stage. I kept telling him he's too young – he's only fifteen – and must pass his exams first, but he takes no notice. Only last week he went in for a competition at some cinema in Chelsea, and he's been upset ever since because he didn't get a prize.'

'Did you have much difficulty in getting him to go back to school?' asked Temple.

'Yes, he kept saying he'd run away and join a theatrical

company of some sort. But surely they'd never want a boy of his age.'

'You are sure he went on that train?'

'Yes, I saw him off myself at Waterloo, but he never arrived at the school. The Headmaster telephoned the same evening, because apparently two boys said they had seen Clive on the train.'

Promising to keep in touch with the distracted Mrs Wayman, Temple returned to his flat. Some time later he picked up an evening paper, and a headline caught his eye.

MARMADUKE BAILEY IS MISSING
VENTRILOQUIST CONSULTS PAUL TEMPLE

Temple flung down the paper with an exclamation of annoyance. He wondered how the news could have leaked out. Probably Ivor Mount had mentioned it casually to some actor friend or perhaps a journalist he had met at his Club.

An hour later, the telephone rang, and after Temple had said 'Hello' twice, a squeaky little voice came over the line.

'Is that Mr Paul Temple?'

'Speaking. Who are you?'

'I'm Marmaduke Bailey.'

Temple frowned. Obviously, he thought, this was someone's idea of a joke.

'Where are you speaking from?' he asked.

'Never mind that, Mr Temple. Will you tell the boss that I'll be back on Saturday for certain? Tell him I'm just having a bit of a holiday.'

Temple looked puzzled. The voice was obviously very like that of the celebrated dummy, as known to millions of radio listeners and TV viewers.

'You can't be Marmaduke Bailey,' he said; 'what's your real name?

There was a characteristic little chuckle from the other end. 'That would be telling, Mr Temple! That would be telling!'

There was a click as the receiver was replaced. Temple immediately flashed the operator and asked for the call to be traced. After a few minutes' wait he was told that it came from a call-box in Bickerton, a small town in Sussex.

Temple went to his bookshelves and found a guide to Sussex, which informed him that Bickerton had two cinemas, the Regal and the Luxor. Taking a chance, he telephoned the latter and asked if by any chance they had a talent contest on the stage that week.

'No, sir,' came the prompt reply, 'but they hold one every Wednesday at the Regal.'

Temple thanked his informant politely and replaced his receiver.

He thought for a few moments, then dialled the number of Ivor Mount's flat. When the ventriloquist came to the telephone. Temple said:

'I think I'm on the trail of your doll. But I want you to give me your word that if I recover it for you, you won't take any action against the person who stole it. And I think I can guarantee you won't lose by the bargain.'

'All right, Mr Temple, whatever you say,' agreed Ivor Mount at once. 'As long as I get Marmaduke back, that's all I'm really worried about.'

'Splendid.' said Temple. 'Then keep tomorrow evening free and call for me here at about six o'clock.'

They found the Regal Cinema, Bickerton, packed with an eager audience.

'Talent contests seem to be popular,' said Temple. Ivor Mount shrugged his shoulders.

'I went in for them myself once,' he recalled. 'That's the hard way of getting on the stage.'

He seemed very bored with the proceedings, until the compère suddenly came on and announced:

'The next act will be Master Clive Wayman, presenting an impersonation of Ivor Mount, the well-known ventriloquist, and his celebrated doll, Marmaduke Bailey!'

Mount sat bolt upright in his seat, and Temple had to restrain him when the curtains opened to reveal Clive Wayman holding what was unmistakably the genuine Marmaduke Bailey.

'It's all right,' whispered Temple. 'He won't run away.'

Indeed, Master Wayman obviously had every intention of remaining right in the centre of the stage, where he proceeded to retail Ivor Mount's 'patter' with all the assurance of a veteran. He was obviously too young to give more than a sketchy imitation of Mount's normal voice, but his mimicry of Marmaduke was quite uncanny, and he was presently adjudged second prize-winner on the strength of the audience's applause. As he came off, clutching an electric toaster, Temple and Mount were waiting for him at the side of the stage. He recognised the ventriloquist immediately, and his eyes bulged.

'I haven't hurt Marmaduke, Mr Mount, honest I haven't,' he gasped before they could say a word.

Temple steered the boy into a convenient corner, while Mount took possession of his doll and examined it.

'What made you do this, Clive?' he asked.

'Well, I went in for that competition at Chelsea and did an impersonation with an imaginary doll. But the audience

226

didn't like me. I was feeling very fed up about it when I saw Mr Mount on the train. Then it suddenly came over me that if only I had a real doll I could do the act properly. I waited at the corner of the corridor till I saw Mr Mount go into the restaurant-car, then I took the box and put it with my own luggage. All the boys had stacks of stuff, so it wasn't noticed. I'd read about this competition being held here every week, so I caught the next train to Bickerton.'

'You've certainly got a nerve, young man,' said the ventriloquist, 'and if it wasn't for Mr Temple you might have found yourself in the hands of the police.'

'It was a lucky thing you phoned me, Clive,' smiled Temple. 'After that remarkable impersonation. I couldn't be too hard on you. I'm sure your headmaster will see you are punished, but you've caused Mr Mount and your mother a lot of worry; I hope you realise that.'

'I'm sorry, Mr Temple,' said the boy, looking very uncomfortable.

'All right. Well, I'm going to telephone your mother, then we are going to take you straight back to school.'

In the car they were silent for a while. The ventriloquist was figuring out the useful publicity he would get when this human little story was reported in the papers. Presently he said:

'I'm thinking of putting on a special show for the youngsters during the next holidays, Clive. I could probably use a bright young boy like you.'

Clive positively bounced on the seat in his excitement.

'Could you really, Mr Mount? I'd work like a beaver – I promise.'

'I'll drop you a line at school when it's all fixed up,' promised the ventriloquist.

227

As the car drew up at the school, the boy thrust a small parcel into Temple's arms.

'If you see my mother, Mr Temple, would you please give her this?' begged Clive. 'And tell her I'm sorry she's been upset.'

'Fair enough, Clive,' smiled Temple, and placed the electric toaster carefully on the seat beside him.

BY THE SAME AUTHOR

Beware of Johnny Washington

When a gang of desperate criminals begins leaving calling cards inscribed '*With the Compliments of Johnny Washington*', the real Johnny Washington is encouraged by an attractive newspaper columnist to throw in his lot with the police. Johnny, an American 'gentleman of leisure' who has settled at a quiet country house in Kent to enjoy the fishing, soon finds himself involved with the mysterious Horatio Quince, a retired schoolmaster who is on the trail of the gang's unscrupulous leader, the elusive 'Grey Moose'.

Best known for creating *Paul Temple* for BBC radio in 1938, Francis Durbridge's prolific output of crime and mystery stories, encompassing plays, radio, television, films and books, made him a household name for more than 50 years. A new radio character, *Johnny Washington Esquire*, hit the airwaves in 1949, leading to the publication of this one-off novel in 1951.

This Detective Club classic is introduced by writer and bibliographer Melvyn Barnes, author of *Francis Durbridge: A Centenary Appreciation*, who reveals how Johnny Washington's only literary outing was actually a reworking of Durbridge's own *Send for Paul Temple*.

BY THE SAME AUTHOR

Another Woman's Shoes

It was an open-and-shut case: Lucy Staines was murdered by her hot-headed fiancé Harold Weldon. But something about it is troubling ex-Fleet Street crime reporter Mike Baxter – why was one of Lucy's shoes missing from the crime scene? When an identical murder occurs while Weldon is safely behind bars, the whole case is re-opened – and everything revolves around another woman's shoes . . .

Another Woman's Shoes is Francis Durbridge's rewrite of his radio serial *Paul Temple and the Gilbert Case*, in which Mike and Linda Baxter take the places of Paul and Steve Temple in pursuing the killer. This new edition is introduced by bibliographer Melvyn Barnes and includes the short story 'Paul Temple and the Nightingale'.